BLUE RIBBONS

Also by Kim Ablon Whitney

The Perfect Distance

Blue
RIBBONS

Kim Ablon Whitney

ISBN 978-0692338087

Cover design by Margaret Sunter
Interior design by Anne Honeywood
Cover photo by Caranine Smith/www.bigeq.com
Text set in Sabon

for Maggie

Chapter 1

"I WANT THIS LAST SUMMER."

I was in my usual eavesdropping spot when I heard Mom. In our apartment there's a hallway right outside Dad's study and it has this little nook where someone can stand unnoticed and listen in.

"Don't say 'last summer.' We don't know anything yet," Dad said.

Although I couldn't see into the room, I could picture the scene: Dad behind his desk, glasses resting on the table, his right hand rubbing his beard. Mom would be standing—she never liked to sit still—looking at him with her intense blue eyes.

"It's true," Mom said. "He's for sale. Susie texted me."

A moment's silence, and then Dad's voice again: "Don't you think two ponies are enough? She's only thirteen."

"This one's different. It's the best pony in the country. They're only selling it now because the girl shot up in height and has to move on to a horse. You can never buy a pony like this at the beginning of the season. And plus, she'll be outgrowing Drizzle after this year so we'll have three just for the summer."

I leaned closer to make sure I was hearing right. The best pony in the country. Woodland's Tried and True. Everyone on the show circuit had heard the rumors that he was going to be for sale.

Mom hadn't mentioned buying him to me, but we'd watched Tyler, a beautiful bay, win over and over at all the shows we went to. He'd won the grand pony hunter championship at Devon just a few weeks ago. I'd gotten good ribbons in the smalls with Drizzle and the mediums with Sammy, but Mom lingered ringside, watching the award presentations. And I'd seen her talking to Susie after one of my lessons last week. Even then I'd already known. Now, almost shaking as I strained to hear more of their conversation, I wondered how I could be feeling absolute dread. How could I not want something that anyone else would have loved to have? Who wouldn't want to own Tyler? Who wouldn't want to win at every show? It was every pony rider's dream to show a pony like that. So it had to be mine, too. Plus, it was my mom's dream.

* * *

My gift. My blessing. My miracle. My baby. My angel. These were just some of the things Mom called me. She wasn't like every mom. For one thing, she was this amazing businesswoman. All that money that bought my ponies? Most of it Mom made. She worked for a big skincare company for a long time before founding her own line of cosmetics, ProduX. She grew ProduX until it was in almost every department store and then sold it for millions back to the company she had left. How cool was that? In her office were framed photos of her featured in all the big business magazines: *Fortune, Business Week, Working Woman.* Of course she was so busy working all those years she never had time to get married or have kids. And then when she got around to it and met my father, she wasn't, as she likes to say, "a spring chicken any-more." Or as I heard her say to her best friend, Wendy, when I wasn't supposed to be listening, "a fertile myrtle." And people who aren't fertile myrtles don't always have the easiest time having babies. To make matters worse my dad was six-teen years older than her. That's why I was her gift, her bless-ing, her miracle, her baby, her angel. And that's why she'd do anything to give me what I wanted, which sometimes seemed more like what *she* wanted.

Chapter 2

"I WANT TO GO LOOK at the pony next week," Mom told Dad.

"What about Regan? Have you even asked her?"

"Of course she'll want to. Are you kidding?"

Dad sighed. "What if we didn't show that much this summer? What if we enjoyed some time away from the shows? Maybe we could take a few trips as a family, go to the Vineyard, or even Europe if you want to. Remember that place we stayed in the South of France?"

"You make it sound like we can just take off for Europe for weeks at a time," Mom said. "You know we can't—not *now*."

Not now. I wasn't supposed to know what they were talking about, but I did. Mom was sick again. I'd had my suspicions from whispered conversations, late night phone calls, and the way Dad kept asking Mom how she was feeling and giving her concerned looks, but now I knew for sure. I pushed my back up against the wall, letting the molding edge dig into my shoulder, to feel something other than scared. Moms weren't supposed to be like a pony, owned or leased for a few years until you outgrew them. They were supposed to be for life.

"So we could go for a few days at a time," Dad tried. "Or the Vineyard? We'll rent a place?"

"This late in the season? We won't find anything. Just say yes to this so I can make the arrangements."

"Do I even have to sign off on this? You're going to do what you want anyway." Dad's voice wasn't angry, just resigned. He had endless patience, especially with Mom.

"So say yes," Mom said. "Be on my side."

"How could I be anything but on your side?" Dad answered.

I didn't have to listen any longer to know Mom would get her way. She always does. Plus, I didn't want them to come out and see me. Then we'd have to have the what-did-she-hear-how-much-does-she-know conversation. I might do something heinous like cry. Any good eavesdropper knew the trick was to vamoose before the conversation got even close to wrapping up.

I tiptoed back to my bedroom and texted Hailey right away. I typed as fast as I could, pushing Mom's reoccurrence out of my mind: **u won't believe it. mom wants us 2 go look at tyler...**

Hailey wrote back: **woodland's tried and true????**
yup.

It was a moment till she texted back. **wow.**
will u come with?

It took a lot longer for her response: **have 2 ask my mom, but want 2.**

I felt like there was more Hailey might be thinking, but maybe they were things she felt she couldn't say to me. Hailey had a really nice pony, but he wasn't fancy like my ponies, and certainly not fancy like Tyler. She never said as much, but I knew Hailey wished she had a different, fancier pony to ride. But her younger sister rode, too, and her parents were divorced and they didn't have all that much money to spend on ponies. And there was also Hailey's singing. She had an amazing voice and had been taking voice lessons since she was eight. Someday she wanted to have a career as a recording artist.

cool, I typed back. **c u at the barn 2moro.**

I crawled into bed, knowing I wouldn't be able to sleep for a long while, and also knowing Mom would be coming in soon. She came in every night to kiss me. Sometimes I pretended to be asleep so I didn't have to talk to her. Sometimes I *was* asleep, but I still knew she'd been there. Sometimes I thought if I didn't need her it wouldn't hurt as much if she died, but that was probably entirely stupid.

This time it was a half hour later. I didn't pretend to close my eyes.

"What are you still doing up?" she asked.

"I don't know. Just thinking."

"About West Salem?"

"I guess." West Salem, our first big show after Devon, was two weeks away. But if anything, I'd been thinking about Mom's doctor's appointment this past week and how from listening to her and Dad I now knew for sure she'd lied to me about what her oncologist had said: "You know, the usual, a few things to keep an eye on..."

Would it be so wrong to just be honest with me? Every day the headlines were filled with terrorist plots and school shootings, what was a little cancer?

Mom leaned close to me now and I could smell peach from one of the ProduX wrinkle reducers. "I have something to tell you, but I'm not sure I should tell you now because then you'll never be able to sleep..."

I wondered, could Mom actually be about to tell me the truth? I sat up a little and looked straight at her. I took a deep breath—did I really want to know?

"Your father and I've decided we should go look at Woodland's Tried and True." It was pretty dark in the room, but I didn't need to see her to know she was smiling. She grabbed my hands. Suddenly she seemed more like Hailey than my mom. "Can you imagine? Riding Tyler?"

"That would be amazing," I said, but I wasn't sure my voice was excited enough. I should have been squealing, almost bursting. Like she was.

"You're scared of the pressure," Mom said. "I know the pony's won a lot..."

"That's not it."

"Then what is it?"

"Did the doctor really say everything was fine?"

"Regan, come on, you're always so serious. Let's talk about ponies, okay? Don't you want to try Tyler?"

"I guess so."

"See," she said, poking me gently in the side. "I knew it. And if we end up buying him you'll have so much fun. Just think—you and Tyler? You'll be unstoppable! This summer is going to be the greatest ever."

I let her kiss me. I could have called her on it. I could have demanded she tell me the truth. I could have said I knew this summer wasn't going to be the greatest ever. That, at best, it would be the summer the cancer came back. That, at worst, it could be the summer my mother died.

Chapter 3

MOM ARRANGED TO USE the company's private plane to go try Tyler. When she sold ProduX, they hired her to stay on in a consulting role, which means she still gets some of the perks. We drove from our apartment on the Upper East Side of Manhattan to the barn in Pound Ridge where we picked up Hailey and my trainer, Susie.

The moment I got out of the car all the barn dogs, mostly Susie's, came running. A few initial barks turned into wagging tails. I patted heads, accepted lick-kisses, and picked up Squirt, a dachshund-pug mix. I had fallen in love with Squirt when he was a rescue dog Susie was fostering. I'd begged my mother to let me have him. I'd even snuck him home once in my backpack. But she said no and Susie ended up keeping him, so at least I got to see him a lot.

Jane was already on a pony, even though it was just past eight o'clock on Saturday and most kids were still under the covers. Hailey and I went to say hi to Jane while Susie got her stuff together. Jane rode up next to us and swung her leg forward in front of the saddle to tighten her girth.

"What time are you supposed to be there?" She pulled her girth up a hole.

"Eleven."

"Did you see the photo of Ike on *The Chronicle* website?" Jane asked.

I exchanged glances with Hailey. We'd both seen the photo and agreed not to say anything to Jane about it. Jane had brought Ike, whose show name was Impromptu, along from a ragged green pony that had a bad habit of veering left at the jumps, trying to jump the standard, to a polished, consistent winner who always jumped the middle. She had her heart set on showing him at Devon, but her dad had sold him weeks before. With his new rider, Ike had been medium pony champion. In the photo, his new rider was grinning and the championship ribbon fluttered from Ike's bridle. There was no mention of Jane and how hard she'd worked with Ike anywhere in the article that went with the photo.

"Yeah, we saw it," I admitted.

"That should have been me." Jane shrugged, but I could tell that she was just trying to act strong.

Jane's dad, Tommy, came out of the barn and called to Jane as he walked into the ring. He had on his usual Tommy uniform—he always wore jeans and a polo shirt, a different color for every day. One time when we were hanging out at Jane's we snuck into his room and looked in his dresser and there they were, about twenty different polos in a rainbow of colors. Today's was a deep blue.

Jane's dad was a trainer and also worked out of the farm. He and Susie started sharing some clients and now they worked together a lot. Jane's father bought green ponies really cheap and brought them along, had Jane show them, and when they got good he sold them for much more than he bought them for. Riding lots of different ponies had made Jane a really good rider, but she never got to keep a pony very long—the minute it started winning, they sold it. Like Ike. I would have invited Jane to come with Hailey and me, but Tommy would never let Jane take a day off to go look at a pony he wasn't going to buy.

Tommy dropped a vertical down a few holes. "You ready to jump, Janie?"

"Have fun," Jane whispered before she moved off the rail and departed into a canter.

From the barn, we drove over to the Westchester airport. Hailey had never been on the plane before and I saw her eyes get real big as we stepped aboard. Sometimes I forgot that things I was used to were totally 'wow' to other people. Inside it was not like a regular plane. Instead of aisles of cramped seats there were just two rows of chairs facing each other. There was also good food like fresh fruit and really yummy chocolate-chunk cookies.

"Do we have to put on our seatbelts?" she asked.

"Just for takeoff and landing," I told her.

Susie sat down next to Mom in the row across from us and they started chatting. Since I'd started riding with Susie, she and Mom had become pretty good friends. Mom said she and Susie had more in common than people thought. Even though Mom graduated from one of the top business schools in the country and Susie didn't even go to college, they both started their own businesses. Susie had been renting stalls at the barn in Westchester, but she hoped to someday buy her own barn, and Mom often counseled her on how she could get the funds together. I wondered if Mom would tell Susie about the cancer before she told me.

The engine started and we headed off down the runway. The pilot's voice came over the PA, but it was nothing like being on a real airplane with stewardesses demonstrating how to pull down oxygen masks or making sure your seat belt was on and your seat was in the upright position. All he said was, "Cleared for takeoff. It'll be about forty-five minutes till we land. Relax and enjoy it."

"That's it?" Hailey said.

"Yeah, isn't it cool?"

She looked a little nervous and her voice quivered as she said, "I guess."

"Are you scared?"

"Nah," Hailey said.

It seemed impossible that Hailey was scared. Hailey was the bravest person I knew. She always said whatever was on her mind, which sometimes wasn't so nice, and she had sung the national anthem at last year's Pony Finals, the biggest championship show for ponies each year. When it came to riding, Hailey was equally fearless. Susie said she was probably going to be a great jumper rider. Her only problem was that sometimes she was too bold and overrode things. Susie was always trying to get her to calm down and be subtler.

"You are totally scared. I can't believe it!"

Hailey frowned. "Okay, maybe a little."

"If you're going to be the next Beyoncé, you better get used to flying."

Hailey shot me a look and stuck out her tongue. "Beyoncé? More like Debbie Harry."

Hailey was really old school when it came to music and Blondie was one of her all-time favorite bands. That was the only reason I even knew who Debbie Harry was. "Okay, well, Debbie must have flown everywhere, too."

"I know," she said. "It's just this plane's so small. Ever heard of the song 'The Day the Music Died'?"

"Nope."

"It's about the day Buddy Holly, Ritchie Valens, and The Big Bopper died in a plane crash after a concert."

"The big who?" I asked.

Hailey shook her head. "Forget it."

She put her hand onto the seat next to me and even though it felt kind of dorky, I grabbed it. "Squeeze as hard as you want," I told her. "If you're scared just squeeze, okay?"

Hailey squeezed really hard, jamming my fingers together. "Ow!" I squealed.

"You said squeeze hard!"

"Yeah, but don't kill my hand so I can never ride again."

"Then *I'll* have to ride Tyler," Hailey said, still squeezing.

We both started laughing and pretty soon we were in the air.

Chapter 4

FOR THE REST OF THE PLANE ride I kept Hailey's mind off the fact that we were a few thousand feet off the ground by going over the details for the raffle baskets we were organizing to raise money for Hailey to enter the lip sync at Pony Finals to benefit Danny and Ron's Rescue.

Danny Robertshaw and Ron Danta were two trainers and judges, who were also life partners. After the big hurricane down South, they helped find homes for lots of displaced dogs. Then, they turned those first few hundred adopted dogs into a full-fledged rescue organization. That's where Squirt came from. Since they'd started, Danny and Ron placed thousands of dogs. Hailey had two dogs from them and Jane had one, and I would have had at least one if there was any way on this earth to convince my mother to let me get a dog. Believe me, it wasn't for lack of trying. I'd begged, pleaded, argued, negotiated, and no luck. Mom liked horses, but she'd been bitten by a dog as a girl and was terrified of them. When Mom got sick the first time I stopped bothering her about a dog for a while. Then she got better and I started in again. I guess now I needed to lay off.

Everyone goes to watch the lip sync during Pony Finals. Hailey had been runner-up in it last year in her age group. In order to be in it you have to get sponsors and in addition to a trophy for the best act, there's also an award for the most money raised. An amateur rider, Kim Kolloff, came up with the idea for the lip sync as a way to encourage kids, especially the privileged ones of the show circuit, to learn about giving back. I loved doing work for Danny and Ron's. There was nothing I cared about more than animals and it was so cool to be able to raise money to help them. You might think that kids would have a hard time getting donations, but so many people in the horse show world are well-connected, and when kids ask them to help out they have a hard time saying no.

Hailey, her face white, was looking out the window as the plane climbed higher.

"Let's go over the raffle baskets." I pulled out my notes. "Basket one is the iPad, iPad case, and iTunes gift card. Basket two is the gift card to the spa and the collection of ProduX. Basket three is a pair of Pikeurs from Hadfield's, a pair of Roeckl gloves, and one of those really cool crops. Basket four is the Belle & Bow basket with two pairs of custom bows, a belt, a T-shirt, a saddle pad, a tote bag, and a charm necklace."

Hailey looked away from the window. "Those are all good."

"Yeah, but basket five is hurting. So far all we have is a bunch of horse treats and a few grooming products. Lame."

"What if we make it horse and dog? Like try to get dog treats and dog grooming products, or a gift certificate to the mobile dog grooming place?"

"Great idea." I started scribbling. "And maybe a matching horse and dog blanket? Like Bakers or turn-out sheets?"

"Or at least a really nice halter and a really nice collar?"

"Brilliant!"

I started jotting down a plan of action, feeling a bit like Mom when she plots out ideas for a new face cream. "Let's ask the grooming place for a gift card and The Clothes Horse if they'd do the blankets." The Clothes Horse made custom blankets for horses and dogs, too, and Mom happened to be a big customer. If my ponies were people, they would need walk-in closets for all their clothes.

"And if The Clothes Horse doesn't come through, we could hit up Beval for the halter and collar. Is that all the baskets?"

"One more, and I was thinking maybe riding lessons for that one. Get Susie to donate a lesson, and maybe Hugo."

"Or a free stall at a show," Hailey suggested.

"Great idea."

"Are we selling tickets at West Salem?"

"West Salem, Old Lyme, and Montclair. The drawing will be at Montclair."

"You'll probably have two mediums and a small to show if Tyler works out," Hailey said.

I shifted in my seat. If we bought Tyler, I'd have him and my other medium, Google Me (barn name Sammy), and my small pony, Playdate (barn name Drizzle). Although I was thirteen, when my birthday fell meant I was actually twelve for my riding age so I could still ride small ponies. But this was my last year with Drizzle. I didn't really want to talk about what that would be like, having three ponies, since Hailey just had Donald, so I said, "Do you think you can beat Dakota this year?"

"Uh, yeah, this year Dakota is so going down!"

Last year Hailey lost the lip sync to Dakota Pearce, a girl we really don't like. Dakota won just because she dressed and danced like she was a teenager. Some people loved it but it made me cringe.

"Jane's getting a new pony, too," Hailey said. "She was telling me about it while I was waiting for you."

"Is she excited?"

"Not really. It's another Tommy special."

The pilot's voice came over the cabin: "We're cruising over D.C. right now and should be landing at Winchester Regional in about twenty minutes."

"I might have to hold your hand again," Hailey said.

"Okay," I said.

Chapter 5

ASHBURN FARM WAS IN UPPERVILLE, Virginia, which was probably the most beautiful horse country in the whole world. Or at least the most beautiful I'd ever seen. Miles of green pastures, towering oak trees, and stone walls. It was also prime foxhunting country so you could see the hunt jumps—stone walls and log piles—on the fence lines between the farms. The trainer at Ashburn, Judy Ford, had been turning out top ponies for decades. She was a short, perky woman with a thick Southern accent.

"Welcome, y'all!" she called to us as we got out of the rental car and came into the barn. "We're just getting Tyler tacked up."

Tyler was inside the barn on the crossties. Even just standing there, he was gorgeous. Beautiful shiny coat, cresty neck, and wise eyes. He turned his head to look at us and it was like *he* was checking *us* out, seeing if we were worthy of owning him. The groom put Tyler's bridle on and led him out to the ring. Bethany Sowles, Tyler's owner, was already in the ring, riding a horse. She was one of the best pony jocks in the country and I'd watched her win on Tyler and her other ponies many times. She brought the horse she was on down to a walk and Judy told her to come get on Tyler.

"Y'all know Bethany?" Judy asked us.

"Yes," Mom said. "Nice to see you again."

Hailey and I said at practically the same time, "Hi!" and then looked at each other and giggled.

Bethany was definitely too tall for Tyler—her legs almost reached past his belly. When she picked up a trot, it felt like we all—Susie, Mom, Hailey, and me—took a deep breath. Tyler was an awesome mover. He barely flexed his knees at all, his toes gliding across the ground. He always won the under saddles, but unlike many ponies who were good movers, he jumped amazingly, too.

If Tyler had been green or unknown, we would have wanted to watch him do a lot, but we'd seen him go plenty at the shows. Bethany jumped one course and then she came into the middle of the ring and hopped off. She slid off her saddle and held Tyler while Susie and I put on my saddle.

"You're going to love him," Bethany said. "I'm going to miss him so much. You'll win everything on him." She said it like it was already set that we were buying him.

Susie gave me a leg up and I tightened my girth. Tyler felt big for a medium pony, bigger than my other medium, Sammy. "Just trot around a bit, and get used to him," Susie told me.

I shortened my reins and picked up a trot. My shoulders felt tight and I tried to tell myself to relax. I hated that

Bethany was watching. But soon I pretty much forgot about her. Tyler had the nicest trot and his canter was like sitting on a cloud. He was so smooth and comfortable. He also carried his head and neck in just the right spot, not too low and not too high. I didn't have to work at all to get him framed up.

"Looks good," Susie said. "How's he feel?"

"Really nice," I answered.

Susie changed one of the jumps to a cross-rail and told me to start over it. Tyler was just as smooth to the jumps. His pace never changed, which made it easy to find the distances. Usually it took me a little while to get used to a pony and to put in a good round, but the first course I jumped with Tyler felt like it could have won at any big show. In the air over the jumps he was slow and smooth, and getting down the lines was easy because he had a big stride.

Susie had me jump two more courses. It wasn't a fluke—those were just as good as the first. But instead of feeling excited, I felt like I was an actress in a movie about a girl who's excited because she's getting the pony of her dreams.

"Great job riding him," Susie said. "Do you want to do any more or do you think you've gotten a good sense of him?"

"I think I'm okay," I said. "He seems really straightforward."

"You look beautiful on him," Judy said.

I looked over to where Mom and Hailey were standing at the side of the ring. Hailey was a wisp of a girl, really small and skinny. She hated being small because everyone always assumed she was younger than her age. Sometimes people even asked if she was my little sister because we both had the same medium brown hair color. But Hailey made up for her small size with her big personality.

Mom was beaming at me. She looked perfectly healthy. Her hair was thick and shiny and for a mom she wore pretty cool clothes. Today she wore designer jeans and a flowy black shirt. No one would know she was sick. Cancer was like that—it ate you from the inside out.

I forced myself to smile back and tried to tell myself that I was crazy for not wanting Tyler. I had hoped that, when I rode him, I'd realize how much I wanted him, but it felt like the opposite was happening. I wanted him even less now that I knew how easy he was to ride.

I got off and patted him. It wasn't like I didn't like him—of course I liked him. Who wouldn't like him? It was just that he wasn't what would save this summer. No pony could do that.

The groom came to get him and take him into the barn. Hailey and I followed with some carrots Mom had brought.

"That looked amazing," Hailey said. "What did it feel like?"

"It felt really good. He's got such a huge stride you land into a line and don't even have to move up at all."

Hailey looked back to where Mom and Susie were talking to Judy. "You're totally getting him. Wow."

"I don't know," I said. "We'll have to see what my mom says."

But I already knew. Hailey was right. Mom was talking about setting up a pre-purchase vet exam, wiring the money, and how soon we could get Tyler to the farm. I knew she wanted me to have him before West Salem.

Hailey kept looking at Tyler, but I was sneaking glances at Mom. I wondered when she would start chemo.

Chapter 6

I WENT TO THE PROFESSIONAL Children's School. Last year I went to a regular private school but Mom decided we should switch to PCS because they were really accommodating to students' schedules. At my old school, I was sort of special because of my riding, but at PCS *everyone* was special. There were dancers, singers, musicians, figure skaters, actors, models, athletes. In one classroom you had someone who won an Olympic Medal, someone who played at Carnegie Hall, and someone who just shot a movie with Brad Pitt. And I wasn't the only rider either. Caitlyn Rogers, who rode with Susie, and does the big eq, went to PCS. And so did Olivia Martin, who rode with Hugo Fines, and who showed against me in the ponies.

Most weekdays Mom picked me up and we drove out to the barn. Sometimes, if Mom had meetings, my babysitter, Lauren, drove me. Dad didn't drive me much except on weekends because he had to be at the office. On weekends we were usually at our other house in Darien. After Mom sold ProduX,

I overheard her telling Dad he should quit his job as a patent attorney if he wanted to. She said plenty of people in their sixties retire and start doing things they always wanted to do.

"I like my work," Dad had said.

"But you could do anything you wanted now," Mom had replied.

Dad smiled. "I think I'll keep doing what I'm doing, thank you."

When Mom got sick the first time, he suggested he quit so he could be around for her 24/7. That time she said no way was he quitting.

It's a fifty-minute drive to the barn if there was no traffic and I usually did some of my homework in the car.

"Hi, Mom," I said as I jumped into the passenger seat.

"Good day?" she asked.

"Fine." That was about all there ever was to say about school, unless I was complaining about a test. I didn't have many close friends at school, but that wasn't the biggest deal because going to PCS wasn't about making or having friends. It was about getting what you had to get done so you could live your other life. Olivia was probably my best friend at school and once we were out of school she would much rather hang out with the kids at her barn, and I'd much rather hang out with Hailey and Jane.

"Are you excited?" Mom asked.

Tyler had arrived at the farm the day before. We'd let him rest from the trip from Virginia, but today I was going to ride him. Jane's new pony was arriving, too, so it was going to be a busy day.

"Definitely," I said, trying to be that actress in the movie again.

"I talked to Susie this morning and we both agreed we'll just see how it goes—no pressure. If you ride him as well as you did when we tried him, you'll show him at West Salem, but if not, there's no rush, we have the whole summer."

Before I thought about it, I blurted out, "If there's no rush, then why did you kill yourself to get him here so fast?" I regretted how ungrateful I sounded, but more than that I regretted the words I'd used—*kill yourself*. When your mom had cancer, throwing around phrases like 'kill yourself' or 'I'd rather die' wasn't recommended.

"Regan," Mom said sharply. "I got him here so fast for you."

We were quiet for a while before I decided to ask, "Do you have to have more chemo, or another surgery?" The words spilled out, surprising even me that I'd said them. So much for the benefits of remaining in the dark.

Mom glanced sideways at me and then quickly back to the road. "How did you know it's back?"

"I have ears."

She sighed. "We're not sure about the treatment yet. I have to have another CT scan."

"Were you just not going to tell me?"

"Of course I was going to, honey."

"And now you're going to tell me it's no big deal, right?"

Mom checked her side-mirror and then switched lanes. "No, I'm going to tell you I'm going to be fine."

That was Mom's attitude on everything—if anyone could

do it, she could. Start a successful business—check. Sell business for millions—check. Find man to marry—check. Have child at age 43—check. Beat cancer...

"But I read on the internet that sometimes when cancer comes back it's worse than before." I still didn't quite understand how you could even get the kind of cancer Mom had again when she'd had everything removed that had cancer in it. Her first surgery had taken out her ovaries, uterus, fallopian tubes, cervix—everything you saw on that inside-of-a-woman diagram in human development class. But I guess the cancer was like dogs you hear about that get separated from their owners on a trip and somehow make it home months later, having traveled thousands of miles to get back.

"Listen to you, all gloom and doom. And sometimes it just needs one more quick dose to knock it back for good. I beat this once and I'll beat it again. Will you promise me you'll stop googling ovarian cancer?"

"I googled ovarian cancer recurrence," I said.

"Stop googling period!"

I glanced at Mom. After the chemo her hair had grown back kind of different. It had a curl to it now. She also kept it much shorter—it reached just barely past her ears where before the cancer it had been shoulder-length. If it had been me, I would have grown it back as long as possible just to prove I could. But it was like Mom knew that it was just a matter of time before she would lose it again.

Chapter 7

WHEN WE GOT TO THE BARN, Mom headed right to Tyler's stall. "Aren't you coming?" she asked when I didn't follow.

"I'm just gonna throw my stuff in the tack room first."

"Okay."

Jane was in the tack room, putting away clean saddle pads. "Tyler's so beautiful! You're so lucky!"

"Thanks," I said. Although I didn't feel lucky. How could anyone whose mother had cancer be considered lucky? I was the complete opposite of lucky, actually. There was a poster somewhere of a girl sitting next to her mother getting chemo and underneath it were the words: COMPLETE OPPOSITE OF LUCKY. But Jane didn't know the cancer was back.

"I bet you can't wait to ride him."

"Yeah."

"I can't wait to see him go."

I tried to change the subject. "You're getting another pony today, too, right?"

Jane made a face. "Dad says he's nice, but he always says that."

"You must miss Ike."

"Yeah," Jane said, not meeting my eye. "I mean it would have been awesome to have him for the summer... or part of the summer anyway."

"Hailey's not here yet?" I asked.

Jane shook her head. Hailey went to a public school a few towns over and didn't get out until three-thirty. And on Tuesday and Thursday she didn't come to the barn at all because she had her voice lessons. I hated those days. Lessons were no fun without her.

"I guess I'm going to go see Tyler," I told Jane. "See you in the ring."

It was time to start being the movie actress again. I'd decided it was a TV movie, probably on the Disney Channel. Mom had a friend who produced those kinds of movies. Like any other horse movie, they would get all the horse stuff wrong. Like the pony who would play Tyler, the ultimate show pony, would be a skinny Arab with a dish face. And they'd have him wearing a Western rope halter. That kind of stuff drove Hailey, Jane and me crazy.

Mom was still at Tyler's stall talking to Martha. Susie had different grooms that worked for her, but Martha worked only for us. Mom said it was better for our ponies to always get full attention. All I could say is it was a good thing I loved Martha.

"Martha says he's really sweet and very clean in his stall," Mom informed me.

"Great," I said, trying to perfect my TV movie girl smile. TVMG would care about every little cute thing Tyler did, even where he pooped in his stall.

"Hi, Martha," I said.

"He's beautiful, Regan," she said. "You are one lucky girl."

"I know," I said, not sure how many more times in one day I could stand to be told I was lucky.

I hadn't even looked at Tyler yet and I turned toward him. If Hailey or Jane were me, they would have felt something powerful when they looked at him. They would have felt like owning him was a dream come true. TVMG would run to him, wrap her arms around him, and breathe in the smell of his fur. TVMG would imagine all the blue ribbons they would win. But when I looked at him I didn't feel anything but a little sad. We were like those arranged marriages you read about in books about long ago times, or other countries. Forced together and not in love.

"Look," Mom said, pointing to the nameplate on Tyler's door. I hadn't noticed it yet. It read: WOODLAND'S TRIED AND TRUE, OWNED BY REGAN STERNLICHT.

"How did you get that made up so fast?"

Mom smiled. "You know I work quickly! The second I heard he was for sale I knew we would have this pony."

I looked away from the nameplate and Tyler, feeling sick to my stomach. The more Mom wanted me to want Tyler, the more I *didn't* want him. Was she doing all this so fast because she knew she only had a few months to live?

Hailey and her mom walked into the barn and thank god

Hailey didn't tell me how lucky I was. I don't think I could have stood that. She had to hurry to get on because Susie was really strict about us being on time.

Hailey's mom stayed for a few minutes before she went off to her afternoon shift at the hospital, where she worked as a nurse in the maternity ward.

"Full moon last night," she said to Mom. "We had twelve delivering, including two sets of twins!"

"Busy night," Mom said.

"That's for sure." Mrs. Mullins turned her eyes to Tyler. "So... this is the new pony?"

"Woodland's Tried and True," Mom said, lighting up. "Isn't he gorgeous!"

Martha was tacking up Tyler. She had a spotless baby pad on his back and was about to put on one of my saddles. I listened to Mom and Mrs. Mullins, trying to hear any hints about Mom's condition. Maybe Mom would say something revealing by accident. Like, you'd buy a pony like this for your daughter, too, if you knew you were dying.

Mrs. Mullins patted Tyler on the neck. "Wow. He *is* pretty."

Martha slid my saddle on and tightened the girth. Martha had a bad burn on the side of her face that reached up onto her head and so most of the time she wore either a baseball hat or a bandana to cover up her patchy hair in that spot. Today she wore a pink bandana. Most people didn't know how she had gotten the burn and were too afraid to ask, but Mom had asked her so we knew it was from getting too close to a wood-burning stove when she was really little. I guess in that way Martha was the complete opposite of lucky, too. I wondered what was worse—being burned as a child, or your mom having the really bad kind of cancer. I say really bad kind, because I'd learned there were many types. Cancer people liked to be all cancer-solidarity-rah-rah, but the fact of the matter was some people had the faint, curable kind and others, like Mom, had the nasty, Satan-inside-you kind.

Martha put on Tyler's bridle and led him to the mounting block outside the barn. I followed, leaving Mrs. Mullins and Mom to chat for a few more minutes.

Hailey came out behind me with Donald and Jane was getting on Coco, another one of her family's "project" ponies.

Susie was already in the ring, helping Francie Martinez with a young mare that Susie had imported from Europe and was working with to sell. When Francie was a junior rider she used to train with Susie at the farm Susie worked at before she started her own stable. Francie had just finished her junior year at Skidmore College. In a few days, she was headed to Los Angeles for the summer to work for one of the biggest trainers on the West Coast. Susie had helped Francie get the job so she could see a different part of the country and be with her longtime boyfriend, Colby, who lived out there.

"Once more," Susie told Francie. "And this time don't help her so much. If she wants to pull you down to the jumps, let her figure it out herself a little. She's not always going to get such an accurate ride and she has to get used to that."

Francie picked up a canter and started the course. It was a straightforward hunter course with two jumps set on a line on both of the long sides of the ring, two jumps set on a line across one diagonal of the ring, and a single oxer across the other diagonal. The jumps were set at three-foot six-inches, higher than I'd ever jumped in my life, but not that high for someone as good as Francie. The mare was a bay with a big head. She was probably going to be an equitation horse or a jumper if she didn't turn out to be calm enough for the equitation. Francie hardly ever made a mistake and it was amazing to watch her ride. I could only hope that someday I'd be as good as she was.

"Great," Susie said. "Perfect ride."

Francie brought the mare down to a walk. "Hi, girls," she said to us. "Regan, what do you think of your new pony?"

"He's great," I said.

"Don't let your head get too big, okay?" Francie loosened her reins, letting the mare stretch her neck. "Just because you've got a super fancy pony doesn't mean you're automatically going to win on him. You still have to ride."

"I know," I said.

I didn't mind Francie talking to me like that. Sometimes it felt like even Susie could be too easy on me, like she was afraid if she ever yelled at me, it might make Mom mad and she'd risk losing us as a client. After all, we were her biggest client. Just because I was thirteen didn't mean I didn't know how much my ponies cost or what it meant to someone like Susie. Although I didn't ask outright how much Tyler cost, I heard people mumbling that he was for sale for $350,000, which meant a $35,000 commission to Susie, not to mention all that we paid in boarding and training fees. Francie never seemed to think about how what she said would go over with

Mom or me. I liked her even more for that and I wished she were working for Susie for the summer instead of going to L.A.

When Jane came into the ring, Susie told us to pick up a trot. She worked us on the flat first. Her big thing, when it came to me and Tyler, was telling me not to overdo things. "He has a big trot but that doesn't mean you have to post so high," she said.

As we were warming up, Francie came back into the ring on foot to help lower the jumps.

We trotted a small cross-rail and then cantered a single vertical on a circle. Tyler felt just as easy as when I tried him. I kept waiting—almost wishing—he'd speed up or maybe spook at a jump, but he was perfect. It might be more fun if I had to work at it to figure him out—if it didn't come so easily.

Next, Susie came up with a course and we rode it one at a time. Hailey went first and overrode the first line. It was five strides and Hailey pushed Donald so much she almost left out a stride and did four.

"Hailey, he has a *huge* stride," Susie told her. "You always book down that first line. You don't need to, okay?"

"I know." She shook her head at her mistake. "I don't know why I always do that."

Susie continued, "You know your pony doesn't do well in the hacks so if you want a shot at champion or reserve you have to do it from being consistent over fences. That's just the bottom line."

Donald, whose show name was Imagine Dragon, was a big-hearted pony. He never stopped or spooked but he was plain looking, a downright bad mover, and a flat but good jumper.

"Jane, you're up," Susie said.

Jane picked up a canter on Coco, a chestnut pony with four white socks. All of Jane's ponies had issues and Coco's issue was her lead changes. She jumped everything great, but when she landed on the wrong lead after the jumps, she raced through her changes, practically bolting. Tommy thought that Coco's previous owner had practiced too many changes on her so for the first few months they had Coco, Jane would trot through every lead change instead of doing a flying change. They had only recently started doing them again.

"Remember not to make a big deal of the changes," Susie warned Jane. "Just ease her over with a little inside leg and once you feel her in your outside rein, ask with a subtle out-side leg."

Jane jumped the first line and Coco landed on the correct lead. She continued around the course and after the oxer down the diagonal, Coco landed on the wrong lead. Jane did just what Susie had told her and Coco changed leads flaw-lessly.

"Perfect," Susie said. "That's her harder one, too, left to right. The next one will be even easier."

Susie was right—after the next line Coco swapped like an old pro. Jane brought her down to a walk and patted her.

"Awesome," Susie said. "All that hard work and patience is paying off, isn't it?"

"Yeah," Jane said, still patting Coco.

"You just need to remember to do the same thing at the

show—easy-does-it or you'll get her all worked up. Your dad's going to be psyched when we tell him how good she was today."

Usually Tommy would be in the ring, but he was picking up the new pony.

Susie turned to me. "All right, Regan, same course."

Chapter 8

THANKS TO HAILEY GOING FIRST and serving as an example, I knew not to move up to make the five strides down the first line. I turned to the diagonal line and found the distances just right. I was maybe a touch deep to the oxer on the other diagonal, but I finished off well on the other outside line. I was still cantering my circle when Jane's older brother, Alex, roared up on his motorbike. Most of the horses at the barn were used to Alex riding around, but Tyler wasn't. He spooked and jumped away from the noise. It was the first thing he'd done wrong and I found myself almost happy about it. Maybe he wouldn't turn out to be so easy after all.

Susie yelled at Alex, "How many times have I told you not to come flying up to the ring like that?" Susie didn't mind Alex riding around the farm—she said it was good for the horses to get used to everything so they wouldn't spook at the shows, but he was always supposed to go slowly when he came up to the ring and barn.

Alex cut the engine and took off his helmet. "Sorry."

Alex's hair reached almost to his chin and got all tangled under his helmet. He was three years older than Jane and competed in motocross events like we competed in horse shows. He actually used to ride ponies, too—he was the family "pony jock" until Jane got old enough to take over. But Alex wasn't into riding like Jane was. He did it because he had to. That was the thing about Jane and her family—riding wasn't just for fun. It was their business.

"It's a good thing your dad's not here," Susie said to Alex.

"And you're not going to tell him, right?" Alex grinned and I got the feeling he had come up to the ring so fast because he *knew* his father wasn't around. As I looked at him, I found myself smiling, too, and I only caught myself when Susie said, "Regan, pick up a canter and do the course once more with Alex standing there with his bike. Just to make sure Tyler's okay with it."

The first time I cantered past Alex, Tyler still shied a little bit, but after that he was fine. I sighed as I brought Tyler down to a walk. That was all he was going to do and now he was going to be perfect again?

"That's good for today," Susie said. "Actually, I think that's enough for all of you. We'll jump again on Friday, but otherwise I think you all look good. Why don't you take them out for a walk around the back field."

We rode side-by-side on the path around the back pasture, passing trails that went off into the woods. There were supposed to be miles of awesome trails but we weren't allowed to go on them. When you were riding a $350,000 pony, or even a $75,000 pony like Donald, you couldn't chance it getting hurt from stepping on a rock or twisting its ankle in a groundhog hole. Hailey's mom used to ride some growing up and she always talked about how she and her friends galloped wildly through the woods. Once on vacation in France, I rode bareback on the beach and it was amazing. When we passed the trails, I always looked down them, wondering where they led.

"So what's he feel like?" Jane asked as we walked. "Does he feel as nice as he looks?"

I shrugged. "I'm sure you'll ride him." When I couldn't make it out to the barn, a lot of times Jane rode my ponies. Susie was pretty small, too, so sometimes she even rode them. "You can ride him sometime, too, Hailey. He's fun, I guess."

"You act like it's no big deal," Hailey said. "You just got the best pony in the country!"

"Hailey," Jane said.

Hailey glanced at Jane. "What?"

"Don't be so—"

I cut her off. "It's okay." I paused and then added, "I didn't really ask for him. My mom just sort of went ahead with it." I wanted to tell them that it was hard to be so excited when you knew your mom was buying you this pony because she was really sick again. But I didn't want Hailey and Jane to know yet. I didn't know enough of the details myself and it had been so nice this past year and a half not being the girl whose mom had cancer.

"You mean you don't want him?" Jane asked.

"How can you not want a pony like Tyler?" Hailey said.

I thought my friends were supposed to understand everything about me. I thought they were supposed to get it. But they couldn't get this because I was clearly crazy.

We turned back to the barn and I was relieved to see Tommy pulling in with the two-horse trailer.

"Your new pony's here," I said to Jane.

"You mean my new *project*," she said.

Chapter 9

WE RODE OVER TO WHERE Tommy had parked the trailer. As he hopped out of the truck, Jane asked, "Is he cute?"

"In an underweight, wormy kind of way." Tommy grinned at Jane.

"Dad!"

Hailey and I shared a look—poor Jane. This was going to be another extreme makeover, Tommy edition.

"But he moves great and we'll see how he jumps. I bet he—"

Jane didn't let Tommy finish his sentence. "*We'll see* how he jumps? Really, Dad?"

"Janie, have a little faith, okay?"

Tommy let down the ramp of the trailer. He looked so young and was so physically active—so unlike my dad. Tommy was always lifting the trailer ramp, moving heavy jumps, and carrying hay bales. My dad specialized in reading, working, and drinking coffee. Sometimes my dad went for long walks through Central Park, but he never went to the gym or went jogging like my friends' dads. Sometimes there would be another older dad at a school event or horse show and I'd meet eyes with the other dad's daughter and it was like we immediately knew we shared something. When Dad and I went places together, people always looked hard at us, like they were trying to figure out how we fit together. Sometimes I just wanted to call out, "Yup, I know he looks too old, but he's my dad."

Susie had come over to the trailer. She got the butt-bar and Tommy backed the pony out.

"Where did you find this one?" Susie ran her hand over the pony's dusty, white coat. The pony glanced back at Susie suspiciously. One of his eyes was blue, the other brown. I don't think I'd ever seen a pony with one blue eye before. Susie said, "Needs a few groceries, huh? But I like the blue eye—that's kind of cool."

You could see the pony's ribs. Even its hipbones stuck out. I tried not to gasp.

"Virginia Kroll bred him."

"This pony's one of Vi's?"

Virginia Kroll had once bred some of the country's best ponies. She had a famous sire that threw a lot of winners back in the eighties and nineties. But that stud died and Virginia was said to have gone more than a little batty in her old age, carelessly breeding too many ponies and not really taking care of them. I looked at the pony's feet. His hooves were long and one was split.

"Watch him trot," Tommy said.

He jogged the pony down the dirt driveway. He spooked at a shadow, skittering away and Tommy had to pull him back. But once he got him going again he did have a beautiful floating trot, almost as nice as Tyler.

"Well, Janie?" Susie said. "You might win some hacks if we can get him not to spook."

"That's good because apparently Dad's never even seen him jump," she said.

"Janie," Tommy said, leading the pony back. "Look at him. Look at those lines. He's bred to jump. It's just his brain we need to worry about."

Jane forced a smile. She slid off Coco and led her into the barn. Jane's shoulders were a little rounded and I felt even worse, sitting there on glossy Tyler.

The pony's coat was inches thick from living in the fields all winter. Tommy said the best thing to do was to body clip him—no amount of currying would get him shed out quickly enough. Martha was the expert body clipper in the barn and she said she had time to clip him, but the pony had to have a bath first. "I'm not ruining my clippers on layers of grime," she told Tommy.

"Jane'll get him nice and squeaky clean," Tommy said. "Don't worry."

Jane wasn't exactly pumped to give the pigpen pony the bath of a lifetime or face Martha's wrath, but Hailey and I said we'd help. I texted Mom to come a little later to pick me up, promising I'd get all my homework done.

The pony's name was Frankie. "I get it, like Old Blue Eyes," Hailey said. "That's kind of cute actually."

Jane and I gave her blank looks.

"Old Blue Eyes? Frank Sinatra?" She looked exasperated.

I shrugged. "I still have no idea what you're talking about."

"Me neither," Jane said.

Hailey sighed like she didn't know what to do with us. "Frank Sinatra was a famous singer from the fifties. Like the Jay-Z of today. People called him Old Blue Eyes because he had really blue eyes."

In the wash stall, we filled up two buckets of warm sudsy water and then we each took a sponge to a part of Frankie's body. I started on his hind end. Especially because he was white, the dirt showed up even more, quickly turning the suds brown.

"Oh my god is he gross."

"I know." With her forearm Jane wiped suds off her cheek. She shook her head. "What a mess. Thanks, Dad."

I didn't mind dealing with Frankie and Hailey didn't seem to either. So without saying anything we worked extra hard, soaping and rinsing, and letting Jane slack off a little. Hailey sang a song called "New York, New York," which Jane and I had actually heard before, and Hailey told us that Frank Sinatra had made it famous. Hailey's voice was gorgeous—I loved listening to her sing. Each time we sprayed Frankie off the water ran brown. He was surprisingly good about being bathed and even let us soap up his face. He lowered his head so I could get his forelock.

"He's really good for a pony who hasn't had many baths," I said.

"No kidding," Hailey said as she went to get a sweat scraper.

We rinsed him off for the third or fourth time; I had lost track. This time the water ran clear. Hailey scraped off the extra water with the sweat scraper and I handed Jane a towel. She worked on his legs while I dried his face. He leaned into me as I toweled him and then he sneezed into the towel. He seemed grateful for the attention.

"I think he likes being taken care of." He poked his nose out to me again. "Do you want me to rub your face more?" I rubbed under his jaw and he stretched his neck out, loving it.

We took him for a walk in the sun to dry off and when he was bone dry we presented him to Martha. She had her big clippers out and oil to periodically clean them. "He better be super clean," she said with a smile. "The clippers don't lie." She plugged the clippers into the extension cord. "Don't put him on the cross-ties yet. Hold him while I turn them on. Let's see what he thinks."

She switched on the clippers. Frankie didn't even flinch at the buzzing sound. Martha held them up against his neck so he could feel the vibration. He looked at us with a funny expression, like he was wondering why we were making such a big deal about clippers. Again, it was weird. Why would a pony that was used to living in a field, probably only pulled in every once in a while to have a saddle thrown on his back, be so calm about being clipped?

"Now for the real test."

Martha started with one line on his neck. I wasn't sure whether the test was seeing whether he would be good when she clipped him, or seeing whether he was clean. But we passed on both fronts; he remained happily still as the pure white strip of hair fell to the ground.

"Spick-and-span. Good job, girls. You can probably put him on the cross-ties if you want."

"I don't mind holding him," I said. "Just in case." I didn't really think he'd need to be held, but I liked him. It was almost like he'd singled me out the way he'd asked me to keep rubbing his face. I should have been spending my time with my new pony, but that was the last thing I wanted to do. Hailey and Jane hung around with me. We liked Martha a lot and she was really good with the horses. She knew things no one else did and every time we were with her we learned new things, like how to poultice a hoof or how to make an emergency twitch out of a lead rope.

I asked her, "I don't think we've ever had a horse with a blue eye in the barn. What's the deal with that?"

"It's usually only in white or paint horses, horses with a bald face."

"Can they see just as well?"

"Yup. People used to think it meant they were blind in that eye, but it's not true. Some horses have two blue eyes."

Martha wielded the clippers like a chef at a Japanese steak house. Before long, half of one side of his body was done. He was good for all of it, even his stomach, which could be ticklish. Martha moved to his hind end, pausing after she did a strip. She stopped and peered closely at what she'd just done. I was sure she'd found a patch of dirt we'd missed.

"Look at this," she said.

I took a hesitant step closer, bracing myself for the grubby, brown patch we'd missed. Martha was running her finger over the spot.

"A brand," I said.

"Yup."

Jane leaned over my shoulder. The brand was a small, half-moon with what looked like a tiny triangle over it.

Hailey wiggled between Martha and me. "Vi's ponies don't have brands, do they?"

Martha dusted some loose hair off Frankie. Her shirt was covered in white hair. "Not that I know of."

Jane went to tell Tommy, who was in the ring teaching Hailey's sister and another younger pony kid. He must have been with Susie because, a few moments later, they both came to take a look.

"Strange," Tommy said, examining the brand.

"What do you think it means?" Jane asked.

"That he isn't one of Vi's crop, I guess."

"Did she give you paperwork?" Susie asked.

"She said she was going to try to find his registration papers."

I couldn't stop looking at the half-moon. It was pretty, but also sort of ominous looking, almost like he was owned by people who had practiced witchcraft, which I knew was a ridiculous thought. "If he isn't one of Vi's, then where's he from?"

"I don't know," Tommy said, shrugging. "I'm not sure it matters either."

He and Susie headed back off down the aisle. Martha started the clippers again. I reached out one more time and ran my finger along the outline of the brand, the size of a small plum. How could we not find out where he was from?

Chapter 10

THE NIGHT BEFORE WEST SALEM Mom and Dad sat me down. Dad did all the talking. Mom was clearly annoyed to be telling me. She had probably tried to convince him that they should wait till after the show and he'd insisted they tell me now.

Mom's CT scan results had come back and the docs had formulated a plan. They were going to do a course of chemo to see if they could reduce the tumors. The problem was the tumors were on her intestines and to get to them they might have to remove too much of her intestines. If the chemo worked it might shrink the tumors and get them to pull away from the intestines enough so they could just remove the tumors. She'd have chemo once every three weeks for a few cycles and then they'd do another CT scan to see if they could do the surgery.

"Okay," I said.

"Questions?" Dad asked.

"I guess not."

"I want you to put all this aside," Mom added. "It's not your job to worry. You focus on the show."

I nodded. "Yup, okay."

I went back to my room, feeling paralyzed. I didn't feel like telling Hailey. I didn't feel like crying. I didn't know what I felt like. I lay on my bed for a long time, wishing I had a dog to snuggle with. Then I wouldn't feel so alone. I wondered if other only children felt lonely or if it was just only children of cancer patients. Finally I got up, brushed my teeth, and put on my pajamas. I went back into the family room and told Mom and Dad I was going to bed.

I told my mom, "I really want to get my sleep so I thought I'd say good-night and then you wouldn't have to come in later, you know? I just want to get my rest for tomorrow."

"Oh," Mom said, clearly pretending not to be hurt. "Sure. That makes total sense."

I slunk back to my room, feeling awful for what I'd just done.

* * *

West Salem Farm is an hour from our apartment—it's one of the closest shows we do all year. Mom had to work late so we stayed in the city on Friday night instead of going out to Darien. We left our apartment at six in the morning. Manhattan at that time was totally dead. The streets were empty except for the occasional yellow streak of a cab. It was so quiet that if you listened you could actually hear the streetlights clicking from green to yellow to red. The only people out were the dog-people, men and women dressed in sweatpants and fleece vests trailing their labs, boxers, and pugs, and the joggers.

"Shoot," Mom said, as we pulled onto FDR Drive. "I forgot the carrots. I bought a whole bunch for Tyler... that is, if he's good."

"I'm sure Susie has some for the whole barn." Usually Mom's devotion to making sure my ponies were well-carroted seemed really sweet, but right then it was annoying.

We got to the show at just after seven. Lots of people were already out riding, preparing their horses for the day of showing. Most riders had Patagonia or North Face windbreakers on, some in bright colors. It would warm up by midday, but the temperature still hovered around fifty, the air brisk. A few of the warm-up rings out front were open for lungeing, and horses and ponies cantered circles around grooms.

At Susie's stalls in one of the temporary tents, Martha was grooming Tyler. Country music played in the background. Martha was originally from Tennessee and had made her way east following grooming jobs.

We'd stopped at Starbucks and picked up coffees for everyone, including Martha's double espresso and Susie's skinny latte.

"You are my savior," Martha said as Mom handed her the coffee.

"How's Tyler doing?" Mom asked.

"Oh, this old pro knows his way around a horse show," she said. "He got off the trailer yesterday and *yawned*. He's done this a few times all right."

While Mom and Martha were chatting, I slipped into the

tack room to get my helmet out of my tack trunk. Jane's trunk was open, which meant she was out riding. Hailey didn't have to come until nine since Donald was her only pony and he didn't need to be ridden before he showed.

"Do you think Regan's nervous?" I heard Martha ask Mom from the grooming stall.

"Probably a little. You know everyone's going to be watching today."

"She'll do great—she always does."

"I hope so," Mom said.

There was a pause and then Martha added, "I hope it's all right to say something... Susie mentioned about the cancer being back. I'm really sorry to hear it."

So Mom had told Susie. It was officially public, which meant Jane and Hailey either already knew, or would soon.

"Thank you, Martha," Mom said in what I recognized as her professional tone. She had a way of talking about her cancer that made it seem like she was talking about someone else, her sister or a friend perhaps.

We were in a really weird phase of cancer treatment, where Mom would look fine for a while, like nothing was wrong. I remembered this phase. It was the pretend-this-won't-change-our-life phase, now with an added dash of is-this-really-going-to-be-it-this-time?

I walked back to the grooming stall. Martha dipped a brush in water and was flattening down Tyler's mane.

"When's the braider coming?" Mom asked.

"Right after the lesson."

Jane rode up on Coco, and Susie and Tommy whizzed up

in the golf cart seconds behind her. Katie Whitt, an amateur rider, rode up to the barn after them. Katie went to NYU and had two really nice hunters with Susie. Hektor came and took Katie's horse.

Sweat covered Coco and steam was rising from her neck and back.

"How was she?" I asked Jane, although it was pretty clear she hadn't been that good.

"A little fresh," Jane said.

"Let's get Tyler tacked up," Susie said to Martha. "And where's Manuel?" She called out to one of the other grooms, "Manuel?" He appeared and Susie said, "Jane needs help with Coco because she's got to get on Drizzle." To me, Susie added, "I thought Jane could get on Drizzle and Sammy so you could concentrate on Tyler."

"Sure," I said, even though I hated the idea of my friend getting my ponies ready for me. It made her seem like she was another employee, like Martha. And like everyone at the barn's job was to make the Sternlicht family happy, or else Susie would lose her biggest client.

Mom handed Susie her coffee and Susie thanked her. Then Susie came and put her arm around my shoulder. "Let's take this pony out for a spin, huh? Make sure he doesn't have any tricks up his sleeve."

Chapter 11

OF COURSE I WOULD HAVE BEEN happy if Tyler had a few tricks up his sleeve. If he'd been spooky or fresh. If I'd had to work him down like Jane had to with Coco. But Tyler didn't have any tricks up his sleeve. He was a perfect gentleman in my lesson. After a few jumps Susie asked me how I was feeling and when I told her I felt good—not exactly the truth, but for a different reason other than whether I felt I was clicking with Tyler—she said we might as well save him for the classes ahead.

Once the horse show starts, you could find me, Hailey, and Jane at the pony ring. We stashed our backpacks with everything we needed for the day—boot polish, hairbrush, hairnets and bobby pins, crop and spurs, gloves, ChapStick, sunscreen, cell phone, protein bars and bottles of vitamin-enhanced water—at the tent next to the ring. From then on out we were either riding or watching.

The days we spent at the pony ring were the best. I wanted each day to go on forever. I loved watching pony after pony and listening to the trainers at the in gate.

I rode Sammy in the pony equitation class. Sammy was a great pony, but he wasn't completely easy. He loved to cut the corners to the jumps and you had to work really hard to keep him from diving in. Hailey was third in the Pony Medal, which was a really good ribbon since in the Medal the small, medium, and large ponies competed against each other and the older, more experienced kids on the large ponies often won. I finished seventh and I was happy with that since I didn't usually do that well in the equitation classes.

The first division of the day was almost always the small ponies. I placed third in the first class and second in the second class over-fences with Drizzle and I won the hack. Jane catch-rode a pony to good ribbons, too.

When it came time for the mediums, Martha had Tyler up at the ring. Susie decided that I should ride him first and then Sammy. Tyler was all braided now—his mane and tail beautifully done up. We had bought the fake tail from his previous owner because it was one of the custom ones and it matched his hair color exactly. With the fake strands braided into his real hair, his tail looked thick and full. Tyler was the kind of pony that was so gorgeous that people walking by stared at him. If ponies were people, Tyler would have been one of those guys in the Abercrombie & Fitch ads. I should have been so happy he was mine but just looking at him, I had that small sick-to-my-stomach feeling just below my ribs. There was another big problem—when I looked at him, I immediately thought of my mom and of the cancer—the one thing I was trying hard not to think about.

Hailey and I warmed up together. The schooling area was

busy. Hugo Fines was calling out to Olivia Martin, telling her to get her eye on the jump right out of the turn. Hugo ran Autumn Ridge Farm, the top show stable on the East Coast. He was tall and skinny and always impeccably dressed. Today that meant chinos and a navy quilted Polo jacket with Maui Jim sunglasses. His dark hair was perfectly styled. Autumn Ridge was what people called a factory barn because they had something like seventy horses, tons of clients, and multiple assistant trainers. I'd never been to their barn, but I'd heard it was like a palace with fountains, statues, and shaped hedges. Their set-up at shows was always amazing, with incredible shrubs and flowers done by professional landscapers, and their horses' stalls were always bedded with the shavings banked nearly all the way up the walls.

Patti Dayton was hovering next to the vertical Olivia was jumping, waiting for Hugo to finish so she could claim the jump. Susie had just gotten the second of the two jumps in the schooling ring for us to work over. A few trainers and riders stood on the sidelines, watching the warm-ups. I could feel everyone paying particular attention to Tyler and me, waiting to see how I'd ride him.

Susie put the jump down to a small vertical and we cantered it a few times before she raised it. Hugo finished with Olivia, and Patti started schooling Ava Higgenbotham. Ava's parents were really into boats and all of her ponies had nautical names. Right now she was on Leeward. Her other medium was named Windward, and she had a large pony called Coastal. Sometimes when we were bored we invented silly names she could name her next pony or horse, like Shipwreck or Titanic. The Higgenbothams had family money. Ava's grandfather had opened a chain of department stores that had made millions. From what I could tell, her parents didn't seem to work. Patti was Ava's private trainer and Patti was always praising Ava, like if she didn't she might lose her cushy six-figure salary job with the Higgenbothams.

We jumped the vertical a few more times at the new height and also jumped an oxer before Susie declared us ready to go.

At the in gate, Martha and Manuel rubbed our boots with a rag, cleaned off the ponies' mouths, and polished their hooves. I loved the sooty smell of hoof-oil, kind of like the same way I liked smelling gasoline when we filled up the car.

"Who wants to go first?" Susie asked us.

Hailey looked at me and shrugged. Jane had this thing about always going first, but Hailey never cared when she went.

"I will," I said, wanting to get it over with.

"Okay, you know where you're going?"

"It's the outside going away in five strides, diagonal in six, outside in five and then home over the diagonal in a four to a two."

"You got it," Susie said. "Ride him just like you have been."

Olivia finished to lots of Hugo's trademark high-pitched whoops. Hugo's first assistant, Alison, was standing next to him clapping.

Susie said to me, "Okay, kiddo, you're in."

I entered the ring at a walk and listened to the announcer's voice. "Now on course is number 1748. This is Woodland's Tried and True, owned and ridden by Regan Sternlicht of New York, New York."

I didn't have to glance at the sides of the rings to know that people had stopped to watch us. Of course they wanted to see Tyler with his new owner. They wanted to know if I'd be able to ride him—if we were going to be a winning combination. Dad had arrived a half-hour ago and was standing with Mom on the sidelines.

I put my leg on Tyler and asked him to trot. Tyler was such a beautiful mover—his legs sweeping over the ground—that Susie told me to be sure to show off his trot. Once the judge had enough time to watch him trot, I pressed him into the canter. I made sure to get him going forward and out in front of my leg on my opening circle and then relaxed and stayed the same as I came out of the turn to the first line. Tyler's stride was so even that it was easy to see the right distance and we jumped into the line perfectly. I counted the strides to myself and made sure to give Tyler a nice release over the oxer out of the line.

The rest of the course went just as smoothly and each jump felt better than the last. I knew everyone watching was realizing that from now on we were the team to beat. But I couldn't enjoy the ride. It felt like I was watching someone else ride Tyler—like I was just going through the motions, numb to it all. I landed off the last fence and Susie clapped and whooped loudly. I could hear Mom and Dad clapping, too.

"Good job," Susie said as I came out. I was glad when she didn't gush, but instead turned her attention to Hailey.

"Don't override the first line!" Susie called to Hailey as she entered the ring.

This time Hailey didn't. She was a little deep coming into the second line, but Donald still jumped it well. Susie clapped and whooped for her, too.

When Hailey came out of the ring, we all went over the next course and then I went first again. This time you finished over an oxer on the long side of the ring. As I approached it, I saw that I needed to press Tyler forward a little bit to make the distance work out. For what must have been just a split second I wondered what would happen if I didn't press him forward? Or if I didn't press him forward enough? Maybe the distance would be a little long and he'd have to stretch over the jump. Or worse, he'd fit in an extra stride. A chip like that would keep us out of the ribbons completely.

But I put my leg on him and he jumped it perfectly.

Chapter 12

MY ROUNDS ON SAMMY were good, too. I had to hurry slightly down the first line in the first class because I forgot that Sammy didn't have the huge stride that Tyler did, but other than that I didn't have any real mistakes. Hailey and I watched the rest of the class together, including Jane on Coco. Coco went okay—she did her changes, but she was still fresh and she got quick through them, which would probably be enough to keep her out of the ribbons.

Hailey, Jane, and I watched the rest of the class from the spectator tent alongside the ring. When Dakota Pearce came into the ring, Hailey made a show of shielding her eyes. "I can't even look at her. Please tell me she just chipped."

Dakota was a pretty good rider, which made things worse. If she were horrible and never got any ribbons, she wouldn't be so hate-able, but she won a lot. Her parents were both renowned cardiac surgeons and in addition to practicing at New York Presbyterian, they spent weeks in third world countries doing volunteer surgeries on children with heart problems. It was pretty ironic that their daughter had no heart. Since her parents were often in faraway lands saving lives, she spent a lot of time living with her trainers, which might have been okay if she didn't ride with Lenny and Kitty Lowe. Lenny and Kitty were cutthroat and often borderline unethical husband-and-wife trainers who were hard on their horses and cruel to their riders. Hillside Acres (people joked and called it Hell's Acres) was like a cult—once people started riding there, no matter how mentally abusive Lenny and Kitty were to them, they wouldn't leave.

As Dakota rode, I prayed for her to mess up. Of course, she didn't. Hailey heard Lenny and Kitty whooping like she'd just nailed the test at the Maclay Finals, not put in a decent round in a pony hunter class.

Hailey took her hand away from her face. "Was she *that* good?"

I shook my head. "She was good, but they were definitely over-clapping."

There were eighteen ponies in the mediums, so the division took hours to complete. Toward the end of the classes, the grooms brought up the ponies again and they stood in clusters near the in gate, ready for the jog. Only the ponies that had really bad mistakes and had no hopes of getting a jog stayed back at the barn. Even Jane brought up Coco—just in case she got a jog. The weather still hadn't warmed up completely and all the ponies wore wool dress sheets in their farm colors with each pony's owner's last name monogrammed on the middle of the blanket.

There was always this tension right before the jog was

called. Everyone had an idea of who would get what ribbon, but nothing was certain until the numbers had been called out loud. Until then everyone had a hope that they might win. There was a breathless anticipation as everyone waited, wondering and wishing.

Jane, Hailey, and I crowded around the girl who worked the in gate, Elena. Hailey slid onto the table Elena sat at and she barked at her, "Hailey, get off, you'll break it."

"Hailey break it?" Jane said, giggling. "She weighs like forty pounds."

"I weigh more than forty pounds," Hailey said, sliding back off the table.

We stood close to Elena, hoping to hear the jog before it was officially announced over the P.A.

"Who's winning today, girls?" Elena asked.

Hailey and Jane both said at practically the same time, "Regan on Tyler."

Elena glanced at me. She had multiple piercings in her ears and lots of tattoos on her arms, which made her stick out a little in the preppy and conservative horse show world. "Looks like it's unanimous."

"They don't know what they're talking about," I said.

"Come on," Hailey said. "You were perfect."

"Hailey was good, too," I tried. "And there were other good trips. What about Olivia? She was really good."

"She was kind of deep to the in-and-out," Jane pointed out.

"Still, she could win. You just don't know yet."

"You sound like you don't *want* to win," Hailey said.

Before I could figure out how to answer that, the judge's voice came over Elena's walkie-talkie: "Ready for the jog order?"

"Go ahead," Elena said and we all leaned closer.

I held my breath, my heart thumping away. Everyone else was hoping their number would be called first, but I was hoping mine wouldn't be the one called. Maybe if I finished second or third, it wouldn't seem automatic that Tyler and I should always win. The first class felt like it meant so much about what the next few months would hold for me. I glanced over at Mom and Dad. They were sipping coffees and chatting with the other pony parents, including Hailey's mom. I knew my winning would mean so much to Mom, especially after how I'd pushed her away the night before, so why couldn't I want it?

Elena poised her pen on her pad of paper. The judge called the first number and I let out a small sigh, not loud enough for anyone to hear.

Chapter 13

I WAS ON TOP. Hailey and Jane both shot me looks that said, "See?" Olivia was second; Sammy was called third; Dakota fourth; and Donald sixth. In the second class Tyler was on top again. I had won both classes. Dakota was second; Sammy was fourth; and Donald was fifth. Coco hadn't gotten a jog in either class.

"Congratulations," Hailey said.

"Yeah, congrats," Jane added.

Since Coco didn't get a jog in either class, Jane jogged Sammy for me. It was an unspoken rule that I would jog the higher placing pony, but I would have been just as happy jogging Sammy and letting Jane jog Tyler.

I led Tyler through the in gate. I didn't even have to cluck to get him to trot as I ran next to him—he knew exactly what the jog entailed and he probably had spent most of his life getting the top call. Dakota came in behind me, then Olivia, Sammy, and so on through tenth place.

Once the judge saw each pony trot and declared them

sound and the class to be pinned as is, the announcer called out the results. "Winning our first medium pony hunter class today is Woodland's Tried and True with Regan Sternlicht." My name sounded too loud in my own ears. It felt like the whole horse show heard it even though there were two other rings with their own classes going on.

A woman in a ruffled skirt paired with cowboy boots presented me with a blue ribbon and I led Tyler out of the ring. I kept my head down, trying not to make a big deal of it. I glanced up once and saw Mom talking with Hugo. He always tried to chat up Mom, I'm sure hoping that someday I'd switch from Susie and go ride with him. But Mom would never want me to ride with a factory barn, even if Hugo won the Finals year after year. She liked the family feel of Susie's program. She said it was like ProduX before she sold it. I loved Susie and I never wanted to ride with anyone else either, but if I did ride with a barn like Autumn Ridge at least I wouldn't be the only rider to have so many ponies. Hugo specialized in kids whose parents were billionaires. At Autumn Ridge, I wouldn't be the richest kid in the barn.

The second class was conformation, but it didn't matter. There was practically no pony on the planet that would be moved up over Tyler. So it was no use hoping I'd finish second or third—I was winning the class whether I liked it or not.

When I came out of the ring after getting my second blue, Mom and Dad met me at the in gate. I tried to manage a smile. I was TVMG again. TVMG would be so happy to win for her poor, dying mother. It would all be so tragic and TVMG would rise above it all.

Dad wore a pink button-down shirt and khakis. Not many guys could pull off wearing pink or purple, but Dad did. I didn't notice his clothes or his age at home, but I noticed them when we were in public. Dad never seemed self-conscious about his age. I remembered one time he took me to Dylan's Candy Bar for ice cream and the waitress said, "Special time out with Grandpa?"

"I guess I really should shave off this beard," Dad joked with her while I was dying of mortification. "My wife keeps saying it makes me look too old."

When the waitress left to make our sundaes, I asked Dad, "Mom wants you to shave your beard?"

Dad shook his head. "I didn't want the waitress to feel badly for what she said." He was busy thinking about *her* feelings.

Now, Dad said to me, "You rode great. Was it fun?"

"I guess so," I said.

Dad furrowed his brow slightly, but before he could say anything else, Mom piped up, "I knew this was the right pony for you. Didn't I tell you how amazing he was?"

I turned away from her. What she never understood was that, whether I won wasn't just about what pony I had. No matter what, I still had to ride well. Even though Tyler was great and a lot of riders would win with him, there were plenty that wouldn't. But when you had expensive ponies, everyone assumed you won because of the pony. They never talked about how well you rode. With Jane people were always saying how well she rode—and even Hailey, too. But with me it was always about what a great pony I had.

"You better get back on," Mom said, looking over to where Martha was putting my saddle back on Tyler for the under saddle. Martha gave me a leg up and I walked into the ring with all the other girls on their ponies.

I gave Tyler a loose rein and pushed him forward to show off his movement. Even though he was such a good mover, I still had to make sure to have good passes in front of the judge's booth before the announcer asked us to line up in the center of the ring. Hailey and Jane and I always tried to line up next to each other, although sometimes it was hard to do.

This time I managed to line up next to Hailey, but Jane was down at the end of the line.

"You guys were so awesome today," Hailey said. "It's like you've been riding him forever."

"Maybe it was just luck," I said. "You were great, too."

"You wouldn't even have to show tomorrow and you'd probably still be champion," Hailey said.

I didn't know what to say since it was true. I couldn't explain to Hailey that I didn't want to be champion. Hailey had ridden well, too, but she'd only gotten a fifth and a sixth. Sometimes at smaller shows Donald ended up sixth in the hack, but in this company he wasn't even going to place. Also, Tyler was already qualified for Pony Finals, but Donald wasn't. She *needed* to be champion or reserve—I didn't.

"You're still sleeping over tonight, right?" Hailey asked.

"Of course." I couldn't understand how Hailey could still want to be friends with me since I beat her week after week. But she never complained and she was always the first to congratulate me. Then I remembered—the cancer. Maybe she knew and that was why she was being so kind. But Hailey wasn't good at saying nice things unless she meant them. So maybe it wasn't all about the cancer. I sighed. Cancer messed with your head, even when it was your mother who had it. It made me suspicious of everyone's motives and never sure whether people were acting normal around me.

The announcer called out: "And I have the results of the medium pony hunter under-saddle... winning our class today, the third win in a row today, for Woodland's Tried and True. Regan Sternlicht in the irons. Congratulations, Regan."

I moved Tyler forward and forced a smile as the same woman pinned the blue ribbon on Tyler's bridle.

At the in gate I slid off Tyler. Mom came and hugged me, but I barely felt her arms around me.

"Great job," Susie said.

"Thanks," I managed.

"Let's go get lunch," Dad said. "I'm starving."

"And we have to get the carrots out of your car," Mom said to him. "I called Daddy and asked him to bring them," she explained to me.

"I have to get my backpack," I said. I couldn't wait to leave. Most any other time I would have wanted to stay and watch the large ponies, but right then I wanted to be anywhere but at the ring.

I had left my backpack under Elena's tent. Elena was still there, taking numbers for the large ponies.

"I guess they were right. Congrats, girl," Elena said.

"Thanks," I said.

It was when I leaned down to get my backpack that

Dakota Pearce walked by with another girl from her barn and said, "Yeah, the only reason her mother bought her that pony is because she's, like, dying."

Chapter 14

HAILEY'S MOM IS A REALLY good cook. For dinner that night she was making Wienerschnitzel. It's an Austrian recipe she learned to make in a cooking/dating class she took through community education called The Right Meal/The Right Match. She learned some good recipes, but none of the men she met were keepers.

Hailey's parents got divorced when she was eight and her father remarried a woman Hailey and her mother called "the Carrot" because she used a spray-on tanner that made her skin orange and because she was constantly on a diet and snacking on mini carrots. Hailey's father and the Carrot lived in New Jersey and Hailey only went there one weekend a month.

"You had a good day today, huh?" Mrs. Mullins said to me as we were helping her with the Wienerschnitzel.

My three blue ribbons were hanging up on the banner with Susan Charles, Inc. on it. "Yeah, definitely."

Wienerschnitzel was actually really fun to make. Mrs.

Mullins bought this special plastic tray with three sections just for making it: one section for flour, one for egg, and one for breadcrumbs. Hailey and I manned the tray and coated the cutlets in the flour, then dipped them into the egg, and finally rolled them in the breadcrumbs. As we cooked, one of Hailey's dogs, Milo, came over and sat at our feet, looking up hopefully. Whenever I'm at Hailey's, I try to soak up the feeling of living with pets always underfoot, so when I went home to our way too clean and quiet apartment, I could remember how it felt. But being at Hailey's made me long to have a dog. It was a yearning so big at times that it felt like a physical emptiness, like I needed a dog to complete me. My mom had offered to get a cat but I didn't yearn for a cat. Cats seemed like only children themselves, independent and aloof. Maybe if we got a cat, I'd come to feel it was enough, but I worried, if we got a cat, I'd never have any hope of getting a dog.

My mom didn't cook at all, except for omelets. When people asked her if she cooked, she said, "No, but I'm really good at take-out." We also had a person who came in and cooked for us, which didn't seem weird to me until I was over at Hailey's and her mother was cooking. Then it seemed really weird.

Two parakeets squawked from their cage in the corner of the room. One hopped onto a perch and pecked at a birdseed bell.

Mrs. Mullins poured oil into a frying pan and turned on the burner. "Your mom certainly seems excited about Tyler."

"No kidding," I said, rolling my eyes a little.

The oil started to sizzle and Mrs. Mullins turned down the burner. "One of the keys to making perfect Wiener-schnitzel is getting the temperature exactly right," she explained. "They said it's just like starting a relationship—you can't come on too strong or it'll burn out." She made a face and changed the topic back to riding. "Sometimes I think Jane's got it the easiest. No pressure because the ponies she rides are so green."

"Are you kidding?" Hailey said. "Have you seen how intense Tommy is? Plus when she catch-rides there's so much pressure. Not that I wouldn't love to get catch-rides like she does..."

"That's true. I hadn't thought of that." Mrs. Mullins moved over to the tray to take the first cutlet to put in the pan. She was heavy-set, but pretty. It was always hard to believe tiny Hailey was her daughter, but Hailey's dad was short and slender. Mrs. Mullins always seemed to be smiling and I liked her smile, even though her two front teeth overlapped a tiny bit.

"What's the weather for tomorrow?" Hailey asked.

"Kind of like today," her mom said. "Cool, but more sunshine."

Hailey sighed and dusted another cutlet with flour.

"Honey, you don't need the rain. You can win on a sunny day."

Donald was a total mudder—he marched around any course in the thickest slop. So when it was really raining hard and other ponies were misbehaving, Donald won.

Mrs. Mullin put the first cutlet in the pan and it sizzled.

When all the cutlets were prepared for the pan, Hailey and I set the table and poured drinks.

Hailey's mom bellowed for Hailey's younger sister, Anna, and her brother, Owen, to come for dinner. The sound of Owen's thundering feet on the stairs followed, which made the dogs start yapping.

"Quiet!" Mrs. Mullins yelled at them. "And you too, Owen. You're not an elephant."

Owen insisted his snake be able to eat with us and the compromise was that it got to be in its travel case under the table. Owen kept sneaking down to see it and Anna called him a freak and Owen said he was going to feed her hamsters to his snake. Anna was wearing the third place ribbon she'd won today in the children's ponies hooked on her pajama top. Hailey told her she was a dork and to take it off and she started crying. Then Mrs. Mullins made Hailey apologize to her.

The dinner conversation was loud and rapid and I loved it. I loved everything about Hailey's house—her mom, the animals, even Owen and his gross snake.

"So tell me about Jane's new pony," Mrs. Mullins said.

"It's got this funny brand," I said. "In the shape of a half-moon."

"Does that mean something?"

"I don't know. I don't know anything about brands really. But it means it wasn't one of Vi's ponies, which Tommy thought it was."

"Hmm," Mrs. Mullins said. "A mysterious past... I've met many men with those."

I glanced at Hailey to see if she was interested in the pony. "I wonder where it came from. I mean, how did it end up in one of Vi's fields?"

"That part is totally weird," Hailey agreed.

After dinner Hailey and I moved her mother's half-done scrapbooking project and Owen's Legos from the couch to watch last year's live stream of the Medal Finals. We've watched it a bunch of times but it never got old. We knew each of the two hundred plus trips and just what happened. There were some really terrible rounds where riders crashed and fell off and we always replayed those again and again.

"Here comes the first jump fiasco," Hailey said, reaching into the bowl of popcorn on the coffee table and spilling some on the floor that Milo rushed in and snarfed up. Hailey's cat, a tiger striped one with a partially ripped ear, walked along the couch. At my feet lay their other rescue dog, Chopper. All told Hailey's family had three birds, two dogs, a cat, two hamsters, and Owen's snake.

The rider on course looked okay in the opening circle and then at the first jump the horse did this really lame little refusal and the rider went straight over the horse's head, taking the bridle with her. We started laughing and Hailey replayed it again.

"Seriously, though," I said, as the poor girl stood up and brushed the dirt from her breeches. "You go all the way to Harrisburg and then you fall off at the first jump? That stinks."

"Yeah, I know," Hailey said. "I'd die if I did that."

Hailey and I both stopped at her choice of words. The live

stream kept playing and both of us stared at it, barely watching. Hailey looked down at the laptop as if she was considering whether she should stop it.

"You know about my mom," I said. "About the cancer being back."

Hailey nodded. "I should have just said something."

"It's okay."

"I'm sorry."

I wondered if she was sorry for not having said something, or sorry for the cancer. Probably both. "It's like all of a sudden everyone knows. I overheard Dakota say that's why Mom wanted to get Tyler."

"She's the devil in breeches." Hailey made a disgusted face and then paused. "Do you think that's why your mom bought Tyler?"

I was sort of shocked Hailey asked that question, but I shouldn't have been. This was Hailey, after all. But instead of being annoyed by her lack of tact, for once I was kind of glad she was honest. She wasn't just being nice to me because my mom had cancer.

"Sort of, yeah. Like maybe it'll make up for it."

"My mom says your mom's strong—if anyone can beat this, it's her."

"Yeah," I said. But it wasn't that easy. Before my mom got cancer I believed in everything happening for a reason, the best man winning, what goes around comes around, and all those reassuring clichés. But they didn't work in cancer land. People who didn't smoke got lung cancer. Strong people who vowed to fight ended up dying anyway. I couldn't blame Hailey for what she was trying to do—offer hope and support. Like everyone else, she was just trying.

Chapter 15

AFTER WATCHING THE LIVE STREAM, we decided to google Frankie's brand. We took the laptop into the kitchen so we could get snacks at the same time. Hailey's mom was on her computer and pots, pans, and dishes still covered the stove and counter. Anna was at the kitchen table with markers spread out around her, drawing horses with rainbows in the background. A few markers had fallen to the floor. Owen had gone to his room, but his leftover ice cream was melting in its dish on the table.

"What do you think of this one, girls?" Her mom read out loud: "Divorced Dad looking for fun, upbeat woman to enjoy the rest of my life with. Enjoys jazz, documentaries, and ethnic food."

I stepped closer to get a better look at the photo. It showed a guy with a receding hairline and gold glasses.

"He looks kind of cute, right?" she asked.

"I guess so," I said to be nice. I mean, he was fifty or something—how could I tell if he was cute?

"Or there's this one—"

"The second one has more hair," I pointed out.

"If it's real," Hailey said. "You should see some of the guys with disgusting fake hair Mom's gone on dates with."

Her mother laughed. "Remember that one guy with the hair sprouting out of his forehead?"

"There have been some real winners over the years." Hailey shook her head.

"I swear I should just give up." Mrs. Mullins closed the screen.

"No way." Hailey's voice was mocking. "True love is out there waiting for you!"

"Okay, that's enough out of you." Her mom playfully poked Hailey in the ribs. "What are you guys up to anyway?"

I said, "We're going to google the brand on the new pony."

"Can you cut up some apple slices for us?" Hailey asked.

"Anything to stop me from browsing Petfinder—the last thing we need is another animal."

Hailey opened up the screen to Google. "What should I type in?"

"Half-moon pony brand?" I suggested.

A slew of hits came up. There was a farm called Half Moon Farm in California and we clicked on that, but it didn't say anything about brands. A few were for products—a handbag with a half-moon stamp on it, and, of all things, a makeup brush made from horsehair. We tried "half-moon brand" and got a bunch of different sites, none of which had anything to do with horses.

Mrs. Mullins slid a plate full of apples next to us, sliced thin the way Hailey liked them. "Maybe just type in equine brands," I said. "We could start there."

Behind us, Mrs. Mullins sang a Top 40 song as she started in on the dishes.

"Mom! Can you please shut up?"

Mrs. Mullins shut off the water. "Sorry, was I being too loud?"

I was cringing—why did Hailey talk to her mom like that? And why did her mom *let* her?

Mrs. Mullins turned the faucet on again. For a minute or two she was quiet, but then she started humming.

"She is so embarrassing," Hailey whispered to me between bites of apple.

"It doesn't bother me," I whispered back.

I pointed to the first entry under equine brands. "What about this one?"

It was a site with a list of many common brands and images of the brands, a few of which looked familiar.

"That's what Daria has," Hailey said, moving the cursor over an image of a crown. "She's a Danish warmblood."

There were all sorts of icons. Letters of the alphabet, circles, stars, shields, but no half-moons. Most were horse breeds, but there were a few pony breeds like the Dartmoor, Exmoor, New Forest, and American Sport Pony breeds. But again, no half-moon.

Mrs. Mullins ran the disposal and then turned off the faucet. The pots and pans were now all piled up in the dish rack and looked like at any moment they might come crashing down. She dried her hands and came over to the computer. "Find anything?"

"Not yet," I said.

Hailey stood up. I wasn't quite ready to give up, but I guess Hailey was. "Come on, let's go watch some TV," she said.

"And then it's off to bed." Mrs. Mullins looked at me. "Your mother will have my head if you don't get a good night's rest. I can't have you riding terribly tomorrow."

We made ice cream sundaes with extra chocolate chips on the theory that if we ate chocolate chips we wouldn't chocolate chip in the ring the next day. Mrs. Mullins went upstairs to tuck Owen in. In the TV room, Anna was watching something lame and Hailey made her change it. Mrs. Mullins came back down and we all sat together. Chopper and Milo climbed onto the couch, too. I loved how it felt, all of us smushed together on the couch.

Chapter 16

HAILEY GOT EXCITED BECAUSE the next morning it was sprinkling. But by the time the mediums went, it had cleared up and was actually kind of warm. I finished up champion with Drizzle and I put in really good rounds with Sammy, too. My first round with Tyler was perfect and Susie whooped loudly. I entered the ring for the second class, which was the handy hunter class, knowing that, if I put in another good trip, I would probably win both classes again, which would mean a clean sweep of the division.

Mom was standing on the sidelines and I met her eye, but she didn't smile at me or give me a thumbs-up. She was always so serious when I was riding, like she didn't want to ruin my concentration. Mom had been a competitive swimmer when she was a girl. She'd spent hours in the pool after school and entered meets on weekends, but her parents never came to watch her, not even in the championships. Her parents had died when I was younger and I'd only met them a few times. They'd lived in a tiny house in a tiny town in Michigan and

Mom hadn't liked to visit them. Everything she did seemed to be the opposite of them—she lived in a big city, had a big corporate job, and had a big apartment and a big country house. And it felt like she was going to do the opposite with me, too—she gave everything to my riding and never missed a show.

I entered the ring and picked up a canter and it was like I had a ringing in my ears. I did my opening circle and rode the first line and the rollback to the oxer perfectly, but I didn't quite feel like me. I almost couldn't feel my hands on the reins. I rode up the outside line, made a neat turn to the trot jump, rode the single fence on the outside of the ring, and then it was down the diagonal home. As I turned the corner, I saw the distance, but instead of flowing up to it, I pulled on the reins and fit in another extra stride. It wasn't a straight-out chip, but the distance was tight and Tyler had to try extra hard to still jump in good form.

Susie clapped for me. She didn't whoop. When I exited the ring, she was making a face. "What happened? You were right on it and then you just pulled."

"I know. I don't know what I was thinking." My face felt flushed and I was hot under my show coat.

Susie smiled. "No worries. It was still a good trip."

As I walked Tyler away from Susie and over to Martha, I saw Mom coming over from the side of the ring. "What was that?" she said when she reached me.

I slid off Tyler and pulled the reins over his head. He lowered his head and sighed.

Martha took the reins and started pulling off his saddle for the jog.

I patted Tyler's neck. "I don't know. I just made a mistake."

"Are you tired?" Mom said. "Did you stay up too late with Hailey?"

I peeled off my gloves. "No, we went to bed at ten just like you said."

Mom made a clucking sound under her breath. "You could have won all five classes, you know."

I turned toward Martha. I could tell she was trying to act really busy with Tyler so we'd forget she was there. "Can I take him for a little walk to cool him down?"

"Let me just rub his saddle mark off and get a fly sheet on him," she said.

I waited while Martha brushed Tyler's back and threw on a scrim. Then I led him away from Mom. When I was further away I glanced back and saw Martha and Mom talking. Hopefully Martha was talking some sense into her.

I had missed Hailey's first round. I saw her go into the ring for her second round and walked Tyler over to the end of the ring to watch her. She went straight from the walk to the canter so the judges wouldn't see what a bad mover Donald was at the trot. His canter was passable and she found a great distance to the first jump. In my head I willed her not to over-ride the lines. She must have been listening to my ESP because she rode out the first line perfectly and headed around the corner. Donald didn't always round his back like Tyler, but he gave a really good jump, pulling his little knees up to his chest.

Hailey nailed the first seven jumps and was headed down

the diagonal home. I held my breath for her—this was turning out to be a really good trip. Donald had never changed his pace with every jump coming up right out of stride. He wore his ears well, too, eagerly looking through the bridle for the next jump. Hailey saw the distance and nailed the last jump. Susie erupted in whoops and Hailey left the ring with a huge smile on her face. I was smiling, too.

I walked Tyler over to the in gate and waited for Hailey to finish talking to Susie. Susie just kept saying how great Hailey had ridden and that she was really proud of her for trusting herself and not overriding the lines.

Hailey jumped off and I gave her a huge hug. "That was awesome!"

"Thanks! I was so nervous to the last jump and then I finally saw the distance. Have you seen any other good trips?"

"Olivia was good but her trot jump was weak. Ava was really long to one jump."

I gave Tyler back to Martha, and Hailey and I watched the rest of the trips from the in gate. When Dakota came into the ring we exchanged a look and I knew we were both silently putting the hex on her. Dakota's pony, Smitten, was a fine-boned chestnut mare that did well in the hacks, but tended to jump flat. Outside of the ring she pinned her ears and in the jogs she always tried to bite Dakota's show coat. I guess I couldn't blame her for being such a witch since she was stuck with Dakota for a rider.

Dakota was putting in a really good trip. On the approach to the single oxer she saw a really long distance and kicked for it. Her pony tried to leave the ground, but ended up doing a Superman, front legs flying straight out. Her pony tried hard, but couldn't quite get over the jump, knocking down the top rail. Hailey and I shared a second, excited look—that would put Dakota out of the ribbons.

Usually I was a generally nice person, but when there was someone I didn't like, it was scary how strongly I could root for them to screw up and how much satisfaction I felt when they did mess up. At least I knew I wasn't alone—Hailey felt exactly the same way.

When it came time for the jog to be announced Hailey looked more nervous than she had before she went in the ring for her rounds. I kept thinking how exciting it would be for her if she won. Hailey had never won a class at a big show like this. She'd been second a few times in the rain but that was the best she'd placed.

The first jog was called and Tyler was on top. I could have predicted that one. But with my tight jump in the second class there was no way I was going to win. Olivia might beat Hailey, but I wouldn't. I reached out and grabbed Hailey's arm as the second class was announced. The first number called was mine again. "Wait, what?"

Hailey's number was called second, Olivia third. "Congratulations," she said, turning to me. She was trying to smile, but I could tell deep down she was upset. How could she not be?

"But that can't be right," I said.

"Come on—" Hailey said. "We have to go jog."

"You got totally robbed," I told Hailey as we went to get our ponies. I gave Susie a pleading look and she just shrugged.

She put her hand on Hailey's shoulders, though. "You nailed that second round."

We jogged in as called for the first class, picking up our ribbons. Hailey finished sixth. Jane jogged Sammy for me in fourth place.

Before I went in for the second round I thought about not jogging. Hailey would win if I didn't jog. But that would be bad sportsmanship. So I had no choice but to collect my second blue of the day, with Hailey right behind me in second. I had won all five classes after all.

The announcer asked me to stay in the ring for the championship and made a big deal about announcing how it had been a clean sweep.

At the in gate I asked Susie how I could have possibly won. She said that maybe my tight jump didn't look that bad from where the judge was sitting.

"Sometimes you win some you shouldn't," she said.

"And sometimes you lose some you should win," I said, looking hard at Hailey.

It must have been awful to be friends with me sometimes. If I rode at another barn and this had happened she could just hate me, the way we hated Dakota, and that would be so much easier. She smiled back at me and I hoped it wasn't a cancer-pity smile. Like she was thinking I needed to win more than she did right now. I had to count on Hailey being Hailey, honest no matter what.

Chapter 17

IF HAILEY WAS MAD AT ME, I couldn't tell. We spent the afternoon cruising around with Danny in his golf cart, along with two of the dogs available for adoption: Peanut, a poodle-mix, and Major, a lab-hound mix with the cutest brindle ears. Jane was busy riding other ponies—schooling some, showing others. It seemed like she spent most of every show day in the saddle. It was almost weird to see her on her own two feet.

We had three of the shrink-wrapped baskets in the cart, too: the iPad basket, the horse-dog combo basket, and the Belle & Bow basket. The Clothes Horse had totally come through on the blankets, donating a gorgeous plaid Baker horse blanket and matching dog blanket. We parked at the different rings and Hailey and I walked around with Peanut and Major, asking people if they wanted to buy tickets to the raffle. Sometimes people would ask about the dogs and we'd tell them all about how sweet they were. Usually I was shy about approaching people, but when it came to the dogs I would do anything. It was like I became a different person and could just walk up to someone and ask them to open their wallets. I got one woman with two purebred corgis talking and ended up asking her why she'd ever pay thousands of dollars for another corgi when she could have a lovable dog like Peanut who needed a home. Peanut crawled into her lap and licked her face and by the end of our conversation she'd bought five raffle tickets and taken Danny's number so she could think about Peanut more.

We sold tickets to Hugo, Patti, and Olivia's parents, too. Danny parked the golf cart by the jumper ring at one point so he could go over and look at a horse he was thinking of trying. We watched Tara Barnes ride a cool-looking young horse in the 1.30 Meter class. That's when I saw Dakota walking toward us. I elbowed Hailey. "Uh oh."

"Hi, girls," Dakota said when she reached us. Most of the girls at the horse show had their hair back in ponytails or wore baseball hats, but Dakota's long, no-doubt highlighted, blond hair was loose. I hated how she said "girls," like she was so much older than us when she wasn't. She wore a gleaming Rolex watch on her wrist and her phone in its bejeweled case was clipped to one side of her Louis Vuitton belt. On the other side of her belt was a small walkie-talkie. Big barns had walkie-talkies for trainers to call from the ring back to the tents to the grooms or other trainers. Sometimes Jane wore one so Tommy could reach her when she was out riding, but it was so ridiculous that Dakota had a walkie-talkie.

"So what are you selling?" she added, as if she didn't know, or that we were raising money for ourselves.

"Raffle tickets to raise money for the lip sync."

"Oh, my parents just pay my sponsorship," she said, eyeing Hailey.

"My mom is matching what we raise," I said. "So we could really raise a lot."

Hailey said, "There's an award for most money raised—that's what we're going for. If you win, you get a golf cart for WEF, too."

"I have a golf cart," Dakota said. She glanced at me. "Congratulations on being champion."

All I could think about was how I'd overheard her say Mom had bought Tyler just because she was dying. "Thanks," I murmured.

"Are you qualified for Pony Finals?" she asked Hailey.

"Pony Medal," Hailey said.

"Hunters?"

"Not yet."

I could feel Hailey's annoyance building to anger.

"What can I win?" Dakota flicked her eyes over the baskets. "Anything good?"

"There's an iPad," I said.

"Already have one." She peered in the back of the cart at the other baskets.

Hailey looked away and I could tell she didn't care whether Dakota bought a hundred dollars worth of tickets—she wanted nothing to do with her.

"There are really nice matching dog and horse blankets from The Clothes Horse..." I tried.

Dakota scrunched up her nose. "My dog already has a Gucci one."

"There's one from Belle & Bow with lots of fun stuff and two pairs of gorgeous bows," Hailey said.

"I have a million of their bows," Dakota said.

That was when Hailey let loose. "It's for charity. Do you even know what charity is? It's when you help a worthy cause."

"Of course I know what charity is. My parents are in Honduras as we speak." Dakota took some cash out of the pocket of her Pikeurs. She peeled off two twenties. "How many tickets can I buy with this?"

I made change for her. It was as if just because her parents did good deeds, she could be a total jerk. "Two tickets. Which basket do you want to bid on?" I handed her the list of all the baskets. "Here are the others."

She scanned the list. "The spa one, I guess."

"Figures," Hailey muttered under her breath.

"I'm glad you're doing the lip sync again—you were third last year, right?" Dakota asked her when I was sure she knew Hailey hadn't been third.

"Second," Hailey said.

Dakota stuffed the ten dollars I'd given her back in her pocket. She looked to the ring. The 1.30 Meter class had finished and the course was being set for the Children's Jumper Classic. "Well, gotta go. I think the course walk is about to start."

As Dakota walked away, Hailey said, "I am so winning the lip sync."

Chapter 18

AT FIRST FRANKIE JIGGED AT THE WALK, which made Jane want to tear her hair out. She'd never win a hack, no matter how beautiful he moved, if he couldn't walk in a relaxed way. But after a week of patience, long walks on a loose rein, and a lot of kind words and patting, he was walking calmly. Jane got him trotting and cantering well, too—that actually came easier because he liked to be in motion. Jane couldn't lesson with us yet, but Hailey and I usually watched her ride Frankie. We were leaning against the fence watching one of the first times they jumped him. It was hot out, low eighties, and it felt like summer was just around the corner. I was almost out of school. Jane and Hailey went to public school so they had more school left than I did.

A lot of ponies Jane rode had spooks or stops so she was used to giving a strong ride. Frankie didn't ever think of stopping—his problem was that he ran at the jumps.

"We need to get him to slow down and relax," Tommy told Jane. He pointed to a simple vertical-vertical in eight strides that Hailey and I had ridden earlier. "Jump the in, land, and bring him back to a halt. Not harshly. Just nicely."

Jane picked up a canter, circled and headed to the in of the line. Frankie started to tense up and get quick the moment he turned to the jump. Jane's immediate reaction was to sit back in the saddle and take a firmer feel on his mouth. Frankie got even quicker, hurdled the jump, and refused to stop afterward. Jane pulled harder and Frankie shook his head and dragged her toward the second jump. He popped over it and it took Jane halfway around the end of the ring to get him to stop.

"He's tough," Hailey said, as Tommy explained to Jane that she couldn't get so defensive.

I wondered what made him want to run away like that. It was like he was trying to escape.

Jane cantered by us on the way to try it again. She was sweating under her helmet and she looked exasperated. I tried to imagine what it would be like to be her. Each pony she rode had some problem she was supposed to be able to fix. Sometimes it probably stunk for Jane, but to me it looked like fun. People would see a pony, not its wealthy rider.

She had ridden the line again and instead of being easier to stop this time, Frankie hurtled toward the second jump. Jane gave up and let him jump it. "I can't stop him!" she said to Tommy. "I'm pulling as hard as I can!"

"That's the point," Tommy said. "You can't just keep pulling and pulling. He'll dig in and fight you. You have to half-halt and when he relaxes, you relax so he learns to be good."

"He's not ever relaxing," Jane said. "He's like a runaway freight train."

"Try it again," Tommy said. "Don't just grab his mouth and pull. Give and take."

Jane had jumped the in of the line again. She'd gotten Frankie to stop this time before the second jump. Then she cantered the out and halted.

"That was better," Tommy said.

"Barely," Jane said.

I didn't know who was sweatier, Jane or Frankie. The back of Jane's polo shirt was as dark with sweat as Frankie's neck.

"We'll get to him," Tommy said. "Don't worry."

"Are we done?" Jane asked.

"For today."

A group of children's pony riders were waiting for their lesson with Tommy, including Anna. As he turned to them, Jane walked over to us.

Jane let the reins slide through her hands till she was on the buckle. Frankie reached out his head gratefully. "Did you hear Ike was champion at Kentucky Spring?"

"Really?" I said, although I'd seen the results posted online already.

Hailey motioned to Frankie. "He looked psycho."

"Dad keeps telling me to relax. It's hard to relax when you're seeing your life flash before your eyes." Jane dropped her feet disparagingly out of the stirrups and hunched back in the saddle. "And now look at him. It's going to take forever to get him cool."

"I'll help you give him a bath and get him put away," I told Jane.

"Really? You don't have to. You're clean—" she eyed my breeches and polo shirt. "You'll get all yucky."

"So what?" I said.

I helped untack Frankie while Jane took off her helmet, threw on a baseball hat, and glugged a bottle of water. We sprayed Frankie down and sponged him with a bucket of warm water mixed with liniment. The mint smell of the liniment filled the air. He stuck his neck out and sighed as we worked on him. We toweled off his legs and then I offered to take him for a walk while Jane cleaned his tack. I walked him all around the front field. He walked quickly, like he wasn't sure where I was taking him. I talked to him and told him to relax. He wanted to rub his face on me and, even though it was bad manners, I let him. It felt like he was telling me he trusted me, even just a little. The back of my polo shirt was now wet and full of little white hairs but I didn't care.

When I brought him back to the barn, Hailey was cleaning out her tack trunk, singing while she was pulling out crops, bits, packets of hair nets, boot polish, saddle soap, old horse show programs, ChapStick, sunscreen, and loose change. I didn't recognize the song—it must have been an old one by someone like Patti Smith. It was really pretty and it struck me as it did every time I heard Hailey sing how amazing it was that such a pipsqueak of a girl could have such a soulful, moody voice.

I walked Frankie down the aisle. Hailey had her back to me and turned when I was coming up behind her. Seeing that it was me and not Hektor or Manuel she kept singing, even louder now, putting her emotions into the finale. Even Frankie, standing next to me, seemed like he was listening and enjoying the music, like it relaxed him.

She held the final note and then I clapped and cheered like I was watching her in concert. Hailey gave a formal bow, dipping her head and spreading her hands dramatically.

Frankie tossed his head once and then lowered his head and moved one of his front feet back. Suddenly I was sure he was about to fall down. What was happening? Was he having a seizure? But it soon became clear he was copying Hailey, bowing himself. He balanced on three legs and tucked his head down. He was doing a trick. So not only had he been bathed and clipped so much that he was perfectly relaxed about it, but someone had taken the time to teach him tricks. Who? I wanted to know more than ever.

Chapter 19

"Did you just see that?" I said to Hailey.

"He bowed, right?"

"Yeah."

We were both wondering if we were seeing things.

"Do it again," I told Hailey. "Bow again, like you did."

She spread her hands and dipped her head. Right on cue, Frankie followed.

"Oh my god," I said. "Let's go tell Jane."

We put Frankie in his stall and burst into the tack room. Finishing each other's sentences we explained what had just happened. Jane wanted to see it for herself so back out into the barn we went. Jane slid open Frankie's door. He popped up his head, eyes bright, a wad of hay in his mouth, like he was surprised to see us again so soon.

Hailey bowed and Frankie did, too. "See?" Hailey said.

"I can't imagine Vi teaching him tricks. I mean her ponies are lucky if they get their feed."

"I know." First the brand and now this. I had to know

where Frankie came from, and Jane and Hailey seemed interested, too. "We should call Vi."

"And ask about him bowing?"

"About the brand, the bowing, what she knows about where he came from. Did she ever get your dad his registration papers?"

"No, she said she couldn't find them. We did a search online for his criteria—white, 13.1 hands, blue eye—and nothing came up. Dad thinks Vi forgot to ever register him."

"We need to talk to her," I said.

"I don't know," Jane said. "She's pretty loopy—we can't just call her up."

"Why not?" Hailey said.

"Yeah, why not?" I echoed.

"I mean we could, but..."

I had my hand on Frankie's door. "Let's go over to your house. Your dad's busy teaching. My mom isn't coming for another hour."

Jane shrugged. "I guess... okay. But I think this whole thing is kind of crazy."

Jane's family lived in a small farmhouse on the property, not far from the barn. Her whole house was probably smaller than our apartment. It had a pretty wrap-around porch, but the paint was chipping off and a few shutters were missing. I didn't love spending time there like I did at Hailey's, but sometimes we'd go over just because it was so close to the barn. The few times that we slept over there I loved being able to walk to the barn at night and see the horses dozing in their stalls. They always looked so surprised to see us. They'd look up from their hay, like, what are you doing here this time of night? Sometimes we'd catch them lying down, snoozing, which was the best of all.

Jane's mother was at the computer in the kitchen. Horse show programs, feed and vet bills, and a check register were spread around her. In between teaching up-down lessons on two ancient appaloosa school ponies, she handled the show entries, the barn supplies, the vet and farrier scheduling, and the client billing for Tommy.

"Hi, Mom," Jane said.

Her mother took off her glasses. She was very plain looking. As long as I'd known her she had her hair cut to her chin in a bob. She wore faded jeans that sat too high on her hips and flannel shirts. Sometimes it was hard to believe she was married to Tommy. She didn't come to the shows often, only the really big ones. Sometimes it seemed like Tommy and Jane lived a different life from Mrs. Hewitt and Alex. Like, Mrs. Hewitt and Alex stayed home all winter while Jane and Tommy were in Florida.

She always talked really slowly and softly. "Hi, girls, what are you up to? Your dad need something?"

"Nope. We're just going up to my room."

The stairs creaked as we went upstairs. There were only two rooms on the second floor, Jane's and her parents' bedrooms, and no bathroom. There was a room in the attic that was Alex's. The only bathroom in the whole house was on the first floor. I couldn't imagine living with only one bathroom and it not even being on the same floor as the bedrooms. My mom and dad had a huge bathroom in the city and his-and-her bathrooms in Darien. When Hailey first saw the his-and-her bathrooms in Darien, she had stopped, and said, "Wait, your mom and dad *both* have their *own* bathroom?" I wished I could have said the house came like that, but it wasn't true. If I could have chosen I'd live in a house like Hailey's, not Jane's. But I guess that was the point—you didn't get to choose. Jane probably felt embarrassed about her house sometimes, the way I felt embarrassed about mine.

Hailey and I sat on Jane's bed as she found Vi's number.

"Who's doing the calling?" she asked.

Hailey and I both looked at each other and then at Jane. "You."

"Why me?"

"Because you're really good with grownups." Of the three of us, Jane was the best with adults. Catch-riding ponies and tagging along with Tommy had made her act like she was older than us. Sometimes it irritated Hailey and me, but now it might come in useful.

"Plus you've met her before and you're Tommy's daughter, so it makes more sense," I said.

"Fine." Jane dialed and a few moments later, she whispered, "It's ringing."

I was sitting on the edge of her bed. Jane's room had old, faded floral wallpaper. Over her dresser she had a wall of photos of the many different ponies she'd ridden over the years. There were so many that some I couldn't remember. I wondered if Jane could name them all.

"Hello?"

Even though I wasn't on the phone I was startled by the

creaky voice of the woman on the other end of the line and how well I could hear her sitting a few feet away from Jane.

"Oh, hi, um, Mrs. Kroll, this is Jane Hewitt."

"Who?" the woman nearly shrieked. It was as if since she couldn't hear very well, she was going to scream.

"Jane Hewitt. I'm Tommy Hewitt's daughter."

She responded in an outraged voice, "I don't know who you are, or what you're selling, but frankly I'm not interested."

Jane held out the phone. "She hung up."

"Really?" Hailey said.

"Yeah."

Jane shook her head. "I don't think this is going to work."

"Just call back," I said. "We need to try again."

"She probably won't answer."

"Just try."

Jane sighed and pressed redial.

"Get ready—in case she does answer," I said.

After a moment I heard the creaky-shrieky voice again. "Who is this?" she demanded.

Jane spoke loud and fast. "Don't hang up please this is Tommy Hewitt's daughter Jane my dad bought one of your ponies—a white medium with one blue eye."

"One of my ponies?"

Jane's eyes lit up. "Yes!"

I inched forward on the bed.

"A white pony, you say?" Vi Kroll asked.

"Yes, a medium."

"I had a pony get loose yesterday. That the one you're calling about? I already apologized for the trouble to your garden."

Jane's expression flattened. "No, no, this is one my dad bought from you."

"My father bought me my very first pony," Vi said, her cackly voice softening. "It cost fifty dollars, which was a lot of money at the time. I came out on Christmas morning and there was a bow around its neck. A big red bow."

"That's really... Wow." Jane made a shrugging motion to me and Hailey, as in, what now?

I whispered to her, "Ask about the brand."

"We were wondering a few things about the pony my dad bought from you. We body clipped it and it has a brand."

"A brand?"

"Yes, it's a half-moon with a triangle over it."

"I don't brand my ponies. There must be some mistake. It's not one of mine."

"Do you remember the pony you sold my dad?" Jane asked.

"Good-looking man, am I right? Quite dapper?"

Jane held back a giggle. "Yes, I guess he's dapper."

"Of course I remember him. He bought one from the six-year-old crop out of Legend. She's giving me some nice foals, that one."

"Legend? Is that her registered name?"

"Legend Has It. She was first on the line at Devon."

"Do you register the foals?"

Vi's outraged voice returned. "What kind of a question is

that? What kind of a breeder do you think I am? What kind of establishment do you think I'm running? This isn't a hog farm. My ponies have won at every top show in the country."

"I know," Jane said.

"Ask about the bowing," I mouthed.

"One other quick thing... Do you ever teach your ponies tricks?"

"Tricks? Parlor tricks?"

"We just wondered because the pony knows how to bow on cue."

"I don't think this is very funny," she said. "Now you're playing a trick on me. Shame on you."

"We're not," Jane said. "I'm sorry if you thought—"

Vi cut her off. "Do say hello to your father for me. Quite a dapper young man. I have to be going. Ta."

"Okay," Jane said. "Thanks!" She took a deep breath. "Ta?" she said to us.

"She's weirder than I thought," Hailey said.

"I tried to tell you."

"Dapper?" Hailey made a face. "What century is she living in?"

Jane laughed. "Quite dapper."

I chuckled, but I was more interested in what we'd learned. "So we need to look up Legend's foals. See if we can find one that fits Frankie's description. I guess he *could* be one of Vi's. But the brand still doesn't make sense, or the bowing."

"Maybe someone's sneaking into pastures and randomly branding ponies and then teaching them tricks," Hailey said.

Before I had the chance to laugh, Alex opened the door to Jane's bedroom. "Have you seen my red shirt?" he asked.

My face flushed just seeing him. He was totally cute.

"You could try knocking next time." Jane rolled her eyes. "What red shirt?"

"The red shirt I wear all the time," Alex said, like it should be obvious.

"The one you never wash?" Jane made a show of holding her nose.

Alex looked at Hailey and me, as if he just realized we were there. "What are you guys doing anyway?"

When no one answered I said, "We're trying to find out about Frankie—where he's from, what he did before he somehow ended up in Vi Kroll's pastures with a strange brand."

"And how exactly are you doing that?"

"Well, we started by calling Vi. And we've been researching Frankie's brand."

Alex nodded like he was kind of impressed. "You guys are like the pony detectives."

The pony detectives—I kind of liked the sound of that. And Alex didn't seem like he was making fun of us, either.

"What did you find out?" he asked.

"Not much so far," Jane said.

"Got any ideas?" I could tell Alex was losing interest in us. He was about to leave and I didn't want him to.

Alex shrugged. "I can't even find my shirt so I'm probably not the person to ask."

As Alex turned to leave, Jane said, "Check the dryer.

Maybe there's a load that got left in there." To me she said, "So what next, Spy Kid?"

Alex left the room, taking with him what seemed like all the energy. I kept staring at the door, listening to his footsteps as he ran downstairs to the laundry room.

"So?" Jane said.

"Why do you even think Alex wants his red shirt?" I realized I had said something out loud that should have just stayed in my own mind when I saw Jane's suspicious look.

"Wait, why do you care?"

Before I could make up an excuse Hailey blurted, "Because she likes him."

"What? You like my brother? My disgusting, revolting brother?"

I stood up from the bed. "No!"

Hailey was looking at her fingernails. "Oh, come on, it's so obvious." She turned her gaze to me so they both were staring at me.

I said in a low voice, "Well, maybe I think he's a little cute."

"Oh my god, Regan, you can't like Alex!"

"Shh!" I practically tackled Jane, covering her mouth with both my hands. The last thing I needed was for Alex to hear her.

Jane made a dramatic show of shivering. "I'm so grossed out right now."

"Nothing's ever going to happen," Hailey pointed out. "He's three years older and he barely knows Regan exists."

"Yeah, exactly." I wanted to get Jane off my back, but Hailey's words stung. As always Hailey was just calling things as they were. Alex would never like me. But why did three years have to be such a big deal? My dad was two *decades* older than my mother. Plus, Alex was only *two* years older than me. He was three years older than Jane, because she was still twelve, not thirteen like me.

"I guess I'll keep trying to figure out more about Frankie's brand," I said, happier than ever to dive back into the mystery of Frankie.

Chapter 20

OUR NEXT SHOW WAS OLD LYME. The weather was overcast and colder than it should have been for early June and some of the ponies were wild, playing in the corners of the ring. But of course Tyler was perfect. I won every single class with him, got good ribbons with Sammy, and was reserve champion with Drizzle. I should have been super psyched. Hailey got a third in one class and otherwise just got low ribbons, even with lots of ponies misbehaving. To make things worse, Dakota was reserve champion.

School ended for me the next week and the summer was officially here. With it came temperatures that were suddenly in the nineties. I had nothing to do each day but ride and hang out at the barn. In the summer we spent a lot more time in our house in Darien, usually at least from Thursday through Sunday, depending on Mom's work schedule. I liked some things about our Darien house, like how much closer it was to the barn, and my walk-in closet, but it was huge and I often felt lost in it. It was also almost too quiet in Darien. Our apartment was quiet, too, but you still had the outside sounds, the honking, car alarms, and sirens. Darien was just one big hush. Maybe I would have liked our house in Darien more if I had a dog to walk and play with in our ginormous yard. Of course we didn't have a dog. Ginormous yard, no dog.

Mom was making me take a kids' web design class that started in a few weeks and I'd probably spend time at the country club we belonged to, playing tennis or swimming in the pool.

At home, I did endless googling about brands, but couldn't find any brand in any country that matched Frankie's. I did learn about brands themselves and how they began way-back-when as a way for owners to mark their property. It made it possible to graze animals communally and thieves were less likely to steal branded horses. The Romans also used to brand their animals as part of a magic spell to protect them from evil. While most brands consisted of letters and numbers, people got creative and used symbols, shapes, slashes, reversed or upside-down letters, or combinations of a few of these things. One site also talked about how to read brands. You could read them from left to right or from top to bottom, or, when one character encloses another, from outside to inside. By reading them you could figure out who the owner was. There was information about some letters and symbols and what they meant. But there was nothing about either a half-moon or a triangle. I copied Frankie's brand onto pieces of paper and tried reading it from top to bottom. I still couldn't figure out anything beyond that it had something to do with a moon and there was a little triangle involved. It certainly didn't seem like he was any kind of recognizable breed.

Mom had her first week of chemo and for some reason this time the combination of drugs gave her really bad diarrhea. She started losing weight alarmingly fast—the first outward physical sign that something was wrong. She still tried to pretend she was fine and she kept doing everything at full speed, causing Dad and her to have some of the only arguments I'd ever heard them have, when he tried to insist she slow down and take it easy on her body. I felt like Dad, except angrier. How was she ever going to fight this if she didn't conserve her energy?

Different people took Mom to her chemo. She called them her cancer-brigade. Dad took her and her best friend Wendy and some other friends from ProduX. When I found out Susie was taking her, I said I got to go with her next. I'd never been allowed to go last time she'd been sick, but that was two years ago, and I felt old enough now. She and Dad agreed and I felt triumphant until the second we stepped off the elevator at Sloan Kettering, and I wished I'd never asked to come. It was eight o'clock at night—kind of a strange hour to have chemo, but Mom liked it that way. The hospital was quiet and afterward she could come home and go to sleep.

The hospital smelled like the Raid bug killer they used at the barn when they found a hornet's nest above one of the stalls. It was enough to make you feel nauseous, even if you weren't the one having chemo. That was the one thing I knew about chemo before Mom got cancer and had to start having infusions. (That was what they called getting chemo at the hospital—infusions—and that was what Mom liked to call it, too, although it sounded kind of weird to me, like it was a fruit smoothie, instead of a poisonous medical treatment.) All I knew about chemo pre-cancer-in-my-life was that you threw up a lot and you lost your hair. But actually, as I came to learn, not everyone throws up—Mom didn't—and you don't lose your hair right away either.

Mom knew all the nurses by name and chatted easily with them as they put a hospital bracelet on her and took her vital signs and blood. Then we had to wait around for what seemed like forever while they did up her blood work so the doctor could talk to her.

"Does it always take this long?" I checked the time on my phone. Twenty-five minutes felt like hours. I wanted to be back home.

"It's probably worse if you come during the day," Mom said. She handed me the US Weekly she'd just flipped through. "It won't be that much longer. Check out page fourteen... Shailene Woodley uses our new facial peel."

Facial peel? How could Mom be so relaxed? Mom said getting her infusion was no big deal, but I hated even the sight of a needle.

They finally called her name and I stayed in the waiting room while she went to meet with the doctor. When she came out, she said, "Okay, it's show time."

Mom had her own private room with a plasma TV and even a dinner menu to order from. I wouldn't have thought anyone would eat while they got their infusion but Mom ordered us two BLTs.

I gave her a confused face. "You hate BLTs." BLTs were always something that just Dad and I loved.

"It's kind of like being pregnant with you all over again," she said, smiling at the idea of that. "Strange cravings for foods I used to hate, and then there are some foods I used to like that I can't stand all of a sudden, like avocado."

Mom introduced me to the nurse, Shelly, who came in to hook up Mom's IV. Shelly was kind of pretty, but she wore too much makeup—blue eyeliner even though she had brown eyes. Mom always said that if you noticed someone's makeup that wasn't good.

"What's going on with the new guy?" Mom asked her.

Shelly clucked and shook her head. "Didn't turn out to be anything."

"I'm sorry," Mom said.

Shelly shrugged. "I'm beginning to think they're all losers." She worked quickly, setting up the IV. I looked away at first. Then I couldn't *not* look at it. Mom had been right— it really wasn't that bad.

Mom reached out and patted Shelly's arm like she was the one who had the life-threatening illness. "Hang in there, okay? I never thought I would meet the man of my dreams but I did, and—" Mom looked at me. "Now I have my angel here."

Shelly smiled. "I can hope, right? Okay, I'll be back to check on you in a little bit."

After Shelly left, Mom said, "So you want to watch a movie?"

"That's it?" I asked.

"What do you mean?"

"I mean, now you just sit here?"

"Yeah, simple, right?"

"And you don't feel it or anything?"

"In a little while my legs start to tingle and they drive me crazy—it's called restless leg syndrome. It's the same thing that happens to me at night. But otherwise, yeah, that's about it."

"Oh," I said. I couldn't believe I didn't really know about the restless leg thing. Now that Mom mentioned it, I sort of remembered a few mornings where she went straight for the Keurig and moaned to Dad about how badly she'd slept. But I guess as much as I claimed to want to know everything about Mom's cancer, there was a lot of stuff I tuned out.

Mom must have seen me looking kind of upset because she said, "It's not that bad, really."

"Then why didn't you want me to come when I was younger?"

Mom's eyes teared up. "Because you're not supposed to be having to go with your mom to get chemo."

"You mean your infusion," I corrected.

Mom chuckled. "Right."

Then there was this moment when neither of us said anything but still it felt like we both knew what we were thinking. I was thinking how she was right—that I didn't want to be here, that I didn't want my mother to have cancer, that I just wanted to have things back to the way they were before. That it didn't seem fair. But more than anything, I was thinking of how it might have been better if the infusions had seemed worse—if it had seemed like they were really doing something. Because this didn't seem like much of anything and that made me think they wouldn't be able to make the cancer go away. That made me think she was really going to die this time.

My eyes filled with heinous tears and Mom seemed to understand why without my having to tell her. She whispered, "Come here," and pulled me close. "I'm glad you came with me." I hugged her tight, nearly shaking. I'd been able to keep myself from thinking about her cancer all the time these last few weeks. I guess I had bought into the pretend-nothing's-wrong attitude. I'd been able to push cancer thoughts away, which was what she and Dad wanted me to do. But seeing her here, getting chemo, made it seem more real. I gripped her harder than I probably should have, the whole time in my head saying, please let this work. Please fix my mother.

Chapter 21

HAILEY AND JANE FINISHED SCHOOL two weeks later and we all headed to our first away show of the summer, Montclair. When we got to the show Hailey, Jane, and I hacked our ponies around and watched other classes. That night we went out to dinner at our favorite Mexican restaurant and then swam in the hotel pool. When I first started riding with Susie, Mom often booked us into the Hyatt and Starwood Hotels, while Hailey and Jane stayed in the Holiday Inn and Days Inn. But once I became friends with Hailey and Jane, I begged Mom to always book the same hotel that they were staying in. Being with my friends was much more important than the sheet thread count.

Mom and Mrs. Mullins sat by the pool talking while the three of us cantered into the water again and again and then judged each other on handstands. Jane's mom hadn't come to the show and her dad went out to dinner with another trainer so Jane had come back to the hotel with us. Anna was in the pool, too. She was always hanging out with us, which Hailey hated, and the three of us swam to the deep end and hung on the sides of the pool, in part to get away from her.

"Is Dakota showing?" Hailey asked.

Jane pulled her legs up to her stomach. "Yeah, I saw her. Oh my god, I didn't tell you what I heard."

Hailey and I both said together, "What?"

Jane was our source for gossip. She heard things from Tommy and was around more trainers to overhear them swapping stories.

"Dad was talking to Alison, who works for Hugo..."

We both nodded.

"She said at West Salem they were stabled next to Hell's Acres and that they had Dakota's pony in its stall in a bitting rig all day long."

We always heard horrible stories—people not watering their ponies so they'd be low on energy and quiet in the ring, or giving them drugs to make them quiet. It was hard to know what was true, but people definitely did terrible things to win. It was kind of funny to hear it from Alison, because from what we'd heard Hugo wasn't exactly a saint either.

"The poor pony." I shuddered, thinking of Smitten with her nose essentially tied to her chest all day. None of us liked Dakota, but that didn't mean Smitten should suffer.

Hailey pushed off from the wall. "That's animal cruelty."

We swam to the shallow end. Hailey's lips were blue. "I'm freezing."

"That's because you have no body fat," Jane said.

"I can't help it that I'm skinny."

I was actually cold, too, and I knew at any moment Mom

would be saying we should get back to the room. We climbed out and wrapped up in the thin hotel towels.

"Sometimes I'm just dying for a real night out," Mrs. Mullins was saying to Mom. "Remember your pre-kids days when you went out with your girlfriends and did wild and crazy things?" Mrs. Mullins made a face, her eyes wide and suggestive. "Well, you know what I mean."

Mom cleared her throat. "I guess so."

I couldn't imagine Mom ever doing anything wild and crazy. Everything in her world was always planned and reasonable, probably even when she was younger and single.

"We should go out! The two of us." Mrs. Mullins was leaning forward in her seat, her face flushed. "Sometime just you and me. A girls' night out."

Mom glanced at me. We were waiting for them, our towels wrapped around us, warmer now, but still shivering.

"Mom!" Hailey gave her mom a disgusted and disapproving look, like she was the parent.

"There's nothing wrong with a girls' night out." Mrs. Mullins shook her head. "Sometimes I can't believe I have such a prude for a daughter."

Hailey huffed and turned away from her mother. She muttered, "She's so stupid."

I didn't really see what was so bad about her mom wanting a girls' night out. And my mom could probably use it to loosen up a bit, but Hailey seemed horrified.

Mom stood up and so did Mrs. Mullins. "So, what do you say? It would be good for you, with everything going on..."

"Maybe, maybe," Mom brushed her off. "Okay, Regan, we better head up to the rooms."

Rooms. Hailey and her mom always shared a room. Mom and I always had separate rooms. It was colder out of the pool area. We scampered into the elevator and pressed the 'door closed' button five times. Jane had texted her dad and he was back at the hotel so she got off on the second floor. The Mullins and Mom and I got off on the fourth floor.

"See you in the a.m.," Mrs. Mullins said. "Sleep tight— don't let the bed bugs bite!"

Mrs. Mullins laughed and Hailey shook her head one more time. I waved at Hailey.

I took a long, hot shower and laid out my clothes for the morning on the extra bed. I was in bed, reading on my iPad, when Mom came in to say goodnight.

"Don't stay up much later," she said.

"I won't." I looked at her and tried to imagine her going out with Mrs. Mullins. "Do you think you and Hailey's mom will go out sometime?"

Mom made a funny, choking sort of sound. "No, definitely not."

Suddenly I was so mad at Mom. I was offended for Mrs. Mullins, for starters. Was Mom such a snob that she couldn't be friends with someone like Mrs. Mullins? "Why not? It sounds like fun. What's wrong with a girls' night out? Maybe you could use some more friends and some more fun."

Mom frowned. "I have friends."

"Wendy. Mrs. Mullins seems more fun." Mom and

Wendy met up every few months to go to the theater or the ballet. It hardly seemed like a raucous good time.

"Let me worry about my social life," Mom said. "And you need to get some sleep."

"A few more minutes of reading," I said.

She kissed me lightly on the cheek. "Only a few."

She was almost to the door when I said, "Are you going to die this time?"

Mom stopped, her back to me. She stood there for a few moments before turning around.

"You need to stop worrying and get some sleep or else you'll ride horribly and I'll feel terrible that it was all my fault." She smiled a fake Mother of TVMG smile.

It was the biggest non-answer-parental-brush-off ever, which meant I knew the real answer.

"Okay," I said because what else could I say? I couldn't say, sleep in here tonight, Mom. Sleep right next to me so I can wake up and know you're still here. So I can pretend you won't leave me.

I couldn't fall asleep. All I could think of was Mom dying. I made a promise to myself to love Tyler and win everything with him if somehow Mom could be okay. Then I worried about Dad and how he'd ever make it without her. Then I imagined her funeral and what it would be like or how I'd act. TVMG would wear a tasteful black dress and give a touching eulogy, the whole time clearly building massive amounts of character. Finally my thoughts turned morbid and I thought about how if she died, she'd actually be gone—poof, disappeared. Mom wanted to be cremated and I thought about her body burning. I started to breathe rapidly. It was too dark in the room and the TV looked sinister somehow, as did the heavy hotel curtains. I wished I was home. I turned on the light. Maybe seeing the hotel room was worse. I turned it back off. My mom could really die this time. What I'd read online said very few people in her situation made it. I found myself promising God I would do anything, if he just didn't let my mother die, when I'd never prayed to God in my life. I clutched my pillow to my chest, shaking and sobbing.

I don't know when or how I fell asleep. Seeing the light of day made me feel better, but I knew more nights like that one would come.

Chapter 22

THE NEXT MORNING, we parked in the exhibitors' lot and walked to the tent where we were stabled. We passed Vanessa, who owned the mobile tack store, pulling out bottles of fly spray, water buckets, and halters. The stabling manager, Roger, a clipboard under his arm, buzzed by on his four-wheeler. By the tent, the farrier was opening up the back of his truck, revealing hundreds of horseshoes in different shapes and sizes. A groom holding a big bay horse waited nearby, the first customer of the day.

The announcer's familiar voice rang out over the show: "Welcome to day four here at the Montclair Horse Show. We'll be starting off with the green ponies in the pony ring, USEF Medal in ring one, and younger amateur-owner hunters, we're looking for you in the main hunter ring. Eight o'clock start all around the horn today."

Tyler was all braided and Martha was trimming his whiskers with a razor.

"Morning, kiddo," she said.

Mom passed Martha the coffee we'd gotten on the way to the show.

"Thank you," she said, taking a sip.

Susie stopped by and collected her coffee. She told us there were eight green ponies, twelve smalls and thirteen mediums, so she predicted Drizzle would go around ten and Tyler and Sammy closer to noon.

"Tyler was so good yesterday I don't think we need to hack him around," she added. "Martha will take him for a hand-walk and you can just get on a little early, okay?"

"Yup." I smiled, but my stomach felt uneasy. It was weird, though, because I wasn't nervous about doing well. It was something else I was feeling.

Jane picked up a catch ride in the greens and Hailey and I went up to watch her. It was a roan large with a cresty neck. It didn't jump the absolute best, but it moved cute and with Jane's accurate ride she was first and second over fences. Watching her talk to the trainer of the pony, I couldn't help but feel jealous. How cool would it be to be such a good rider that people asked you to show their ponies? Frankie wasn't ready to show yet, but Tommy had brought him so he could get used to all the action. Jane had hacked him around the show grounds and Tommy had grooms take him out for hand-walks.

After Jane rode, the three of us went back to the barn and Hailey and I got dressed to show. Mom braided my hair into two braids and tied them with blue ribbons. I started wearing blue for good luck when I was in short stirrup and it became all I ever wore. My mom bought my bows from Belle & Bow

Equestrian. They made all kinds of beautifully colored bows, but I always wore my blue ones. Hailey changed the color of hers every time, and Jane wore her hair up in her helmet like the bigger kids did.

I did well in the smalls with Drizzle, winning the first class and placing third in the second class. For the mediums, Susie put our numbers in early and Hailey, Jane, and I got started cantering small verticals, then a medium oxer, and finishing over a bigger vertical. We all schooled well and I could feel people's eyes on me again—parents, other trainers and riders—wondering if Tyler was going to be perfect today and if anyone would have a chance to beat me. Maybe they thought West Salem and Old Lyme were flukes, and now that I'd had him several weeks, I'd have messed him up. I wasn't sure what they wanted to see. Did they want me to do badly so they could be happy that buying a high-priced winner didn't mean you'd win? Or did they secretly want me to be perfect so they could hate me even more for it? The only thing I knew was I didn't like the extra attention.

Jane went early in the class, like she always liked to do, and Coco was better through her changes.

I waited at the in gate, watching Hailey, while Martha wiped my boots and Tyler's mouth. Hailey turned in a good round. She had one long spot that Donald had to reach for, but overall it was really good.

"Okay?" Susie asked me. "Just find your rhythm and keep it. Let the jumps come to you."

I glanced over to where Mom was watching from the other side of the ring. Dad was away on business and by the time he got back later that day, it didn't really make sense for him to come. Mom had a big straw hat on so I couldn't see her face. Even though she made a living on cosmetics, Mom always said that the best way to have beautiful skin was to stay out of the sun.

"Go get 'em," Susie said, as I entered the ring.

I passed Hailey coming out and she whispered, "Good luck."

I rode my opening circle and just like Susie said I found a good rhythm. It was easy enough on Tyler. Sometimes in my opening circle everything felt just right and I knew I was going to find every distance. Other times—mostly on other ponies—my canter felt choppy or too slow and I knew every distance was going to be like fighting a battle. But Tyler didn't seem to have any mode but perfect. I felt like my job was not to screw things up, not to get in his way, and that didn't feel much like riding. I wanted to come out of the ring feeling like I accomplished something, not like I was the girl chosen from the audience for a magic trick.

So I decided on the way to the first jump to put my theory to the test and try to let Tyler do everything. But it turned out doing nothing was harder than you would think. I mean, you can't make yourself *not* see the distance. I guess I could have closed my eyes but that seemed like going too far. Still, I did as little as I could, but when I saw a distance, it was nearly impossible not to squeeze him forward or lightly steady him. So I guess riding Tyler wasn't exactly a total piece of cake; still he made it look so easy that no one ever believed I had any part in making it happen.

Susie clapped and whooped as I left the ring. Hailey's second trip was a little better than her first and my second trip in the handy class was really good, too. Of course, I ended up winning both classes. I was also fourth and sixth with Sammy. Hailey did really well, too. The judge must have liked Donald a lot because she was third in the first class and second in the second class, and even Jane got a low ribbon in the first class with Coco. Dakota was second and fifth. Everyone congratulated me and I smiled and tried to act like I was super happy, but I just felt dull inside.

We had the hack, too, so after we jogged we hopped off and the grooms took off the ponies' martingales. Hailey always hacked Donald even though she rarely got a ribbon and if she did it was vomit-colored. There were a few other really good movers in the hack so it wasn't a given that Tyler would win. Susie reminded me to make sure I didn't get lost in the crowd. I had a nice pass down the long side by myself at the trot in the first direction and I could tell the judge was watching me. Out of the corner of my eye, I even thought I saw her jot down my number. When we reversed direction I looked around at the other ponies. I figured it was probably between me and Smitten for the win. As much as I didn't love winning, I didn't want Dakota to win. I couldn't get much of a good pass at the trot in the second direction. I did get a nice pass at the canter. The announcer called for us to walk and line up. I lined up next to Hailey, but then kind of wished I hadn't. It must have been awful for her to always wait in line while my number was called first, or maybe second.

"We have the results of the medium pony hunter under saddle."

At the announcer's voice, I sat up taller in the saddle and scratched Tyler's withers with one hand.

"Winning our class today is number 457, Smitten, owned and ridden by Dakota Pearce of Bronxsville, New York."

Dakota walked her pony forward to collect the blue ribbon. I guess all the time in the bitting rig had done its trick. Her pony had kept his head down. Did Dakota know what Lenny and Kitty had done to her pony? She probably didn't care. She looked annoying just walking out of the ring—the way she held her chin up, as if she'd been crowned queen of the universe. It was only a hack class, after all. I would probably still be second—the one time I wouldn't have minded winning.

"And in second place, number 529, Woodland's Tried and True, ridden by Regan Sternlicht."

I patted Tyler's outstretched neck as I walked forward for the red ribbon. As I left the ring, I listened to the rest of the results, hoping to hear Hailey's number called. Maybe someone had picked up a wrong lead and she'd get a ribbon or the judge would give her a ribbon since he seemed to like Donald. Vomit-colored was better than nothing, and even a half-point for sixth place could help her be reserve champion and qualify for Pony Finals. Jane was fifth with Coco. Hailey didn't place.

I could tell she was disappointed as she came out of the ring.

"Want to wait around and troll the large ponies?" I asked, hoping to lift her spirits. "Abby Wilde's showing so we totally might get rides."

She smiled. "Yeah, definitely."

Chapter 23

THE GROOMS TOOK THE PONIES back to the barn.
We'd have to wait through the two over fences for the large
ponies. There were only eight larges and we liked watching
anyway. Sometimes I thought I could sit all day, watching
round after round and never get bored. Abby Wilde had three
of the eight large ponies, which meant the classes dragged on
because they had to wait for her to switch ponies and warm
up. But it also meant that, when it came time for the under
saddle, we'd have a good chance at hacking one of her ponies.

While we watched the over fences, Hailey calculated the
championship points for our division. "You have twenty-six
points," she said. "Dakota was second, fifth, and first so she
has seventeen points. You'll definitely be champion, no matter
what."

"Not if I don't place tomorrow," I said.

Hailey made a face. "Like that's going to happen. You
don't even need to win. You probably just need to get like one
low ribbon to be champion. But if I get two good ribbons and

Dakota doesn't do well, I could be reserve. The points are really spread out."

"That would be so awesome," I said. "You can totally do it."

"Maybe it'll rain." Hailey looked at the sky, hopeful.

When the over fences classes ended we meandered over to the in gate. We tried to act casual, like we were just hanging out, and not really scoping out rides.

Abby's ponies all got jogs and her trainer, Trish, scanned the in gate for joggers. Her eyes fell on us, conveniently still in our show coats. "Wanna jog a pony, girls?"

"Sure," we both said at the same time.

I let Hailey step forward first and claim Melbourne. I got Summer Solstice. Melbourne was the nicer of the two ponies and I hoped Hailey would get the better jogs. Abby jogged her best pony, Elemental.

In the first class, Elemental won, Melbourne was third, and Summer Solstice fifth. In the second class, Melbourne won so Abby quickly switched with Hailey so she could jog Melbourne. Hailey jogged Elemental in second and I was fourth with Summer Solstice.

When we came out of the ring, Hailey and I exchanged a quick hopeful glance as we waited to see if Trish was going to ask us to hack the ponies.

"You girls want to hack them?" Trish asked.

"Definitely."

"You got a saddle nearby?"

"Yup," Hailey said.

The grooms saddled up the ponies. Trish asked for

Hailey's name and then said, "Hailey, you'll hack Melbourne. She's pretty straightforward. Just watch your canter transitions. You need a good bit of leg to get her going. Do you have spurs on?"

"Small ones," Hailey said.

Trish glanced at her spurs. "Should do." She turned to me. "Regan, right?"

I nodded. Of course she knew me. The girl who'd bought Tyler.

"Summer Solstice can be a little stiff, especially to the right. Try to bend her in the corners when you can but not too much that you get her upset."

I nodded as one of Abby's grooms threw me into the saddle. I patted Summer Solstice and picked up my reins. Riders were already in the ring. There was no time to trot around in the schooling area. I followed Hailey into the ring as the announcer called the class to order.

I felt more nervous for this hack class than I had any of the times I'd shown Tyler. I wanted to prove to Trish and anyone else watching that I could ride, and I certainly didn't want to make a stupid mistake like pick up the wrong lead. That would get *everyone* talking.

At the announcer's cue, we picked up the trot. Summer Solstice was comfortable and didn't seem that stiff to me. Abby had a lot of money and really nice ponies. I wondered if she ever felt bad about being so lucky? She certainly didn't seem to care.

I tried to use the corners of the ring when I could tell the judge wasn't looking to bend Summer Solstice like Trish had said to. I used more inside leg than inside hand like Susie had taught us. Then I let her flow on a looser rein down the long side.

Abby was already doing the children's hunters and three-foot medals, in addition to the large ponies. Next year I heard she'd be starting the big eq and moving up to the junior hunters. I also heard she was in the market for her first jumper. There were plenty of kids like her, who had the best horses and didn't seem to feel badly about it the way I did. What was wrong with me?

We came down to a walk and then picked up the canter. I got the right lead and eased into a little half-seat, letting Summer Solstice stretch out her neck.

I guess one way kids dealt with having really nice horses was to push themselves even harder. Molly Donovan was only fourteen and she was already doing small grand prix classes. Heather Mack went to Europe on a Nations Cup team when she was sixteen.

The announcer called for us to walk and reverse. If this direction went well, I had a chance of being in the top three as far as I could gauge. But this was Summer Solstice's harder direction according to Trish.

So maybe I could do that—push myself to achieve so much more than most people my age. But then I wouldn't be here, trolling for hack rides with Hailey, or hanging out with her and Jane. I'd always be at another ring, at another lesson, riding another horse. I kind of liked being where I was supposed to be.

"All canter, all canter please."

What I really liked about riding wasn't certain wins or doing crazy big classes for my age, it was getting to know a pony and getting it to go its best. Which with Tyler wasn't hard at all. Maybe I was just weird that way.

The announcer called for us to walk and line up. I lined up next to Hailey again. It was funny seeing her on a pony other than Donald. She was staring straight ahead and I could tell the idea of getting a good hack ribbon, even if it was on someone else's pony, was a lot of fun.

I listened for my number but I was still surprised when I heard it called first. I had won? I patted Summer Solstice and stepped forward. I had won. On a pony I'd never ridden before. On a pony that didn't always win the hacks. Abby was riding Elemental for a reason—because that was the pony Trish thought she'd win with. Had Abby made a mistake on Elemental like break or pick up the wrong lead?

As I took the blue ribbon, the results continued. Abby was second with Elemental. If she had made a big mistake, she wouldn't have been in the ribbons. Hailey was fourth.

Outside the in gate I slid off Summer Solstice. Abby's groom took the reins and I handed him the ribbon.

When I turned around, Trish was there. "Really good ride. That's the first hack she's ever won. You got her going really soft."

"Thank you," I said, beaming.

It felt like the nicest thing anyone had ever said to me. I was more proud of that blue ribbon than any I had won with Tyler.

Chapter 24

THE NEXT DAY, THERE WASN'T a cloud in the sky and it was suddenly hot. I was sweaty before I pulled on my show coat.

Hailey had a swap before the single oxer in the first round. Her second round was outstanding. The best, most consistent round she'd had in a while.

My first trip on Sammy was good. I was really long to a jump in the second class. On Tyler, I had a good trip in the first round. The second course started toward the in gate over a single brush, then across the diagonal to an oxer. Susie told me not to start out with too much pace, to keep it quiet to the first two jumps. Tyler had such a big stride that I didn't need much pace to get down the first line. I found the perfect quiet spot to the single and another nice distance to the oxer. I pressed Tyler forward a little more than I needed to, going to the first line coming home. After the long distance in I needed to steady Tyler right away to fit in the seven strides evenly. But I waited three strides, making it look like I forgot where I was, and then steadied him. I fit in the seven strides, but the last distance was very tight.

I rode the last two lines better and came out of the ring saying, "That line got tight. I guess I keep forgetting how big his stride is."

Susie squinted at me. "When you jump in long like that in a line coming toward the in gate you know you have to steady him right away." She shook her head and walked away from me.

I slid off and Martha came to get Tyler ready for the jog. She gave me a puzzled look.

"I made one little mistake," I said.

"One mistake?" She cocked her head.

"Yes, one mistake." I expected Mom would be all over me about right now. I saw she'd gotten caught up talking to Olivia Martin's mother.

Martha spritzed Tyler with fly spray. "Okay, you're still getting used to his stride."

"Exactly."

Her lips were pursed tight as if she was trying hard not to say something else. Was she taking my side? Or was she being sarcastic and she didn't believe that I wasn't used to his stride? I couldn't tell.

I left her with Tyler and went to talk to Hailey, hoping to escape before Mom got away from Mrs. Martin. Hailey was chewing on the tip of her leather glove on her pointer finger, watching Isabelle Rollins. Isabelle let her pony get too strung out to the last line and had a huge chip.

"Nearly everyone's made a mistake in the second round,"

Hailey said. "Olivia chocolate-chipped, Jane had a rough change, and you were tight coming out of the line with Tyler."

I could tell Hailey was wary of saying the logical next part—how she really might win. I didn't want to jinx her so I kept quiet, too. There were five more rounds till the jog. We watched in silence and I knew Hailey was praying just like I was for everyone to mess up. And they did. Even Dakota cross-cantered for a few strides.

We huddled around Elena, waiting for the jog. If Hailey won the second class, she might have a chance at the reserve championship and be qualified for Pony Finals.

The jog came over the walkie-talkie. I was on top in the first class with Tyler and fourth with Sammy. Lily Brennan was second. Hailey was third. Dakota was fifth. That meant the judge today liked Donald, too—he'd given him a fourth *with* a swap. I balled my fists up, waiting.

"Second class goes like this..."

When Hailey's number was called first, I still looked at her to confirm that she had been called on top. Dakota was second and I was called third with Tyler.

Hailey did a little hop in place and said a quiet, "yes!" In the horse show world you weren't supposed to celebrate your wins with high-fives, fist-pumps, or end-zone dances. Riders were supposed to keep their emotions in check—when we won or lost. Only grand prix riders ever held up a hand in the air triumphantly during a victory gallop or cursed another rider's faster jump-off time. Hailey's reserved little celebration seemed justified, though. She had waited long enough to have her number called first.

Hailey hurried to get Donald.

"Second class is conformation, girls," Susie said as I took Tyler from Martha.

Hailey's shoulders sank. Mine did, too. How could we both have forgotten that today was conformation? I did the mental calculations that I knew Hailey was doing, too. I was in third place so it was unlikely I would be moved up to first. Impossible? Unheard of? No. But unlikely. Dakota's pony wasn't a model winner. Still, Smitten had better conformation than Donald. Donald was the boy with the brilliant brain and the scrawny body. He had a long back, a plain head, and lots of jewelry, including a big splint on his right front.

We jogged the first class and I smiled as I accepted the blue. But all I was thinking about was Hailey and what would happen next.

Chapter 25

HAILEY LED THE JOG FOR THE second class, her own knees bouncing up extra high. To me leading the jog was old hat, but to Hailey it was all new. I only hoped she would stay on top.

We lined our ponies up as the judge came into the ring to examine them. I peeked down the line to see Hailey working it with Donald, trying hard to get his ears up and his neck stretched out. Donald yawned, his ears cocked out to the side. He looked like he couldn't be bothered to even try—like he already knew how this was going to turn out.

I would have been happy to let Tyler stand with his legs splayed, but he was a modeling robot and planted his feet perfectly squarely without me even having to try to position him. He pricked up his ears and looked through the bridle as if he was waiting for his close-up. No Victoria's Secret model had as much presence as he did.

The judge started at the top of the line. I kept peeking down to where Hailey was trying desperately to get Donald to put his ears up. She was tapping her palm with the end of her crop and then, when that failed, taking a pinch of footing and rubbing it between her fingers. Still, Donald's ears remained cocked to the side.

The judge walked around Donald, taking in his legs and, no doubt, his splint. She spent enough time on him that it was clear she would be open to moving him down. If she had just zoomed past him, it would probably mean she wasn't going to move him.

She checked Smitten next, taking about the same amount of time she had with Donald. When she got to Tyler she stood to the side of him and I could tell she was admiring him. I didn't try to get Tyler to look good, but he did it anyway. The judge circled around him, making quick notations on her clipboard, all the while wearing a satisfied half-smile like someone who had just had a delicious-looking dessert placed in front of them.

Please, I prayed, just move me up one spot. Not two. Please. It seemed to take forever until she made her way through the rest of the ponies. I didn't dare glance at Hailey now. I didn't want to see her waiting, chewing on her glove.

Finally, the judge walked back toward the top of the line. Damn it. She wasn't going back to her booth and calling over the walkie-talkie that the results were good and to pin the class as it stood. I said one last prayer that she'd move me up to second, or, at worst, swap Hailey and Dakota. Hailey wouldn't win and Dakota would, but it wouldn't be my fault.

"Number 237—" The judge was pointing at me. I braced myself. "Move up a spot, please."

One spot, over Dakota. Hailey still was winning.

I eagerly swapped places with Dakota. She huffed a breath out the side of her mouth and did the riding-equivalent of a stomp back to third place.

Now I allowed myself to look down the line at Hailey. We were first and second! Beating Dakota! It couldn't get more perfect than this. Hailey would be reserve champion and would qualify for Pony Finals. She grinned at me, her shoulders raising in a small who-would-have-guessed shrug.

I noticed that the judge hadn't left the ring. We'd already jogged. What was she waiting for? Why wasn't she calling in the change and why wasn't the announcer pinning the class? Was she considering another swap further down the line?

But she was standing in between Tyler and Donald, still looking at the ponies with her clipboard raised in front of her. A feeling of panic swept over me and Hailey's face looked terrified, too, as she realized what was happening. The judge looked down at her clipboard and then at me. "Up one more."

"One more?" I said, as if I hadn't heard her right.

"You two are swapping. Move up to first."

I stared at her a moment longer, trying to figure out if there was anything I could possibly do to change her mind.

She called over the radio. "237 moves up to first."

Hailey led Donald back behind me. I tried to catch her eye and tell her how sorry I was. She made a point of not looking at me.

I sleepwalked out of the ring and then back into the ring to get the championship ribbon. Dakota was reserve champion. Being second, not first, had cost Hailey the reserve championship. Dakota had beaten her by two points. If the class had stood how it was called or I had been moved only to second place, Hailey would have been reserve. When I came back out of the ring, I looked for Hailey but she was gone.

Chapter 26

I STARTED BY GOOGLING THINGS like "missing pony" or "lost pony" the night we got home from Montclair. I wanted to do anything to make myself forget about getting moved up over Hailey and causing her to miss winning the class and qualifying for Pony Finals. Mom was exhausted from the show and had gone to bed early.

By the time I'd gotten back to the tent at the show, Hailey had left. Martha said Hailey had to go with her mom to pick up her brother, but I knew she didn't want to see me.

"It's not your fault," Martha had said to try to make me feel better. "You can't control the results." She looked at me meaningfully—like maybe she *did* think I was trying to control the results. "She'll qualify."

"But what if she doesn't?" If Hailey didn't qualify for the hunters, it would be unlikely her parents would want to pay for her to go all the way to Kentucky just for the Pony Medal. It would be awful to go to Pony Finals without Hailey, and she also wouldn't be able to do the lip sync.

"Life isn't fair, is it?" Martha reached up and adjusted her bandana, as if she were subtly making the point that she was talking about a lot more than ribbons: her burns, Mom's cancer, the things in life you couldn't control.

"Yeah, I guess."

I sat on the couch with my laptop, hoping the distraction would work. Dad was in a chair reading on his iPad. I hadn't gotten far with the brand research and this was the only next step I could think of. Spending time on Frankie also kept my mind off Mom's treatment. We had entered the second phase—where the chemo drained Mom's health and we prayed like hell it would work. Everything depended on what the next results showed. If the chemo shrank the tumors and they could be removed, everything would be as close to okay as possible. If not, we progressed to phase three. We'd never been to phase three before, so I didn't quite know what it was about yet. All I knew was that it wasn't a place you wanted to be.

I got some hits on "lost pony" but nothing in Maryland or any place that sounded remotely close to Vi's. There was a missing miniature pony in Pennsylvania and a missing Fjord in DC. I moved on to equine websites, checking the classifieds and bulletin boards. But it was also hard to know when Frankie might have gone missing, *if* he had gone missing. It could have been months ago, or years ago. Although it seemed more likely it would be sort of recently since he knew that trick of bowing. Would he remember it on cue like that if he learned it years ago? Perhaps. I'd heard stories of horses remembering people many years after they last saw them, so why not tricks they were taught?

There had to be someone at Vi's who would remember Frankie, I decided. Vi was batty and she might not take the best care of her ponies, but she usually did feed and water them. People rode them.

At the barn on Tuesday I asked Tommy whether Vi had a trainer. He had on a yellow polo today. He was tan from being in the sun so much and I thought how Vi had called him dapper.

"Not really," he said as we walked the ponies around the ring after our lesson. "There's a local girl, Kelly, who helps her with them sometimes."

"And there must be people who feed them and muck the stalls, right?"

"She goes through barn help pretty fast. Most people don't stick around when they don't get paid."

It figured that Vi didn't always pay people. The workers would be hard to track down, but Kelly might be someone we could talk to.

"You and Jane really want to find out about Frankie, huh?" Tommy said.

"Hailey, too," I said, glancing across the ring to where she was walking Donald on a loose rein. I'd said hi to Hailey but not much else and I was worried she was still mad at me from the show. I hadn't seen her yesterday since Tuesday was her voice lesson. I texted her a bunch and she'd barely written back.

"Does Kelly have a last name? Or a phone number?"

Tommy was changing the jumps around now. He and Susie usually set a new course each week. He lifted rails and wiggled standards, no longer looking at me. Maybe he hadn't heard me, or was pretending he hadn't heard me.

"Jane," he called out. "I need you to get on Oscar. He was stopping with Grace and he needs a school before she rides him again."

I walked to where Tommy was adjusting a small roll top. "Um, so do you know Kelly's last name?"

"I need Jane's attention on her ponies," Tommy said, his back still to me. "And I know your mother feels the same way about you. Pony Finals will be here before you know it."

"I know." I stood there quietly for a few extra moments. If Tommy didn't say anything soon, I'd have to give up.

"Kenney," he finally said as he bent over the roll top. "Kelly Kenney."

"Thank you," I said.

The three of us walked the ponies out of the ring and over to the barn. The hay and shavings were being delivered from a big tractor-trailer that was parked to the side of the front door.

Donald and Tyler didn't care—they were used to big trucks. But as we approached, Frankie's head shot up. Jane took a hard feel of the reins. Frankie started to skitter and shy. He let out a shrill whinny.

"What the heck is wrong with this pony?" Jane said.

"He's scared of the truck."

"Thanks," Jane said. "I hadn't figured that out."

Frankie sidestepped, tossing his head. Jane gave a frustrated I've-had-it sigh, hopped off, and started leading him, snorting, into the barn.

"Shouldn't you try to get him used to it?" I called after her.

She said without looking back, "Dad told me to get on Oscar."

Jane disappeared into the barn and I turned to Hailey, hoping to share a sympathetic look. But she was already sliding off Donald and pulling the reins over his head. Suddenly I felt like I was losing both my friends.

"Wait," I said. "I'm sorry."

"For what?"

"You know... getting moved up."

Hailey shrugged and started into the barn. Over her shoulder she said, "It's not your fault you have the best pony in the country and win everything, no matter what."

I stood there after she had gone, considering what she'd just said. While I understood how upset she was, I also felt like she had finally gone too far with her careless words. I certainly wasn't going to run after her and keep apologizing.

When I led Tyler into the barn, Jane had Frankie in his stall. He was sticking his head out the door above the stall chain as she rushed to strip his saddle. Frankie gazed out at me with a still-anxious look. Why are you scared of trailers? I wondered. What happened to you?

Chapter 27

I FOUND KELLY KENNEY pretty easily through postings on *The Chronicle* Bulletin Board. I sent her a quick message explaining that I rode with Susie and Tommy and that we couldn't find the pony Tommy had bought from Vi registered with the USEF, even though Vi had said it was one of Legend's foals. I also explained about the brand and asked whether she remembered whether he'd been at Vi's long. I dashed off the email before bed and checked my messages first thing the next morning, but she hadn't replied. On the ride to the barn mid morning I was still checking my phone constantly.

"What's up?" Mom said. "Waiting for something?"

"We're trying to figure out where Frankie came from and we emailed the girl who rides for Vi, but she hasn't written back." I used "we" pretty liberally since Jane was clearly sick of Frankie and Hailey was barely talking to me. But I didn't want Mom to think it was just me who was obsessed.

Mom took one hand off the wheel and massaged her own neck. "Do Susie and Tommy know you're doing this?"

"Of course," I said as I stared at my iPhone, wishing it would 'bing' with a new message. My phone had been disturbingly quiet these past few days, since Hailey still wasn't texting or FaceTiming me.

It was Thursday, one of Hailey's voice lesson days, and I found myself partly glad she wouldn't be at the barn, although feeling like that also made me sad. Hailey was my best friend, after all.

Mom stayed to watch my lesson. Her hair had lost its shine and body, but it hadn't started to fall out yet. It looked dull and she was skinnier, bordering on frail, even with the flowing shirts she wore to try to make herself look better. I told myself it was good that she looked bad—it meant the chemo was working and would be shrinking the tumors. I hadn't been having such bad nights as I had at the hotel during Old Lyme, but I hadn't been sleeping great. The dark was freaking me out more and more and I had to sleep with a light on. Even so, just the noise of the wind outside made me nervous.

As we rode, I couldn't keep my eyes off Frankie, sneaking glances whenever I could. His neck looked more cresty and his hind end looked stronger, too. Susie had us jumping an in-and-out and while Frankie had gotten calmer about jumping single fences and even long lines, two jumps only a stride apart blew his mind a little. Jane quickly lost her patience with him as he tried to run through the in-and-out. There was something about Frankie that really drove Jane crazy. She usually tolerated all the problem ponies Tommy tossed her up on, but it was like Frankie was the last straw. I could see her face getting more and more flushed and when Susie asked her to pull him up she yanked him harder than she needed to and then gave him another sharp tug when Susie's back was turned. It was only making Frankie more upset and frantic. I wished I could be on him. I would have all the patience he needed. I'd pat his neck and tell him he was going to be fine.

Mom watched me ride from the fence and then after we were done Susie came over to chat with her while we took the ponies for a walk around the outside of the rings.

"I hate this pony," Jane said. "Did you hear back from Kelly Kenney?"

"Not yet." I was itching to check my phone the moment we got back to the barn.

"I hope we find out he's stolen so we can give him back."

I'd thought Jane was interested in where he'd come from, but she just wanted to be rid of him. "Why do you hate him so much? I mean you've ridden lots of crazy ponies. Remember Fifi?"

Fifi liked to ram Jane's legs into the side of the ring. Jane had to school him in awful rubber boots just to give her legs some protection and so she didn't ruin another pair of good boots or half-chaps.

"That's just it," Jane said. "I'm so sick of reject ponies that I'm supposed to magically make better. You know how many times my legs were black and blue from Fifi?"

"A lot."

"But in the end we got her going right and Dad sold her for a lot. I just feel like I deserve to either keep a pony I've made or to get one nice pony for a change. A green pony is fine—just not damaged goods."

We passed the trail leading off into the woods. Tyler turned his head, almost like he wanted to take the path, and I had to pull him back.

"But just think of how amazing you are. How cool is it that you fix all these ponies!" I would have much rather been known for fixing ponies than for riding perfect ones.

"Well, I'm not fixing this one," Jane said.

I said kind of quietly, "That's not really fair to Frankie."

"And it's not fair to me that I do all the work, but do I get anything for it? No. I didn't even get to show Ike at Devon. Did I tell you he's leading the country in points?"

Even though I wished I had Jane's problem, I could still understand what she was feeling. She did do so much of the work—she was like a twelve-year-old professional rider. "Have you ever tried explaining it to your dad?"

"He won't listen." She shook her head.

But it really *wasn't* fair to Frankie. I began to hope, like Jane, that maybe we'd find he had owners who cared about him, who taught him tricks, but something had happened and they lost him and now they wanted him back. Although I didn't want him to leave the barn, either.

Back at the barn, I gave Tyler to Martha and went into the tack room. I pulled a baseball hat on over my sweaty hair and grabbed my phone from my tack trunk. I had three new emails: one junk mail, one from another riding friend, and one from Kelly Kenney. A shiver of excitement tickled my spine as I opened it.

Hi!

Got your email. I remember the pony but I don't know where Vi got him from. I wasn't at the barn for a few weeks back in October and then when I came back there he was. I remember asking Vi about him and she insisted he was one of hers. I didn't think he was but it's no use arguing with her when she gets something in her mind. I guess I figured some crazy friend of hers dumped him on her. That's all I know! Good luck!

Kelly

Jane came in carrying Frankie's bridle. She hung it on the cleaning hook in the middle of the room and picked up the empty tack bucket.

"Listen to this—" I said as she moved to the sink to fill the bucket. I read her the email.

"Great, so we still know nothing." Jane turned on the faucet and filled up the bucket.

"Well, we know he came to Vi's in October."

"What good does that do us?"

"It's something." I put my phone down and started in on my saddle. Martha cleaned the bridles, but it was up to me to take care of my saddles.

Jane had positioned the bucket between us and we both dunked our sponges in the warm water and wrung them out. I ran my sponge along the bar of saddle soap and inhaled deeply—there was nothing better than the fruity smell of glycerin.

Jane cleaned the rubber reins on Frankie's schooling bridle with a vengeance, using the sponge, a toothbrush, and her fingernails to pry off the caked dirt.

I cleaned the flap on the side I was working on and then ran my sponge along the stirrup leathers. "Have you talked to Hailey today?"

Jane dunked her sponge in the water, which had turned a milky brown. "We texted."

"Is she mad at me? Did she say anything to you?"

Jane washed the suds from the reins. She seemed a little calmer now, like she'd gotten some anger out on the rubber reins. "You mean about the show?"

I rolled up my stirrup and wiped a little Supple leather conditioner on my sponge. "Yeah, I feel terrible, but it's not really my fault. I think she hates me."

"She doesn't hate you. It's just.... Sometimes it's hard. I mean, I know what she's feeling."

"Great, so you both hate me."

Jane was scrubbing the green crud off the bit now, but she wasn't as furious in her scrubbing. "We don't hate you. How could we hate you when we love you? Just give her another day or so."

"I guess I'm at least glad you guys are being normal and getting mad at me. It feels like some people are just nice to me because of the mom-cancer thing."

Jane looked thoughtful. "That must suck. Sometimes I can tell people are just being nice to me because of who my dad is and it's so fake. I can always tell and I totally want to call them on it."

"Yeah to me they're all like, 'how are you *doing*?'" I strung out the word 'doing' the way people always did.

Jane said, "And 'oh, you rode *so* well. Your pony is *so* nice.' Um, did you see her bolt through her change?"

Jane and I dissolved into laughter. I guess I hadn't thought people kissed up to her because of her dad.

I rubbed the Supple on my saddle. The leather drank up the conditioner, turning a shade darker. "And you're okay with me maybe kind of having a crush on Alex?"

Jane dunked the bit in the water and stuck out her tongue. "I can't possibly understand it, but, yeah, if you like him, ugh, whatever. Like you said, nothing's going to happen anyway."

"Right, exactly."

"Can you change the water?"

"Yup." I took the bucket over to the sink and dumped it down the drain.

It felt like Jane and I had more in common than I realized. Maybe what we had in common was that we weren't allowed to hold on to the things we desperately wanted to keep. "It stinks that you make up ponies and don't get to keep them," I told her.

She shrugged. "Like you don't want your mom to have cancer?"

"Yeah," I said.

I was refilling the bucket when Mom pushed open the tack room door. "There you are. Jane, Frankie's going better."

Jane put on her polite face and I wondered if she thought

my mom was being fake. But, overall, Frankie really was going better. "Thanks."

"Regan, you almost ready to go?"

I turned off the faucet and brought Jane the clean water. "Yup, I'll be right out."

Mom stood there, waiting for me. I wanted to say something else to Jane, just to make sure everything between the three of us was really going to be okay. I didn't know how I could handle life if Hailey and Jane weren't my best friends, especially if the chemo didn't work. But Mom didn't budge and I'm not sure I would have come up with something to say anyway. So I quickly finished my saddle and slid it back onto my rack.

I closed my tack trunk. "See you tomorrow."

"Yup," Jane said. "Bye."

Mom and I were almost to the front of the barn when I said, "I forgot something. Meet you in the car."

I jogged back inside to Frankie's stall. He looked up at me. It was kind of dorky to make a promise to a horse, something TVMG would say, except I was saying it to the wrong pony. "I'll find out about you," I said. "I promise."

He poked his nose out to me and I kissed him. I was surprised he let me, but it almost seemed like he wanted me to.

Chapter 28

DESPITE HOW MUCH JANE DIDN'T like Frankie, he *was* going better. After a few more weeks, he could canter a course without bolting or leaving out strides. He still often looked quick and tense, but it was a major improvement.

We didn't have a big show one weekend so Tommy took a few pony kids who needed more practice to a one-day show nearby, and Jane took Frankie. I wanted to go and watch Frankie, but Mom said she wanted to take me to get my hair cut and out to lunch and I knew it wasn't optional. I moped nearly the whole time we spent together, barely talking to her, and then felt terrible about how I'd behaved afterwards. I mean, my mother could be dying and I was mad I didn't get to go watch a one-day?

Jane said Frankie was actually really good at the show. She did the special ponies and the regulars and ended up champion in the specials and reserve champion in the regulars.

Hailey hadn't ever said anything else about Montclair, but

Jane had been right—after a few more days things did blow over and we were pretty much back to normal. If she didn't end up champion or reserve at Fairlee, our next show, then Susie was going to take her to a smaller show in Massachusetts where she'd hopefully be able to qualify.

I hadn't gotten any further with figuring out where Frankie had come from, but one night while I was watching TV I had a breakthrough idea. I had one of those forensic shows on and they were doing an autopsy, looking for clues to the murder that the body could provide. The lead CSI was lecturing an intern about how the dead can still speak through their bodies.

We didn't have a dead body in our mystery, but I realized we did have a live one. Frankie had shown us some clues in his behavior, but so far we'd neglected to pay attention to what his body had to say about where he'd been.

The next day at the barn I explained my theory to Jane and Hailey.

"So what are we supposed to do? Look at him under a microscope or send his blood out for labs?" Jane said.

"No, but I thought maybe the next time Dr. Shailor's here we could ask her some questions."

"Wait, his feet," Hailey said.

Jane rolled her eyes. "What about them?"

"We should talk to Joe. I remember in Pony Club we learned about how you can know things about a horse from their feet."

"That's a great idea," I spoke up. "When's Joe coming next?"

"I don't see how this is going to tell us anything, but we can go check," Jane said.

We headed off down the aisle. It felt good to be the three of us together again, after what had happened with Jane learning I liked Alex, and then me getting moved up over Hailey at Montclair.

The list of schedules—farrier, vet, acupuncturist, massage therapist—was posted outside the office. Joe was at the barn at least four days out of each month, since he shod all the horses and ponies in the barn. We were in luck because not only was he coming on Friday, but Frankie was due to be shod.

* * *

On Friday, I led Frankie down the aisle to where Joe was set up. Hailey walked on one side of Frankie and Jane on the other. Joe was glugging from a Gatorade bottle, sweat running down his face. Joe was probably in his late twenties or early thirties, and his father was a farrier, too.

"What's with the posse?" Joe adjusted his Detroit Tigers baseball hat. I'd never seen him without it. It only came off for repositioning on his head.

"We just wanted to ask you something," I said.

"Yes, when you're seniors in high school I'll take each and every one of you to the prom." Joe grinned at us. He reached out to take Frankie's lead rope but Frankie stiffened, planting his toes. His eyes were full of worry.

"Oh, yes, I forgot." Joe pulled off his hat, revealing matted and sweaty hair. "Not many things I'll take my hat off for... Stars and Stripes, sitting down for a meal, and a skittish horse."

I put my hand on Frankie's neck, trying to calm him. "He doesn't like your hat?"

"Nope. Old Blue Eyes does not like hats. He made that perfectly clear the last time I did him."

"But I've worn a baseball hat around him," Jane pointed out. "We all have."

"Well, he either hates the Tigers or he thinks it's just not my best look."

We were learning more about Frankie already and we hadn't even gotten to asking Joe any questions.

With the hat off, Frankie lowered his head and let Joe put him on the cross-ties. Joe picked up his left front hoof and clipped off the nail heads. A few moments later, he was pulling off the shoe.

"So what's up?" Joe asked.

"We want to pick your brain." It was something I'd heard Mom say to people when she wanted to get information on something.

"Go ahead and pick away."

"You can tell stuff from a horse's feet, right?" Hailey said.

"What kind of stuff are you looking to find out?" Joe was holding Frankie's hoof, which looked small in his large and callused hands. He set the hoof against the thick leather apron that covered his thighs, and started filing it with a wide heavy file. Slivers of gray hoof fell to the ground. "By looking at this hoof here I can tell that the Tigers are going to win the World Series in five games."

"Joe!" Jane said. "Be serious!"

Joe set down Frankie's hoof. "What do you want to know about this pony that you don't already know?"

"We want to know where he came from and *he's* the only clue we really have," I said.

One of Susie's dogs, a yellow lab-mix, Darcy, darted in and grabbed some of the clipped hoof. Before Joe could scold him, he'd snuck back outside with his prize. No matter how many times hoof shavings made the dogs sick, they couldn't keep themselves from gorging on it.

Joe rubbed his fingers, which were stained black, over the front of Frankie's hoof. "See these ridges?"

We all moved closer.

"Yeah?" I just hoped this time Joe was being serious and a joke wasn't about to follow.

"Horses get ridges when they've suffered some kind of stress."

"Like what?" Jane said.

Joe stretched back up, bending backward to loosen his muscles. "Depends on the horse. Sometimes it's just something like shipping them to Florida. It could be a big change in feed or weather. But it could also be something worse that happened to them. I don't know what happened, but this pony has a lot of ridges."

Darcy was back again. This time I caught him by the collar. "So he probably went through something really bad. I wish we knew what or, at least, when."

"You can also tell a little bit about *when* the stress occurred." Joe wiped his hands on his apron. "Hooves usually grow about a quarter of an inch every six to eight weeks. A little less in the winter. So if we measure back to the ridges—" Joe put his hand on Frankie's hoof, approximating the measurement. "It was probably about a year ago."

"Wow," Hailey said. "That is so cool."

Joe stretched upright again. He put his hands on his back, pressing on the muscles. "I guess you didn't know just how cool being a farrier is. This is why we get paid the big bucks and work in such luxurious settings."

As Joe moved onto Frankie's other hoof, clipping, pulling off the shoe, we thanked him.

"No problem, girls." Joe began filing the hoof. "That's my job—solving mysteries one hoof at a time."

I took Darcy outside and told Susie he was snarfing hoof. Susie was teaching the big eq kids. The jumps looked huge. She asked me to tie Darcy up outside the barn till Joe was gone. Darcy gave me a pathetic look. I told him it was for his own good. I would be such a good dog-mom. It was a crime I didn't have a dog.

Jane had to go ride another pony. Hailey and I stayed with Joe. It was fun to watch him work, how effortlessly he pulled shoes, and clipped and trimmed the hooves. Frankie was getting two new shoes up front and Joe selected ones from the racks hanging in the back of the truck. He turned on the fire in the portable forge he brought with him and heated up the shoes till they glowed red. The whole time he talked to us, about our ponies and who was winning what these days. He did a lot of the other barns in the area and big barns in other states, too, so he knew all the people we showed against. He did Hugo's horses and told us Hugo had fifteen ponies headed to Pony Finals.

He pressed the flaming hot shoe against Frankie's hoof. "Equines..." Joe shook his head. "He's scared of a baseball hat, but not a burning shoe."

Joe was right—it was weird the things Frankie was scared of. Some things you'd think would freak him out he couldn't have cared less about. Joe made adjustments to the shoe, shaping it by hammering it on his anvil. He stuck it in a bucket of cold water, which let off a hissing noise. All these sounds—the hissing and clanking—and Frankie didn't flinch.

When he was done fitting and nailing the shoes back on Frankie's front feet, he filed down the nails and rubbed black sealant over them. He clipped and filed Frankie's back feet, which were bare.

He unhooked Frankie and snapped a lead rope on him. "He's all yours."

"Thanks," I said.

He picked up his hat. "It's always a pleasure."

As we walked away, Joe put his hat back on and called out, "Don't forget about the prom!"

Hailey laughed. "We won't."

Back at Frankie's stall, I was all excited. "I still can't believe how cool that was."

I led Frankie in and after I came out Hailey slid the door shut. "All thanks to me and my pony club education."

I had the idea of looking at Frankie's body in the first place, but I didn't bring that up. I was just glad Hailey was getting invested in finding out about Frankie, and that we were best friends again.

Frankie stuck his head over the door, like he didn't want us to go away. I patted his neck. I felt all this love when I looked at him. Love I didn't ever feel for Tyler. Tyler was like the guy who liked you and was supposed to be perfect for you, but for whatever reason you just didn't ever feel anything when you were with him. Frankie was the secret guy you couldn't stop thinking about. Complicated, dark maybe, but endlessly appealing.

"So if it was a year ago that he went through so much stress and he arrived at Vi's six months ago then we know that the stress wasn't from arriving at Vi's."

"Which you would think if you were a pony would stress you out—being dumped at Vi's," Hailey said.

"So it had to be something pretty serious that happened to him," I said. "Not just a change in feed or the weather. Something *bad* happened to this pony."

"Or *someone* bad did something to him," Hailey said.

I nodded. Frankie buried his nose in my shoulder, like he knew we were talking about him. "*Someone*, a man, with a baseball hat."

Chapter 29

SUSIE ALWAYS TOLD US HOW, when she was our age, Fairlee was *the* pony barn in the country, turning out national champions and Pony Finals winners year after year. They used to host the Pony Finals, too, back when it switched locations from year to year. Once Susie found all these old *Chronicles* in her mother's attic and we had so much fun looking at the horse show results and pictures. Jumps and tack and riding clothes changed over the years, but a good jumper was still a good jumper. It was cool to see some of the professionals, who win a lot in the hunters and jumpers today, back when they were riding ponies. There were even a few pictures of Susie. She catch-rode to a lot of wins when she was a junior.

Fairlee was one of the last remaining shows where you rode on a huge outside course. I loved riding on the field at Fairlee, but some people didn't go there anymore because they were worried about riding on grass. Susie wouldn't let us miss it—ever. She said it was important to go to different shows and not get stuck in the same rut of going to one place that had shows all season.

The ponies arrived at the show on Friday and we hacked around the rings. After we were finished riding we hung out watching the classes that were still going on. Since Frankie did so well at the local show, Tommy decided Jane was going to show Frankie in the greens. It seemed like a lot to throw Frankie onto the outside course at Fairlee, but Tommy didn't have the time to wait and bring him along more slowly. He needed to get him showing, and sold, as soon as possible. Every month that he put board and training into him sucked the profit out of the sale.

Fairlee was close enough that we could all stay in our homes. On Saturday morning Mom drove me over to the show. It was a gorgeous summer day. Fairlee was an old-fashioned hunt club and people were playing on the paddle tennis courts when we pulled up to the tents. Later, we'd hear splashing and chants of Marco Polo coming from the swimming pool.

The green ponies went first and I was ringside to watch Frankie. I sat on a folding chair under the tent between the two hunter rings watching Tommy give Jane last minute instructions. He had one hand around her back as she sat in the saddle and was pointing to the course with the other hand.

Since talking to Joe, I'd decided to post about Frankie on *The Chronicle* bulletin board. I'd looked for info about Frankie online, but I hadn't posted anything. We had a pony with a blue eye and a brand. This wasn't a bay with two white socks. People were going to remember this pony if they'd seen him. I asked anyone with information about him to write to me.

The outside course was beautiful. There had been hardly any rain so far this summer, which stunk for Hailey. But Weston Joyce was judging the ponies today and he had a soft spot for Donald, always giving him good ribbons when he went well. If the summer stayed this dry, in a few short weeks the grass would be burnt out and the ground hard. But today the grass was still thick and green. The birch rails and blue and yellow flowers, that were the hunt club colors and decorated the jumps, stood out against the grass. It all looked so bright and I wondered how Frankie would react, although he didn't usually care about the colors of the jumps.

The pony on course came out and it was Jane's turn. Tommy patted her leg and she rode Frankie into the ring. His trot was hurried and Jane let him ease into the canter. Jane rode as large an opening circle as possible since there wasn't a dotted line. Frankie sighted in on the first jump. He was quick down the line, but not a runaway like he'd been when he'd first come to the farm. He got a little faster coming home toward the in gate. Jane reeled him back in and finished the course without any big mistakes. In her second trip, Frankie got quick again coming home and Jane pulled a little too hard on him, making him even more upset. It was like every day was opposite day for Frankie—if he sped up, the last thing you wanted to do was pull.

I stayed through the jog. The other greens hadn't been that great and the pony divisions were weak at Fairlee in general. Autumn Ridge didn't come to Fairlee anymore, choosing to go to a generic show with ten rings that offered endless weeks of competition and classes for anyone and everyone. Frankie ended up getting decent ribbons, a third and a fifth. Frankie hacked really well and was second. But when Jane came out she didn't even pat him. It didn't seem to matter if he went well for her; Jane didn't like him on principle.

The courses were the same for the regular ponies. With Tyler I won the first class and was called in second in the conformation class, but moved up to first. Dakota had little mistakes in each round, and she was fifth and fourth. Hailey rode well and was third and second, great ribbons for her. I got low ribbons with Sammy—for some reason he didn't love the outside course.

After the jog we got back on for the hack. Anna hacked Sammy for me now that I had Tyler. I trotted into the ring and brought Tyler back down to the walk. Dakota came in right after me and made a big show of trotting her pony straight down the middle of the ring, trying to get the judge's attention. If I had been Weston Joyce I would have thought it was too showy and knocked her down for it, but not every judge would feel that way.

Hailey was in front of me on Donald and she glanced back so we could quickly share a look about how awful Dakota was. The last few ponies came in the ring and the class was called to order. Soon we were asked to trot.

I was only a few lengths behind Dakota and when I came by the in gate, Kitty was leaning nearly into the ring. "Get seen," she whisper-yelled at Dakota. "Get in front of the judge."

Susie was standing nearby. She didn't say anything to me as I passed her. I had a good pass at the canter in the first direction and I saw Weston write down something, which I guessed was my number.

We reversed direction and picked up a trot. I saw Dakota cut a corner and pass two other ponies, desperate to get another good look from Weston. Then I lost sight of her for a few moments as we finished up the trot and came back down to a walk. I was on the short side of the ring, which meant by the time we were asked to canter I would probably have a great pass down the long side of the ring, right in front of Weston. The announcer asked for the canter and I squeezed Tyler with my outside leg. Tyler had just started to canter when Dakota came up from behind and cut right in front of me. I had no choice but to quickly circle or else Tyler would have broken to the trot. Dakota was unbelievable. It didn't matter if Kitty was yelling at her to get seen—you didn't cut somebody off in a hack.

After circling, I rode down the long side at the canter, but I didn't get the pass I wanted. Before I could get in front of Weston again, the announcer asked us to come back to the walk and line up. Dakota trotted right into the middle of the lineup. I walked Tyler down to the end. At this point I didn't care if I didn't win; I didn't want to be next to Dakota.

Hailey lined up next to me. "Dakota totally cut me off at canter. I almost broke."

"Me, too," I said.

Hailey mouthed something about Dakota that I couldn't

quite make out, although judging from her face I could have probably guessed.

"And the results of the medium pony hunter under saddle," the announcer began. "In first place... Smitten ridden by Dakota Pearce."

Hailey and I watched Dakota walk forward. She patted her pony like she loved him so much. Really we knew all she loved was winning. She gave the biggest, fakest smile to the woman handing out the ribbons.

"In second place... Woodland's Tried and True with Regan Sternlicht."

I accepted the red ribbon and headed out the in gate. I didn't really care about being second, but I didn't want to be second to Dakota.

Dakota was still on her pony at the in gate and said, in a super-cheery voice, "Congratulations, Regan."

"Thanks," I barely managed. "I think you cut off Hailey." I don't know why I didn't say 'you cut *me* off.' I guess it was easier to talk about someone else.

"Hailey? Like she had any chance of winning."

The rest of the results had been announced and the ponies were streaming out of the ring behind us. Anna was third with Sammy and Jane was fourth with Coco. Thanks to Weston Joyce, who did seem to love Donald, Hailey was fifth. It was one of her only hack ribbons of the whole year. Elena waved her hands. "Clear the in gate, girls."

I wish I could have thought of something smart or, at least, mean to say back to Dakota. I wasn't good at thinking fast for comebacks. I walked Tyler over to where Martha and Hektor were standing. Hailey came over to join us. She slid off Donald and made a point of landing hard on the ground. "She is unbelievable."

We spent the rest of the day watching classes, and fuming over Dakota. Who did she think she was? How dare she? Most importantly, how were we going to get even? I didn't tell Hailey what Dakota had said about her. Hailey didn't need to hear that. There wasn't really any way we could get revenge on Dakota in the show ring, except to just ride our best and win. But Hailey vowed that she would practice even harder for the lip sync. She declared, "I'm going to beat that girl if it's the last thing I do."

Hailey calculated the points everyone had in our division. I had twenty-six; Dakota had thirteen; Hailey had eleven. She shook her head. "There's no way I'm going to be reserve tomorrow with Weston judging the other ring, unless it rains and I already checked the forecast—zero percent chance of precipitation."

"Don't think like that. There's the handy and you're awesome at riding handy courses."

Hailey shrugged. "I guess," she said with an air of desperation. "I just want to qualify."

Chapter 30

THE NEXT DAY, BOTH DAKOTA and I put in really good rounds in the first class. Hailey had a good trip, too. Still, I knew there was no way she would beat either of us. The second class was the handy hunter. If there was ever a class where riding counts it was the handy. The course started over a vertical, then you could choose to turn inside an end jump to get to a four-stride line on the diagonal. There was a trot jump after that to a broken line, and then another optional inside turn to an oxer.

If you wanted a shot at a good ribbon, you'd need to do the inside turns. It was how well you'd do them—whether your pony would pivot effortlessly, or whether you'd nearly take your leg off on the standard of the jump you were turning inside of—that would separate the winner.

As we walked up to the ring, Hailey said she wanted to go before me. We stood at the in gate, going over the course. Hailey looked the most serious I'd ever seen her. The rider on course finished to scattered applause and exited the ring. As

Hailey entered the ring her chin was set and determined. The only way for her to be reserve was to turn in the round of her life and win the class. Dakota had ridden conservatively, not opening up her stride and going for bolder distances. If Hailey could really lay it down, there was a chance she could win.

Susie called, "good luck" to Hailey. Under her breath I heard Susie say, "Come on, Hailey."

Hailey rode amazing. I got so caught up in watching her go, I almost forgot I had to jump again. She found every distance and rode the lines just right. Even Donald seemed to try harder than ever, jumping as round and tight as he could, as if he knew what was on the line, too.

Susie whooped loudly and Hailey came out of the ring all smiles. She threw her arms around Donald.

"Perfect," Susie said. "Go get him ready for the jog." She turned to me. "You know your course?"

I recited it once more out loud just so we both could hear it and then walked into the ring. Tyler was also great at handy hunter classes. There wasn't anything I'd found so far that he wasn't good at. I saw a good distance to the first jump and easily slipped inside to the four-stride line. I could feel Tyler tuck his legs up and round his back, giving a great jump out of the line. I settled him back to the trot, hopped the trot jump, and neatly turned back on the broken line. I put my leg on him and squeezed him forward up the line. Other ponies might have had to run down the line to do the seven strides or end up doing eight, but Tyler ate up the distance between the jumps. I glided through the last inside turn, which after the flowing seven could have been challenging, but wasn't for us.

As I headed to the last jump I kept thinking about Hailey and how she had calculated all the points and the scenarios of what would lead to what.

I was probably going to win the first class. Hailey's only hope of being reserve champion was winning one of the classes. Should I circle or pull up? Pretend to drop my reins?

I turned down the diagonal. Instead of heading to the oxer, I headed to the single fence instead. I felt a surge of adrenaline. I could feel everyone's eyes on me. I thought I could hear Susie saying, "What is she doing?" but that was probably just in my head.

I jumped the single fence and I could feel every other rider in the class get a little bit excited. I'd gone off course! How was it possible to be so dumb?

Susie was waiting for me with a quizzical look on her face. "What happened?"

"I don't know. I just spaced, I guess."

I slid off Tyler and walked with Martha over to where Hailey was standing with Donald. Martha pulled off Tyler's saddle and said to me, "Silly girl. Tricks are for kids."

She cocked her head at me and smiled in a kind of wise way. Did she know? How could she possibly know? Except that I wasn't the type who went off course a lot. She didn't seem upset or disappointed, though.

"I just blanked," I told her. "I guess it was the handy—too many turns."

Martha nodded. She didn't say anything else. She started brushing Tyler's back, getting off the saddle mark for the jog for the first class.

I looked at Hailey and shrugged. "I can't believe I did that. One of my dumber moments."

"Remember that time I jumped an oxer backwards?" she said. "At least you didn't do that."

I smiled. She was so happy—I was glad I'd done it. "You were really, really good. That was like your best round ever."

Hailey nearly squealed. "I know. I've been watching and Dakota was pretty good. Emma was really tight to the oxer and no one else has been amazing. If you win the first class and then I win the second I could be reserve. As long as Dakota isn't second in both, or wins."

I saw Mom and Dad walking over from the spectator tent. Hailey and I were along the rail and I braced myself for whatever Mom would have to say. But before she could reach us, Martha took her aside. I kept glancing over my shoulder to try to figure out what Martha was saying to her. Whatever it was, it worked, because, when she and Dad reached us, Mom just said, "Really good ride, Hailey." Still, what she didn't say about my round said enough.

We watched the rest of the class, Hailey hardly able to sit still the closer we got to the jog. With one trip left, Martha and Hektor took off the ponies' flysheets and we walked them up to the in gate. Soon the first jog was called. I had won, Dakota was second, and Hailey was third.

As we came out, Elena called, "Second jog...."

Hailey was chewing on the tip of her gloved finger. I felt more nervous for her than I ever felt for myself.

"319 jogs first..."

Dakota led her pony past Hailey, her head held high.

Hailey's shoulders slumped.

"299 second..."

Hailey was second. A great ribbon at Fairlee. But it wasn't winning and she wouldn't be reserve.

It was strange to watch the second jog from the side of the ring. It was also painful to watch Dakota take the blue ribbon and see Hailey coming in second behind her. Dakota finished with twenty-nine points and Hailey with twenty-one. If Hailey had won and Dakota had been second they would have been tied with twenty-five points and Hailey would have been reserve champion because more of her points were over fences. When would Hailey ever get a break? I had done everything I could to help and it still wasn't enough. Should I have tried to win the class and take the blue away from Dakota? Would Hailey have been reserve then? No, Dakota still would have been reserve.

Hailey came out of the ring and Susie gave her a big hug. "Don't worry, sweetie. We'll get you qualified next weekend. You rode great."

Hailey nodded. "It just would have been nice to do it here." She looked at me and said through gritted teeth, "And to beat Dakota."

"At least you didn't go off course like me," I said. "How could I be so stupid?"

Hailey mumbled, "Yeah, I guess," but I knew it was no consolation. Hailey glanced out over the show grounds and I could tell she was trying hard to hold it together, to not fall apart into tears. Although it had happened to all of us at one point or another, there was nothing worse than being *that* girl—the girl hurrying away from the ring, her face full of hot, embarrassed tears.

Hailey made it back to the barn before she gave in to the tears. I found her in Donald's empty stall. She shielded her face when she saw me. "I came so close. Stupid Donald."

I knew Hailey didn't mean it—she loved Donald. She wiped her face and sniffed back her tears. "I'm so sorry. Here I am crying over a ribbon... talk about insensitive."

"No, you're crying over not qualifying."

"Yeah, but your mom has *cancer*. I'm like such a bad friend right now."

"Please don't treat me different—please weep openly," I said. "That's what a friend does—treat you like your mom doesn't have cancer."

"I just want to blame someone. Donald, Dakota, the judge, but nothing's really doing it for me. I still feel awful and now I have to go to some dinky show and, if I don't qualify there, I'll feel like even more of a loser."

"You'll qualify," I said. "Doesn't it stink when you can't find anything to blame?"

Jane came around the corner, a hand on her hip. "Please tell me you're not having a pity-party without me?"

"No, way." Hailey giggled through her tears. "Come on in. We're just getting started."

That was how we ended up at Fairlee, in Donald's stall, laughing, crying a little, too. I loved my friends. And, in the coming months, I would need them more than I knew.

Chapter 31

SUSIE SAID SINCE THE PONIES WERE so good at Fairlee, we'd give them both Monday and Tuesday off. It rained both days and so I spent most of the time reading and watching TV. Tyler had never been turned out before coming to our barn. Judy Ford and the Sowles family hadn't wanted to risk him hurting himself. Martha had started him off in the smallest turnout and now he was allowed to go out in one of the bigger fields. When I drove up to the barn on Wednesday, he was out in the field and was covered in mud. The field was mostly grass but he had found the one dirt patch that was a puddle from all the rain and rolled in it. He looked so entirely pleased with himself and for once, with the mud caked on his fur—even on his face—he didn't look anything like a fancy show pony. I liked the idea of him rolling in the puddle—of him being able to be a real horse and do something he'd never even known existed. I felt badly that while I was riding Sammy and Drizzle, Martha would be bringing him in and vacuuming off all that hard-earned mud.

On Wednesday and Thursday we hacked the ponies and on Friday we had a lesson again. Afterward, we took the ponies up to the little hill behind the barn where there was lots of shade from the tall oak trees and really nice grass. Tyler was still wet and as the sun dried his coat in patches it made him look like he was two-toned.

He buried his muzzle in the grass and devoured it. Donald was pickier, pulling Hailey away from me and Jane, never satisfied with what looked like perfectly good grass. Frankie kept raising his head between bites, as if being allowed to graze was just too good to be true and the boogey man was waiting in the shadows to get him. When he pulled up his head, he looked far into the distance and I wondered what he was searching for. I'd gotten some replies to my posting, but they were just "good luck" or "hope you get answers." So far, no one actually knew anything about Frankie.

Jane shook her head. "He's making me feel dizzy just watching him. Up and down, up and down."

"Have you decided on your song yet?" I asked Hailey. Beating Dakota was even more of a priority after Fairlee.

"I was going back and forth between Adele and Tina Turner. Then last night I had a better idea." Hailey spread her hands in front of her. "'I Love Rock and Roll' by Joan Jett."

Jane and I looked at her with blank faces.

"You've never heard of it? You've heard of Joan Jett, right?"

We both shook our heads.

"Oh my god, I'll play it for you later. Joan Jett was this totally awesome seventies rocker chick. I could dress up like her—all in black."

"I guess we need to hear the song." Jane touched her hand to her cheek. "Are you guys hot?"

It was mid-eighties and I'd been hot during our lesson. Now that we were in the shade I'd cooled down. "I'm not that bad."

"Hektor came over and made us tacos last night." Jane grimaced. "They were really spicy. I don't know if it was the tacos or what, but I feel gross."

Frankie had finally settled down somewhat when all of a sudden Alex roared out of the woods on his bike. Frankie shied, nearly leaping into Tyler. I took a tighter hold of the lead shank. Tyler jumped away from Frankie, getting his front legs tangled up with each other in the process. I heard the grating sound of metal scraping metal, shoe hitting shoe.

"Alex!" Jane shrieked.

The ponies were standing apart now, heads raised. Tyler was standing what looked like evenly on both his front feet, but that scraping sound hadn't been good.

"Dad is going to kill you. You're not supposed to be riding in the woods. And you don't even have your helmet on!"

I noticed Alex's hair, which was a little sweaty. My stomach fluttered. I should have been worried about Tyler, but I was focused on Alex. I didn't get to see him all that much. Any time I did, I wanted to study him so I would remember what he looked like.

He moved his hair off his forehead with a flip of his head. "You're gonna tell on me?"

Jane didn't answer. Instead she looked at Tyler. "Is he okay?"

Tyler. Right, Tyler. I took my eyes off Alex and picked up Tyler's left foot. The shoe was on and seemed fine. I picked up the other. My stomach sank as I saw the shoe had come off by the heel. He must have caught one shoe with the other and pulled it loose. It was sticking up at a bad angle.

"He grabbed himself. One shoe's a little off."

"I can't believe this!" Jane turned to Alex. Frankie snuck a quick bite of grass and then raised his head again to look at the bike, wide-eyed, while he chewed. Tyler had resumed eating happily again. Donald had pulled Hailey a little ways off.

"I'm sorry." Alex wiped his forehead. "How was I supposed to know you were grazing up here?"

"Because we graze up here," Jane said. "And where's your helmet anyway?"

"I left it in a secret spot."

Jane made a face. "I really don't want a vegetable for a brother. If you die that's one thing..."

"Thanks for the sisterly love."

I chuckled. Sibling fights looked kind of fun. There was always this undercurrent of love. I wished I had a brother or sister to hate.

"So is this the pony that cost so much?" Alex gave Tyler a once-over.

Hailey had pulled Donald closer to us and she laughed, like maybe she was relieved someone else spoke without thinking for once.

"Alex!" Jane screeched. "That's rude."

"He just looks like a pony to me," Alex said. "Four legs, tail..."

"Then why don't you go tell Susie that it's no big deal that Tyler pulled off his shoe? Since you made him do it."

"I didn't *make* him do it."

"Really?" Jane scowled. "You're going to deny you did this? You're not even going to own up to it? You should tell Dad and Susie."

"I'll tell them, but it was an accident."

"An accident that wouldn't have happened if you weren't riding in the woods without your helmet. You just better hope Tyler's okay."

"Whether I had my helmet on or not has nothing to do with anything."

"Yes, it does because it's you breaking the rules..."

Alex and Jane were glaring at each other, like they really wanted to punch each other.

"I'm sure he's fine." I stepped between them. "He's standing on it okay. And I'm not sure why we even need to tell anyone what really happened. We could just say he stepped on himself while he was grazing."

Jane turned to me. Her face looked unusually flushed. "Of course you want to save his butt." She shook her head like she was disgusted by all of us, even Hailey who was just watching and listening.

Tyler was grazing happily—how much discomfort could he be in? "I just don't see the point in getting anyone in trouble. I'm sure it can just be tacked back on."

"Fine. We better bring him back." Jane shot Alex another look. "Wait till we're gone before you start your stupid bike."

On the way back to the barn, Jane said, "It's one thing to have a crush on him. This is going too far."

Hailey and I shared a look—Jane was seriously worked up.

I wondered if Jane ever thought about what it might be like to be Alex. It couldn't be easy the way Jane and her dad had everything in common because of horses. Alex didn't really fit in. Tommy hardly ever took time off from horse shows to watch Alex's races.

Back at the barn, Susie took a look at Tyler's shoe and called Joe. She and Martha discussed whether they should call Dr. Shailor, too. They decided to wait and see what Joe said. Joe arrived an hour later and pulled off the shoe. He said the hoof looked a little bruised and it would be best to leave the shoe off and soak and poultice the hoof. Then, in a few days, he'd put the shoe back on and he thought Tyler would be okay.

"No riding Tyler for a few days," Susie said to me. "I'm sorry, kiddo."

I tried to look disappointed. "It's okay."

Jane came to ask how Tyler was. Her face was really pale now, but she didn't seem as mad.

"He's going to be fine." I tried to tell her with my eyes not to say anything about Alex.

"You don't look so good," Susie said to Jane.

"I don't feel well. I think it was last night's dinner." Jane hugged her stomach.

"Go home," Susie said. "I'll tell Tommy. Regan, you walk her home, okay?"

Jane was too sick to say much as we walked to her house. She did manage, "I can't believe you even like him."

"I can't help it... he's really cute."

Jane shuddered. I'm not sure whether it was from feeling sick or me thinking Alex was cute. I walked with her onto the front porch. She opened the screen door.

"Hello?" her mom called.

"I'm sick," Jane said. "I think it was the tacos."

Mrs. Hewitt came to the door. I told her I was just making sure Jane got home okay.

"Thanks." She put her arm around Jane. "Let's get you into bed."

I walked along the pastures back to the barn. A retiree, his mane long and his back swayed, picked up his head from grazing to see what I was up to.

Hailey was sitting out front of the barn on the bench, scrolling through her phone. I sat down next to her.

"How's Jane?"

"Not good. And she's freaked about me liking Alex. He's cute, right? I'm not crazy for thinking that?"

"He's cute. I don't like him, but he's cute."

"Why can't Jane see that?"

"He's her brother." Hailey said it like she totally understood. I guess not having any siblings I just couldn't relate.

Hailey held out her phone. "Wanna hear the Joan Jett song?"

She passed me her earbuds. I listened for a while and then pulled one earbud out. "I like it."

"I'm thinking maybe I could find some black leather pants, wear a wig. Joan Jett had a spiky black mullet."

I put the earbud back in. The song was loud and bold and

I could picture tiny Hailey, all dressed in black, strutting around the stage. The song ended and I handed Hailey back her earbuds.

Anna came out of the barn and hovered near us.

"So you think I should do it?" Hailey asked me.

"Yeah."

"You're going to do Joan Jett?" Anna said.

"Probably," Hailey murmured.

"Jill and I are going to do Kelly Clarkson."

The lip sync was divided by age groups. Anna and another girl at the barn, Jill, were in the seven-to-nine age group.

Hailey rolled her eyes. "Kelly Clarkson? So predictable."

Mrs. Mullins pulled up in their minivan. Hailey swung her backpack over her shoulder and flashed me the peace sign. She and Anna climbed into the van. Mrs. Mullins rolled down her window to say hi to me and I could hear Owen yelling. Then Hailey yelled, "Shut up!" Chopper jumped into Mrs. Mullin's lap and stuck his head out the window. I waved as they pulled out.

The barn seemed really quiet when they were gone. There was a part of me that wished I was in their loud, crazy car with a dog in my lap, fighting with Owen.

A few moments later, as if he were waiting to get me alone, Alex came out of the barn.

Chapter 32

ALEX HAD HIS HANDS IN HIS POCKETS, shoulders adorably rounded. "Hey, I'm really sorry about your pony. I messed up."

"It's okay."

"But I heard you can't ride him now."

"Only for a few days."

"Still..."

Alex stood next to the bench. His hair had dried kind of crazy. I hadn't been so close to him very often. He had really nice brown eyes and a little scar on his chin from a spill I remembered he took off his bike about a year ago.

I lowered my voice. "I actually don't mind."

Alex gave me a puzzled look. "Why?"

I toed the ground with my foot. "I know this sounds weird, but he's not much fun to ride. He's too easy."

"He's too *easy*?"

"Well, like what if you were doing an easy motorbike course and you barely had to try to win?"

"But I'd still win?"

"Yeah, but don't you get a thrill when you do a really hard course?"

"Definitely. I get totally stoked."

"I don't get that when I ride Tyler. It's boring and everything's supposed to be perfect."

"I don't know." Alex rubbed at his crazy hair. "Still sounds kind of messed up. Jane would love to ride a pony like him."

We both heard a car's wheels on the gravel. I looked up to see Mom pulling in. I wished her Mercedes wasn't so clean and sleek.

"Well, see you," I said to Alex before Mom could see me talking to him and stop and say something embarrassing.

"Yeah, and thanks, for, you know."

"Yup."

As I put on my seatbelt, I watched Alex go back into the barn. Would it really be impossible for something to happen between us? Was there no way he could ever like me? Even if that was the case, I knew I couldn't stop liking him.

Mom said, "It's only a few days and then he'll be fine."

I had almost forgotten that, of course, Susie would have speed-dialed Mom. For a moment there I thought I would need to tell her what happened with Tyler. Mom turned the car around and headed out the driveway.

She continued, "I wish Susie had called Dr. Shailor. I guess if Joe says it's just a bruise, it's just a bruise. A few days off and he'll be back to work."

I took out my phone and scrolled through my messages.

Mom hated it when I did that while talking to her. She was always checking her phone, though, so it was a total double standard.

She raised her voice, like I was listening to something, not looking at something. "But from now on, Susie and I agreed, you're not going to graze him or take him out for walks."

"What?" I looked up from my phone.

"It's just not safe."

"It's not safe to graze a pony?" Had Mom and Susie completely lost their minds?

"Just with Tyler. Take another pony to graze. Take Sammy."

I actually liked grazing Tyler more than riding him. It seemed hard to believe that Susie was in on this one. This seemed like something only Mom would come up with. "Should we get him a padded stall, too?"

Mom turned onto the highway. Her hands on the wheel looked skeletal, a sudden stabbing reminder of how sick she was. Sometimes, for a few moments, I'd forget. "We're just being smart about this. Protecting our investment."

I was silent. Nothing I had to say Mom wanted to hear.

We passed a few exits. The Saw Mill was quiet, no traffic yet.

"Maybe after Pony Finals we can graze him again. It just doesn't seem smart right now."

I still didn't say anything. I just stared out the window at the passing scenery. Sometimes I would pretend I was riding and whatever I saw out the window I had to jump, like stone walls or split post fences. Right then I was too mad to even do that. I turned back to my phone. A text from Hailey. Nothing from Jane. I asked Hailey whether she'd heard how Jane was doing. Then I texted Jane to ask her.

"Regan?"

"What?"

"What's going on?"

"He's a pony." I didn't take my eyes off my screen. "Not an investment."

"He's actually both. You know how much he cost."

"Yes, I do."

"So we have to be smart."

"You keep saying that."

"You can graze any other pony you want."

"It's not about the grazing."

Mom's phone rang. The caller ID came up on the car's Bluetooth. It was her oncologist. She pulled over so she could pick up the handset, so I wouldn't hear. But I could still hear her doctor's voice anyway. She'd had another CT scan. The tumors on her ascending colon and lower bowel had shrunk, but not as much as he had *hoped*. He wanted to do one more round of chemo. He *hoped* by then the surgeon would be able to get to the tumors and leave most of her digestive system intact.

The conversation was over quickly and Mom hung up and smiled. Actually smiled.

"This is good news," she said.

But good news would have been the tumors shrinking so much she wouldn't have to have surgery. Good news didn't include doctors using the word "hoped" repeatedly. Doctors hoping for things was bad.

I swallowed. Grazing Tyler didn't seem important anymore. Why had I made such a big deal about it? Mom had more important things going on and didn't need to be arguing with me about grazing Tyler. Still, I felt so mad. Poor Tyler. He hardly got to be a horse at all. And why did Mom have to be so old anyway? Young mothers didn't get things like ovarian cancer, did they? She had to be stick-thin and career-driven and wait forever to have kids. Why couldn't she be like Hailey's mom? Chubby and messy and loud... and healthy. I took a deep breath, feeling the guilt rush over me for the terrible, selfish thoughts running through my head.

"I won't graze him," I said. "I promise."

Chapter 33

I DIDN'T REMEMBER MOM'S HAIR falling out last time. I just remembered all of a sudden she had a wig. I found out after she'd gotten it. Typical Mom, she'd immediately sprung into action. She'd gotten the name of the top wig-maker in the city from a friend, a TV reporter with thinning hair. With the referral, she'd booked an appointment right away so he could see her hairstyle and take a sample to match the wig to. Once two wigs were ordered, she'd gone out and had her head shaved. This time, for whatever reason, Dad had been enlisted to do the honors, and I was getting a front row seat.

She sat on the marble island in the kitchen, her legs dangling off the side. She looked young all of a sudden, like my sixteen-year-old cousin, Kat. Dad had pinned an old sheet around her neck and it hung down past her waist, a makeshift smock like the kind you get at a hair salon. She touched her hand to her hair, feeling the texture one more time. It hadn't started to fall out until just recently.

I was standing in the corner of the room, unsure if I wanted to watch. It felt like an accident on the side of the road—I'd look for spider webs in windshields and twisted metal even though I was scared of seeing an actual hurt person.

"I'm ready," Mom said. "Let's do it."

Dad had a pair of clippers that Mom had bought specifically for this event. He clicked them on and Mom winced at the dull buzz. Then she straightened up, steeling herself for what came next. Dad moved in slowly, like he was trying to clip the muzzle of a wary pony. I almost expected him to say, "easy now," like Martha did sometimes. Mom trusted Dad, and I did, too. Dad was the kind of guy who never really got flustered. The kind you'd want to have around if disaster struck. He was willing to try his hand at anything—fixing a broken lock, sewing a doll's ripped dress, even shaving Mom's head. I'm not saying he was good at all the things he did, but he was willing to try them without worrying about being embarrassed if he didn't do them well. Perhaps this ability came from being older, from having seen a lot in his life.

Dad paused and then put the clippers to Mom's head. A lock of hair fell. I kept my eyes on the tile floor, watching the hair accumulate.

"Regan, are you still there?" Mom turned her head to look for me and Dad scolded her, "Don't move. I'm making progress here."

"Yeah, I'm here."

"Hey, remember that time, in what was it? Kindergarten or first grade when I got my hair all chopped off?"

"Hmmm."

"I came to pick you up at school and you came to the car and opened the door and said, 'This is my mommy's car, but you're not my mommy, are you?' I had to convince you it was me and to get in the car with me."

I'd looked up from the floor. There was still some hair on Mom's head but it was only stubble now, a quarter of an inch long, like a pony that had just been body clipped. I always loved to run my hands over my ponies when they'd just been clipped. I couldn't imagine ever wanting to touch Mom's bare head. She looked completely different, the features of her face bigger.

"Do you remember?" Mom turned to look at me. Heinous tears were pushing their way out, burrowing up from inside of me, and no matter what I did, I couldn't stop them. I did remember that day and I wasn't sure I'd grown up at all since then because I knew this was my mom, but it didn't look like her at all.

Mom said, "Hey, it's okay. It's still me. Come here—"

But I backed out of the room. I didn't run away, though. I stood frozen, not sure what to do.

"I guess I should have had it done at the salon again." Mom sighed. "I just wanted it to be more private this time. Do I look that awful?"

Dad said, "You want the truth, or should I lie?"

"Lie," Mom said.

"You look awful."

I leaned closer, feeling relieved that I wasn't the only one repulsed. Dad felt exactly the way I did.

Mom's voice was exasperated when she replied, "I said for you to lie."

"I am," Dad said. "How could I ever think you look anything but beautiful?"

And that's when I ran to my room. Because Dad wasn't repulsed. He wasn't scared. He didn't feel like I did at all.

Chapter 34

ON SATURDAY, I CAME INTO the tack room after hacking Sammy. Tommy was changing a bit on a bridle. He had on a blue polo and his sunglasses were tucked into the collar of his shirt. It was just us, a few younger kids Jane's mom was teaching, and a few adults hacking at the barn today. Hailey and Anna were spending the weekend with their father and the Carrot at the Jersey Shore. Jane was still sick. Susie was in Michigan judging a horse show.

"How's Jane?" I asked Tommy.

"Not so great."

"Do you think it's food poisoning?"

"Or a virus. She stopped throwing up, so that's good. But she's totally exhausted."

"Do you think she'll be able to ride again soon?"

"Maybe Monday or Tuesday."

I put Sammy's bridle on the cleaning hook and slid my saddle onto my rack. The baby pad wasn't very dirty so I put it back in the pile of clean ones.

"When are you getting picked up?" He had a funny look

on his face, like he was noticing me for the first time when we'd just been talking to each other.

"I'm supposed to text Lauren when I'm done."

"You want to ride Frankie?"

"Really?"

"I need someone to get on him. I was thinking I might have to put Alex on him."

I giggled at the thought of Alex on Frankie. He could ride—I'd seen him a few times. He actually would probably be good if he wanted to, but he thought horses should be like motorbikes with no-fail gas pedals and brakes, and he didn't like that they had a mind of their own.

"Sure," I said.

"I'll get him tacked up for you."

"That's okay. I can do it." I didn't want Tommy to think I needed special treatment.

I expected Tommy to argue with me. I was relieved and grateful when instead he grabbed a bridle and handed it to me. "Okay, I'll meet you in the ring in ten minutes."

I talked to Frankie as I groomed him. No one was around to hear what a dork I sounded like. He seemed to like my voice, turning his head to look at me as I brushed him over with a medium-bristle brush. When I curried his neck, he lowered his head and let his lower lip hang loose. As I groomed him, I wondered if I'd like Tyler better if I got the chance to take care of him more. Sometimes I wished I could do my own work. With Martha it was hard to ask to tack him up or cool him down. She got paid to take care of my ponies and she had her own way of doing things.

Once I was on, Frankie was more comfortable than I

thought he'd be. Jane made riding him seem like torture. He was actually pretty smooth at the trot. His canter was a little bouncier and uneven, definitely not like Tyler's, but I didn't mind so much. I found it best to alternate between sitting full seat and then getting out of the saddle into a half-seat. I hacked him around and loosened him up while Tommy talked on his phone to someone about another pony. I kept expecting him to say something, but I must have been doing a good job because he just nodded as I passed a few times.

When he hung up he said, "You feel okay to jump a little?"

"Sure." I brought him down to a walk, trying not to let on how excited I was. Tommy made a cross-rail and told me to trot it. I picked up the reins and I could feel Frankie tensing up already. He got even quicker as we trotted to the jump. My instinct was to pull on the reins. He raced over the little jump and landed in a ball of fury.

"Just circle him. Then bring him back down to a walk as gently and calmly as you can."

It took two more circles. I was finally able to get him to walk.

"Here's the thing with this pony." Tommy talked with his hands on his hips. "He's clearly been pulled on and yanked on and he just wants to run away as fast as he can. But you can't pull on him—it'll only make him go faster. Trust him and don't pull, and I promise you he'll slow down. Trot it again."

I knew all this from watching Jane. Still, it was different when you were in the saddle. I had to give Jane credit—it was really hard to fight your instinct and not pull. I trotted it again, using all my willpower and trust to keep my hands still.

"Better," Tommy said. "Again."

By the fourth and fifth time over the cross-rail he was nearly at normal speed. Tommy raised the jump and I cantered it back and forth. It was harder at the canter. I willed myself not to pull as I turned the corner and Frankie lurched forward. Tommy was right—when I didn't pull, he softened. But it was so hard to give up feeling in control, even when feeling in control didn't actually amount to being in control. The other key was not to make too big a move when I saw the distance. Everything with Frankie had to be quiet.

"Really good," Tommy said. "I think he likes you."

He lowered a few jumps and then gave me a little course. "It's the same thing when you land off a jump. Don't grab at him. If you need to circle anywhere go ahead."

I nodded and asked gently for the canter. I turned to the first jump, a little ramp oxer, and didn't pull. Frankie relaxed and luckily the distance was right there. It got easier as we cantered the course. But then at the last jump I saw the distance getting way too deep and I had to take on the reins. Frankie sped right up and went through the distance. I tried to calm him down on the other side, circling until Tommy told me to walk.

"That's okay. Once we get him relaxing he'll be able to tolerate you trying to help him out. Some gymnastics will be good for that but I don't want to fire too much at him right away. I think this poor guy's seen his share of bad rides."

Tommy's phone rang. "Take another minute and we'll try the same course again."

I walked Frankie while he talked and when he was done, he told me to go again. Frankie was even more relaxed and most of the distances came up right out of stride. One time I was a little long and I had to put my leg on. He scooted a bit and jumped flat, but he came back to me better on the other side.

"You're getting it," Tommy said. "Everything has to be done with about one-sixteenth of the pressure and intensity of another pony. Let him walk on a loose rein."

I let the reins slip through my fingers. Frankie shook his head and then sighed. He seemed proud of himself.

"You rode him really well."

He sounded almost surprised. I guess to him I was the girl who only rode the made ponies. He'd probably been doubting himself for even putting me on Frankie in the first place.

"Jane tries to do too much with him a lot of the time," he continued. "You're a very quiet rider and I mean that as a compliment. Jane's really good at riding the stoppers and the spookers. Being subtle is harder for her."

"Thanks," I said. Tommy had no idea how much riding Frankie meant to me, and finding out I was good at it.

"Are you up for riding him again tomorrow if Jane's not better?"

"Definitely."

Chapter 35

THE NEXT DAY FRANKIE WENT even better and Tommy asked me if I wanted to ride him Tuesday, too. By then, Jane was better and came back to the barn. She was still kind of weak from throwing up and not eating anything all week, so at first Tommy kept having me ride him. Susie came back from judging and I guess Tommy talked to her about me riding him because she didn't really say anything about it. I knew I should have told Mom and Dad that I was riding him. I was worried about what Mom would say. She was anticipating that she'd have surgery in July so she was trying to tie up loose ends at ProduX, which meant luckily Lauren was the one to drop me off and pick me up. Susie must have assumed I'd cleared it with Mom.

I wondered if Jane would mind that I was riding Frankie but she said, "He's all yours."

Of course he wasn't all mine. Every day I kept waiting for Tommy to say Jane was completely recovered and that she better get back on him. I wondered if Tommy thought I rode

Frankie better than Jane. It was possible. He had said a couple of times what a good job I did and I felt like I had a connection with Frankie that Jane didn't. I even daydreamed that maybe he'd ask me to show Frankie.

One day after we were done, I took Frankie for a long walk—the kind I was forbidden from doing with Tyler anymore. No grazing and no walking outside of the ring. I rode him around the barn to the back ring. The back ring was pretty small and Susie and Tommy mainly used it for turnout. Today, Martha was lungeing Caitlyn's eq horse in it. Martha was really amazing at doing groundwork and so Susie sometimes had her work with certain horses. She was putting Riley through movements, making him transition from walk to canter, back down to the trot, to a halt, and then straight off into the canter again. That kind of work would build muscle and get his brain tuned in to listening.

I walked closer to the fence to say hi to Martha.

"Hey, there." She kept her eyes trained on Riley as she spoke to me. "How's Frankie?"

"Great," I said with probably a little too much enthusiasm.

Martha gave me a look.

"I just like riding him, that's all."

"Well, that's good, I guess."

"How's Tyler?" I knew I should seem interested in when I could ride him again.

"He's jogging sound. We'll give him a day or so more to be safe."

"Cool." I took a look at Riley. He was really paying attention to Martha. "He looks good."

"This guy is a lazy butt." Martha raised her lunge whip and I heard her start to say can-*ter*. But by the second syllable of the word Frankie had reared up, flinging me onto the ground. If I had expected him to rear I'm sure I could have stayed with him. He had been so relaxed and I was just sitting back in the saddle on a long rein.

The funny thing about falling off was it always happened so fast. At the same time I was always hyperaware of my thoughts. Like I was thinking how I could possibly stay on, or what I did wrong. This time I was trying to figure out what had happened since just a moment before everything had been fine. And then I was thinking that if I got hurt, my mom was going to kill me.

I landed on my right shoulder with a thud, narrowly missing the fence of the ring. Frankie had taken off back toward the barn.

"Oh my god!" Martha gasped.

I thought she was worried about Frankie galloping loose, but I looked up and saw her face and she was clearly only concerned about me. She unclipped the lunge line and set Riley loose in the ring. By the time I was scrambling to my feet, she had climbed between the fence slats and was rushing toward me. "I'm okay," I said although I was still in a little bit of shock and my shoulder ached.

"Sit down," she said. "Don't move."

"I'm fine." I brushed dirt off my shirt and looked toward the barn. "We better go after him."

"Don't worry about him." Martha reached out to sweep some of the dirt I'd missed. "I want to make sure you're okay."

"Stop babying me." My voice turned angry. "Why don't you just pretend I'm Jane?"

I'd seen Jane tossed plenty of times—no one treated her like Martha was treating me. They dusted her off and threw her back in the saddle. One time, a year or so ago, she fell off, rode two more ponies, and only later found out that she'd broken her wrist. She had a cast put on and only missed one week of riding, even showing with her cast. If it had been me, I would have been made to sit on the sidelines for six weeks.

"Whoa, slow down," Martha said.

"No, stop treating me like a princess." I turned and took off toward the barn. My shoulder did hurt a little as I ran. I tried to ignore it.

Luckily, Frankie ran straight into the barn, where Hektor caught him. Martha came jogging into the barn behind me and when I saw her I was overcome by guilt—she'd never been anything but nice to me. She always tried to talk to Mom when I had a bad trip and get her to go easy on me.

"I'm sorry," I said.

"It's okay. We all probably treat you with kid gloves too much. I think we figure you have enough tough stuff to deal with in your life."

I looked at the ground, embarrassed by my outburst. But didn't they treat me like a princess because my mother had so much money? Or was it really because my mom was sick? "I just want to be like Hailey or Jane."

"I know," Martha said. "I know just how you feel."

Martha never talked about her burns and what she'd lived through. She'd probably been teased and stared at and treated differently as a kid. But she never compared her experience to mine. I got enough comparative cancer sympathy from other people. They didn't mean any harm. I knew they were just trying to relate to me. But I'd had my fill of my *friend/relative/ neighbor* had *ovarian/breast/stomach/brain* cancer stories. The stories were either meant to be super inspiring—*and she's alive today!* Or a commiseration—*it's so sad.* Neither made me feel much better because this Momcer (mom with cancer) was all mine.

Chapter 36

HEKTOR ASKED MARTHA WHAT to do with Frankie.

I stepped forward to get him. "I'll take him."

"You're not getting back on," Martha said.

"I guess not," I said. "I wonder why he did that anyway? He was perfectly relaxed..."

"The lunge whip."

I nodded, now remembering Martha raising it. She hadn't snapped it, only raised it, but it had been enough to send Frankie into a frenzy. "He was terrified."

I took the lead rope from Hektor and walked Frankie toward his stall. I wasn't mad at him. More than anything, I just wanted to understand him. He could be so normal sometimes and then, just like that, something would set him off.

Martha walked after me down the aisle. "We should call your mom and tell her what happened."

I stopped Frankie and turned. "Why? I'm fine. She's just going to freak out." Talk about setting someone off. If Mom knew I'd fallen off Frankie? She didn't even know I was riding him. She'd never let me ride him again, that was for sure.

"She'd want to know right away."

I sighed. "She's not even picking me up today. She's busy with work. She's totally stressing out about getting things done before her surgery. I don't want to bother her." Oh, I'd done it all right. I'd played the cancer card. One moment I didn't want to be defined by my Momcer and the next I was happily using it to my advantage.

"Is Lauren picking you up?"

"No, my dad."

"Then you should call him."

"Can't I just tell him when he comes? Please?"

"Promise you will?" Martha stared at me like she knew I would somehow forget.

"Promise."

Hailey and Jane had been riding and when they'd heard what happened to me, they were all concerned.

"I'm totally fine," I told them. "It was no big deal." I wanted to forget the whole thing, especially how I'd told Martha not to baby me. I was glad everyone had been out riding and hadn't heard that part.

When Dad picked me up, my shoulder was aching a little more. I'd definitely be taking some ibuprofen as soon as possible. I just wanted to go home.

Then, instead of getting on the Saw Mill, Dad turned into the parking lot of the diner.

"Wait, what?" I turned in my seat to look at him. "What's wrong? Did something happen? Is Mom in the hospital?"

Tradition with Dad went like this—when something was wrong, he took me out to eat. E.J.'s in the city, the diner in Westchester. We had our spots. He'd order us waffles and egg creams and he'd level with me, in a way that Mom never did. Dad would let me know what was really going on with Mom's cancer after she had essentially kept me in the dark all in the name of protecting me from life's evils.

"No, everything's okay. I just thought we should talk."

Even though I only wanted to go home, I didn't tell Dad that. We parked and went inside. It was 4:30, my shoulder throbbed, and my appetite for whatever dinner Lulu was cooking that night would no doubt be ruined, but it didn't matter.

The menu was on the paper placemat, the same one I used to draw on when I was young enough for the waiter to bring me crayons. I almost wished I could ask for crayons now, just to give me something to do.

The waitress brought our egg creams. Dad took a big sip, like he was fortifying himself. "You know I don't believe in lying to you."

"But Mom does..." Did I really want the truth? I acted like I did to Mom, but maybe the ignorant, over-protected route *was* best. I stared at the placemat. It had a color-by-number butterfly and a small word search with words like bacon and waffle and juice. I knew where every word was from memory, even the backward ones.

"It's harder for her to talk honestly about her own health. It might be different if I were sick."

Sometimes I wondered what it would be like if I could trade a sick mom for a sick dad. Which one would I choose? It was a horrible thing to think, really, but I couldn't stop myself. I guess I always assumed my dad would die first because he was older. I'd never thought I'd lose my mom. Now, with Dad that much older, something could happen to him, too, and I'd be all alone. Who would I live with? Wendy? Susie? Dad's younger sister who lived in California and I barely knew?

"The surgical intervention is going to give her a good shot at going back into remission, but it's going to be tough on her body. She doesn't have much strength now."

"*Surgical intervention?*" I said. "The doctors have gotten to you, too?" Why did doctors always come up with these nice ways of saying the most awful things? Like radiation therapy. Massage was therapeutic. Not radiation. And it wasn't surgical intervention. It was surgery. The kind where they sliced you open and cut up your insides, all in the name of good health.

Dad laughed. "Okay, surgery. After the surgery, she's going to be hit hard."

Now cancer sounded like a contact sport. If ovarian cancer were football, Mom was about to be in the Super Bowl.

"She's weak already so surgery's going to be harder on her this time. She's not going to be up to much so you'll have the pleasure of my company more."

I stirred my egg cream. I wasn't sure I even liked egg creams anymore. When I had one with Hailey once, she got all grossed out because she thought it actually had eggs in it, which, given the name, wasn't that crazy an idea. It was just soda water and chocolate syrup and milk. But soda water and milk was kind of a gross combination. Still, it seemed cruel to tell Dad that I didn't like them anymore. "Okay."

Dad rubbed his beard. "That's it? Questions?"

"What's there to ask?" I wiped my mouth unnecessarily with my napkin. Before he could work harder to get me to open up, I changed the subject. "So, I fell off today."

"Off Drizzle or Sammy?" Dad looked surprised, but not particularly worried. After all, I was perfectly unhurt.

"No, I rode Frankie, one of Jane's ponies."

"Susie had you ride him? Does Mom know?" I could see Dad's brain churning—he was already a few steps ahead, figuring out the goods on this one.

"At first Tommy asked me to ride him because Jane was sick. I rode him really well, so he kept having me ride him. I wasn't riding Tyler because he was hurt. It was just a freak thing. He saw Martha lungeing and spooked at the lunge whip and he reared and—"

"He reared?"

"It wasn't a big deal really." I wished I hadn't said he reared.

"Mom doesn't know yet, does she?"

"Can we keep it between you and me?" I gave Dad my sweetest smile and stirred the bubbles in my egg cream. If you listened closely, you could hear them fizzing.

Dad shook his head.

"I want to ride him again... if Tommy asks me to. I don't want Mom flipping out and saying no."

"She's going to," Dad said, matter of fact.

"Can you talk to her?"

Dad shrugged. "I can, but you know she's going to be upset and protective of you."

I looked out the window. Dad was always so accepting of

Mom's reactions. Did that come with marrying when you were older? Did it come from marrying a powerful professional? Was it because she was sick? I couldn't always remember how it had been when I was younger, before Mom was sick.

"Sometimes I don't love riding Tyler." I felt like I was testing out how it sounded. How Dad would react.

"Hmm."

"I didn't really—" I was going to say, want him, but I stopped myself. Dad had a faraway look in his eye, like he couldn't stop thinking of Mom. I didn't want to be the spoiled brat who didn't like her fancy pony. I couldn't be that girl. Not now.

"So what can I do to help Mom?"

Dad brightened and I knew I'd made the right decision. "We just need to be there for her... tell her how much we love her." Dad trailed off, his eyes moist. "The problem is there's not much we *can* do. That's the worst part of all of this."

His huge love for Mom was embarrassing. It made me uncomfortable. It always seemed like their love was uneven, like maybe he loved her more than she loved him. Or maybe he just loved harder than she did. But it was touching, too, in a way. I mean, he really loved her. I ached for him. Somehow it felt like this was the hardest on him, although I knew that shouldn't be true.

Dad inhaled sharply, pushing back his tears. He wiped at the corner of one eye and took a sip of his egg cream. "We'll be okay, we'll be okay."

It sounded like a mantra. Like something people say again

and again before they go into the ring to make them think positively. Like, I will stay patient and let the jumps come to me. I will stay patient.

He looked at me. "You aren't having much of your egg cream."

I smiled and took a big gulp, even though it made me feel kind of gross as it bubbled down my throat.

Chapter 37

DAD MADE ME TELL MOM about Frankie. That I'd
been riding him and I'd fallen off.

"You're not hurt?"

"No, I'm fine."

She looked at Dad. "Maybe we should take her to see Dr.
Garner just in case?"

"She's fine." Dad rubbed my shoulder—thankfully my
other shoulder because the one I'd fallen on did kind of hurt.
I didn't know if it was because of what Dad said to me at the
diner or whether I was looking at her for the first time in a
while but Mom looked terrible. Her eyes looked too big and
cloudy. Her skin looked thin, like if you scratched at the sur-
face it would flake away. I couldn't imagine how someone
could cut her open without killing her right then and there.

Mom narrowed her eyes. "I'm going to have a word with
Tommy. And Susie? What was she thinking?"

"I think she thought I'd asked you and it was okay."

"Tommy should have never put you on that pony. He's
dangerous."

"He's not dangerous. He's gotten so much better." I wanted to tell Mom how well I rode him, but I didn't think that would matter to her. "His rearing was a freak thing. Please don't get mad at Tommy. It was my fault." It would be horrible if Mom laid into Tommy. He was the only one in the barn who didn't treat me like a total princess and that would be over forever.

"You're not supposed to ride any ponies but your own." Mom leaned her head back on the couch. "I just don't want you getting hurt."

"Okay," I said. I couldn't bear to argue with her given how she looked.

I went to my room and flopped down on my bed. Riding Frankie had been the best thing ever, something I was excited about, and now that was officially over.

I pulled out my phone and checked my messages. I sat upright as I saw I had a notification from *The Chronicle* that someone had responded to my old post looking for information about Frankie. After the initial bunch of messages wishing me good luck, nothing else had come in and I had pretty much given up on finding out anything about him that way. I moved to my computer and pulled up *The Chronicle* site. It took me a moment to find the old thread from my post but then I was there, clicking on the message from a woman named Janette Reese.

My heart raced when I read your post. About a year and a half ago, I sold my daughter's pony, Blue. At the time we were desperate for the money. Both my husband and I had lost our jobs and we were about to foreclose on our house. We couldn't afford the board on Blue and then this guy came to the barn we were at and offered us a few thousand dollars for him. I didn't want to sell him and the guy kind of gave me the creeps. But he had the money in cash and we really had no choice. Ever since I've been wondering what happened to Blue. I've been so worried that man bought him for meat. But why buy a pony, and why pay so much for meat? It didn't make sense. Then I was worried he bought him for some sort of cult sacrifice because he kept saying how perfect it was that he was white and had the blue eye. I know that sounds crazy but you never know about people. I'm so glad he's okay and has a good home. I wonder what happened with that man and how Blue got to your barn. Thank you for giving me peace of mind after all this time.

So now we had a new question: Who was the man who had bought Frankie and what purpose had he bought him for?

* * *

After some Advil and a few days, my shoulder felt fine. Tyler was sound again. Jane had recuperated fully and was now back riding Frankie.

When we were all hanging out by the ring watching Susie teach the big eq kids, I told Hailey and Jane more about what

I'd learned from Janette. I'd already called them to tell them about her reply. Since then I'd exchanged lots of messages with Janette and learned more about Frankie. Her daughter had shown Frankie on the local circuit, which explained why he knew how to jump and do his changes, but wasn't very polished. It also explained why he was used to being clipped and bathed and all that stuff. Frankie had not had the brand when Janette owned him. As far as she knew, he'd also never known any tricks.

"Did you ask her if he was scared of tractor-trailers?" Hailey said.

"Yup. I asked about tractor-trailers, men in baseball hats, and lunge whips and she said she couldn't remember any of those ever being a problem."

Hailey ran the zipper of her half chap up and down. "So whoever the man who bought him was—he taught him tricks, branded him, and made him scared of all those things?"

"He taught him *one* trick. As far as we know there aren't any others." I watched as Caitlyn Rogers, without stirrups, rode the course. Sometimes Susie made us ride without stirrups on the flat and that was bad enough. "How do they even do that?" I said. "Look how tight Caitlyn is."

Jane didn't take her eyes off Caitlyn. "I've jumped without stirrups."

"A whole course?" Hailey said.

"No, but a few jumps. It's not impossible. You just have to get strong enough."

Caitlyn jumped through an in-and-out, holding her position perfectly in the air. She was Susie's best chance at a ribbon in the Finals this year. Susie had been an assistant trainer at West Hills when they had won the Medal and Maclay Finals year after year, but she'd never had a student of her own win. If Caitlyn won or even got a top ribbon, it would be huge for Susie.

I was thinking about how someday it would likely be me, Jane, and Hailey jumping three-foot-six courses without our stirrups. Someday we would be the big eq kids of the barn. If she had a nice enough horse, Jane would be the one who might be able to win it all. It felt predestined like that already—the kids who won everything in the ponies most often became the kids who won everything in the juniors. I couldn't imagine myself jumping courses without stirrups. It seemed as impossible as when we'd seen a vaulting demonstration before a grand prix class at Southampton. Vaulting was where you basically did all these crazy gymnastics like handstands while trotting and cantering on a horse on a lunge line. You didn't use a saddle but instead the horse wore a surcingle around its middle. The vaulters we saw at Southampton were from the Big Apple Circus and it was a cross-promotional thing where they hoped people watching the show would go see the circus.

"So she had no idea what the guy bought Frankie for?" Hailey asked.

I shrugged. "No. He just said he was perfect. But who knows what that means?"

Caitlyn had finished her course and now Jane turned to look at us. "Perfect for what? I can't imagine him being perfect for *anything*."

I rolled the word around in my mind. Perfect. "He liked his blue eye."

Jane said, "But what would you want a blue eye for?"

I thought about the vaulters again and the circus. "Would a white pony with a blue eye be cool in a circus?" I had just said it on a whim. Hailey and Jane looked at me like maybe I was on to something. I continued thinking out loud, "Maybe he knows other tricks. Remember those vaulters in Southampton? Maybe he was a circus pony and he did tricks and someone also did vaulting on him."

Jane shook her head. "But he reared when he saw the lunge whip. A vaulting pony wouldn't be scared of a lunge whip."

"Unless the trainer was cruel to him," Hailey said. "Then he might be. I bet the trainer wore a baseball hat."

We all nodded, our eyes growing wide. Even Jane, who hadn't really cared about where Frankie came from, other than with the hope of getting rid of him, seemed excited.

I said, "Has he been lunged much? If he's a vaulting pony, he would be really good on the lunge line, right?"

"A circus would travel by tractor-trailer..." Hailey said to herself. She looked at me. "Oh my god, I think you could be right."

"Let's go ask Hektor whether he's lunged him," I said.

Hektor was tacking up Katie Whitt's horse. We slowed to a walk once inside the barn.

"Have you ever lunged Frankie?" I said.

"Ever?" Hektor asked.

"Ever. We're just wondering if he's good about being lunged."

Hektor shrugged. "He was okay."

"Just okay?" Jane asked.

"Did he listen to voice commands? Like when you told him to walk and trot?" It seemed like that would be a must for a horse used for vaulting.

Hektor shook his head.

I felt my body deflate. It had finally seemed like we had figured it out but now it wasn't making sense.

"Did you use a lunge whip?" Hailey asked.

"He didn't like the lunge whip." Hektor looked sheepishly at me. I guess he worried I might be mad after what happened when I fell off.

We thanked Hektor and walked back toward the front of the barn. Susie's voice carried from the ring from where she was still teaching the eq kids: "Again! When you see the distance don't shake and bake to get there! Smooth it out."

"So there goes that theory," Jane said.

I let out a half-sigh, half-groan. If he wasn't good at lungeing and didn't know voice commands, he certainly couldn't be a vaulting pony. Which meant we were back to knowing essentially nothing.

"Let's go watch the end of the lesson," Jane said.

Chapter 38

I COULDN'T GIVE UP ON THE IDEA of Frankie being a circus vaulting pony. It was the only thing that made any sense. I watched videos of circus acts with horses on YouTube and on circus websites. The horses were always jet-black or white. A white pony with a blue eye would excite an audience. I could imagine Frankie with a lady in a glittery leotard doing handstands on his back and then afterward he would take a bow. In the videos of vaulters in circus acts, they did amazing things like jumps and flips. I also checked out the website of the American Vaulting Association and learned about what made a good vaulting horse. Attitude and temperament were the most important things and in that way Frankie wouldn't have been a very good candidate since he was nervous and unpredictable at times. But I still wondered if that was because of a mean circus trainer. According to Janette he'd been a great first pony for her daughter—calm and reliable—and at times Frankie did still seem sweet and kind. He seemed like he wanted to be a good pony, but had forgotten how.

On the American Vaulting Association website there was also a section on how to train a vaulting horse. When I got to the part about voice commands, I leaned closer to the screen. It emphasized the importance of working by voice command since a vaulting horse essentially had to be "remote control." My shoulders slumped as I half-heartedly read on. How could Frankie be a circus pony if he didn't know voice commands? Hektor had said he didn't respond to walk or trot. But a few lines later I read something that made me sit up straight:

The verbal commands you will need to teach are:

A tongue click to start the horse out or to move him on faster in the same gait;

"Brrr" (a raspberry sound) or "whoa" for stop; "brrr" is preferred as it is not used in conversation, and you don't want to confuse the horse by using something the vaulter might say.

"Walk" and "trot" with a specific intonation.

"Hup" for canter.

Could Frankie not have been good lungeing for Hektor because Hektor hadn't used the right voice commands? It was possible. I called Hailey and Jane and told them what I'd found.

"We need to lunge him," I said. "Then we'll know for sure one way or another."

They both agreed and the next day Tommy begrudgingly said we could lunge Frankie. Jane told him we thought he might have been a circus pony and he rolled his eyes and said, "Just don't get hurt."

We took Frankie out to the back ring. Jane led him and Hailey and I walked beside her. We didn't bring the lunge whip because that was what had freaked him out in the first place. Hailey and I stood by the rail as Jane took Frankie into the ring. She stood in the middle of the end of the ring closest to us and gave Frankie some slack on the lunge line.

"Okay, what do I do?"

I looked down at my notes. "Cluck to get him to move out."

Hailey and I waited, pressed against the fence, as Jane clucked to Frankie. I wondered if Hailey was as nervous as I was. If this didn't work, I didn't know how we'd ever figure out what had happened to Frankie after Janette had sold him.

Jane clucked quietly and Frankie didn't move. My heart sank. She did it again, louder, and he moved off onto the circle.

"Now tell him to trot but like we talked about. Make it two syllables."

Jane called out, "Tr-*ot*."

And off Frankie went into a trot. Jane shot us a look—it was working! To make him halt the site had said either to use 'whoa' or 'brrr' but had suggested 'brrr' since it was not likely to be used in conversation. After the vaulter did a big flip maybe the ringmaster would say something like, "Whoa, hold on there! Don't fall off." I told Jane what to say. She made a funny face as she did the "brrr" since it did sound silly. The moment it was out of her mouth, Frankie came to a perfect, square halt. He turned his head and glanced at us with what I swear was a smug look on his face—like, finally you guys figure out what I can do.

"Oh my god!" Hailey said. "You were right."

To confirm it Jane asked him to canter with a "hup!" Off Frankie went into a perfect canter departure. He looked happy and relaxed, like he was thrilled we'd figured out his language. Jane put him through a few more paces—it was pretty cool to be able to utter sounds and have him respond perfectly. I think it was one of the first times I'd seen her enjoying working with him. She brought him to a halt and came toward him. I almost couldn't believe when I saw her actually pat him on the neck.

She rolled up the lunge line and led him toward us. "I guess that explains a lot."

Hailey cocked her head. "Except for a few minor details like what happened at the circus and how he got to Vi's."

"One thing at a time," I said.

Chapter 39

IN THE LAST WEEK OF JUNE, Susie and Tommy took a group of riders to a smaller show in Massachusetts. It was Hailey's last chance to qualify for Pony Finals.

I wanted to go along, but it was crazy for me to show my ponies, who were already qualified, at such a small show. I wouldn't have minded going along just to watch and cheer on Hailey. But with Mom's surgery scheduled for three weeks out and me leaving for Shaftsbury to show the following week, I figured I better not ask and just stay home.

Since everyone was at the show, the barn was quiet. I was supposed to just hack my ponies. After I rode Tyler in the ring, I decided to take him for a walk around the ring. I wasn't supposed to but no one was watching, and what could happen, really? On the other side of the ring we came to the trail into the woods. Tyler swung his head to look down the path and it was like he was asking me to take it. I thought about how he looked so happy covered in mud that day in the field. Since his bruise, he was only allowed to go out in the tiny turnout again. He never got to do what he wanted. Before I could think more about all the reasons why I shouldn't, I turned off onto the trail. I immediately started telling myself I would turn around really soon. We'd only just take a quick look to see what the trail was like. But I kept going, wanting to see what was around the next bend and the next. The trail was just wide enough for one horse, single file, and it was surrounded by trees. The ground was safe and even— no jutting rocks or roots. The trail headed up a little hill and I got up into half-seat. Tyler's ears were glued forward and his walk felt very different than his ring walk. He looked with interest at the trees and at a big boulder we passed but he didn't spook at them. The trail leveled out again and I decided to trot. He carried his head higher than in the ring but I didn't mind. He felt alert and alive, like a different pony. He was clearly having fun. He put up with what he was asked to do in the ring but this was what he liked.

The trail spilled out into a grassy field, woods surrounding it on all sides. I had no idea places like this existed. I wanted so badly to canter through the field but I knew I had already pushed my luck and needed to get back. I came back to the barn and slid off Tyler. Before I handed him to Martha he gave me a conspiratorial look that I swear was his saying, "I won't tell if you won't."

* * *

Hailey texted me nonstop from the show. The smalls and mediums were combined with only six total. Even with those stacked odds, Hailey was freaking out and most of my texts were telling her how awesome she and Donald were. The first day Hailey chipped badly in the first class, caving under all the pressure. She still ended up fourth. She won the second class and placed fourth again in the hack. The next day Hailey rode awesome and won both classes. She was champion and qualified for Pony Finals. Jane took Coco even though she was already qualified and was reserve to Hailey. The other big news was that Jane was champion in the greens with Frankie and now he was qualified for Pony Finals, too.

That week Mom said she wanted us to do something fun together. Sometimes we used to drive to upstate New York and go hiking, but that was out of the question. Mom asked me if I wanted to go shopping and go out to lunch, get our nails done, but that wasn't what I wanted to do. We couldn't settle on anything that didn't feel like a forced-bonding-with-your-dying-mother moment and I began to feel badly that the week just might slip by and we wouldn't do anything together. I was even going to relent to the tired lunch/nails/shopping excursion when a few days later Mom said, "I have an idea I think you're going to like. You know how I feel about dogs... but there's a PAUSE FOR PAWS walk-a-thon on Saturday and I thought we could volunteer together. I already called and offered that ProduX have a booth with give-aways for the walkers. They were pretty excited and I won't have to *touch* a dog."

"Really?" I couldn't believe Mom had come up with this idea on her own. It was just the kind of thing I liked to do. It made me feel sick to my stomach that I'd taken Tyler into the woods. What if he'd gotten hurt, or someone had found out?

Still, I couldn't stop thinking about the trail and the field and how different Tyler had seemed.

"Does it sound like something you'd want to do together? Man, or *woman* rather, the booth?" Mom asked.

"Absolutely!"

Mom and I got to the park early on Saturday. Volunteers wearing PAUSE FOR PAWS shirts were flagging the walk-a-thon route, putting up posters, and setting up water stations. Mom found Tania, the event organizer, who thanked her profusely for participating. She led us to a spot near a water station where two other volunteers were setting up a table. Dad drove up a little while later with the boxes of supplies Mom had ordered from the warehouse. He carried the boxes over to the table. Then Mom whispered something to him, which must have been telling him not to stick around so we could have our time together. He snapped a photo of us with his phone and then waved good-bye.

We unloaded the samples of facial cleanser, moisturizers, and sunscreen. We set them up on the table and Tania came over with PAUSE FOR PAWS shirts for us to wear.

An hour later the first walkers showed up, most with dogs. I loved seeing all the different types of dogs, tiny to huge, purebred to mixed breeds. Some walkers carried babies in backpacks or pushed strollers. The weather couldn't have been better, clear skies, but not overly hot. In addition to the walk, there was a diva doggie costume contest and a looks-most-like-its-owner contest. A radio station had a booth and played music, and there were other tables with companies giving away energy bars and doggie treats.

Mom was wrong about not having to touch a dog. Most everyone who came to the booth had at least one dog with them. I'd always bend down and pat the dogs and ask their names. Mom tried to stay behind the booth, handing out samples. I wondered if anyone would guess that Mom was the founder and former CEO of ProduX. They probably just thought she was some salesclerk who had the job of handing out samples at events. Mom was wearing her wig, and if you didn't know her, you probably wouldn't notice it was a wig. But I still wasn't used to it, or her drawn-on eyebrows.

All the dogs were on leashes, but at one point a medium-sized fuzzy bear of a dog got loose and tore across the park. It was heading straight for our booth, its owner running after it. It darted under the table and it must have been instinct over-riding her fear because Mom reached out and grabbed its leash. She seemed to surprise even herself. The dog leaped around by her feet as she tried to remain calm, holding the leash with shaky hands. I was going to take the dog from her, but she looked like she was almost enjoying being forced to confront her fear. The dog sat down and looked up at her and she leaned down to pat his head. His owner came huffing up to the table, apologizing. "She just bolted away."

"No problem," Mom said, handing over the leash. "She's cute."

"Thank you," the woman said.

Mom gave me an infinitely pleased look like this day was working out even better than she'd imagined.

"Mom?" I said.

"Yeah?"

"I know I shouldn't even ask, but what about us getting a dog? You did so well with that one."

Mom sighed. "I don't think now's the right time, honey."

"Maybe this *is* a good time. Dogs can be therapeutic, you know."

"You'll get a dog... someday," she said.

I mumbled, "Like when I'm thirty."

"Before then," Mom said with a faraway look in her eyes.

When most of the dogs and walkers had gone home, we helped pick up the discarded water cups and energy bar wrappers. I could tell Mom was tired. Still, she wouldn't stop helping. Tania came over to thank us again before we left. "You are so great to do this. I don't know many CEOs who take time out to actually do the work."

Mom put her arm around me. "It's all my daughter... she's very inspiring." Mom looked sideways at me, again, the way she had a lot that day, smiling in a kind of strange detached-yet-happy way. I had a weird feeling she knew something about her cancer I didn't know. Like this was the last meaningful thing we'd do together. That feeling of absolute panic I usually only felt at night in bed in the dark rushed over me. It made me feel like I couldn't get enough air. It was a powerful physical kind of scared I'd never felt before Mom got sick.

I tried to shake off the feeling, telling myself I was just tired, too. It was easier to shake it off in the daylight. Mom was having surgery soon. Yes, like Dad said, her recovery would be hard but she'd do just that—recover. She had to.

Chapter 40

THE NEXT WEEK I LEFT FOR Shaftsbury, Vermont for two weeks of the six-week circuit. It was the first show Mom didn't come to. I would stay with the Mullins, which I knew would be so much fun. The show was near several ski resorts so it had cute shops and good restaurants that were happy to have summer customers. It was crazy humid in the city before we left, but in Vermont the mountain air was refreshingly cool.

Now that Hailey was qualified, the pressure was off. Jane was super busy showing lots of ponies for people and Tommy had also gotten her some rides in the children's jumpers and hunters. She was getting tall for medium ponies and Tommy wanted to get her started on horses. Next year he wanted her mostly doing the large ponies, and getting her feet wet in the junior hunters and big eq. The sooner he could get her making up project horses instead of ponies the better, since a big-time eq horse or junior hunter sold for even more money than a top pony.

I felt bad because Vermont was super fun in part because Mom wasn't there. I could almost forget about infusions, de-bulking, and central lines—terminology most kids never had to learn.

We rented a two-bedroom ski condo with a loft. Owen was spending the week with his dad. Hailey and I shared a room and talked forever before falling asleep so I was less likely to have those overwhelming attacks of fear. A few times I woke up in the middle of the night, thinking about death, and things in the room would start to look sinister. I knew that would sound crazy if I told anyone, but that's what it felt like. But I could look over at Hailey and it made me feel better and get back to sleep easier.

Since I felt guilty about how much fun I was having with Hailey and her mom, I texted and called Mom a lot. Mrs. Mullins was so different than Mom. A lot of what she said and did embarrassed Hailey, like how she'd leave the door open when she went to the bathroom.

Mrs. Mullins also came into the kitchen in the morning to get her coffee in only a bra and underwear. Hailey would shield her eyes and moan, "Mom!" According to Hailey she also slurped her coffee too loudly and popped her gum. Nearly everything about her drove Hailey crazy. Sometimes Mrs. Mullins and I would share a sympathetic look behind Hailey's back and one time, when Hailey was in the shower, Mrs. Mullins asked me whether I was so hard on my mother. "Sometimes it's like I can't do anything she doesn't hate me for," she confided.

I tried to console her by telling her my mom annoyed me,

too, just in different ways. And at the end of the day, when Hailey, Anna and I piled into Mrs. Mullin's bed to watch bad TV at night, Hailey snuggled close to her mom and Mrs. Mullins put her arm around her. I lay there loving being a part of their family, even if it was only temporary.

We had spent the week before we left for the show making horse treats at Hailey's and we had a booth by the main hunter ring and spectator tent where we sold them. We were also selling special Danny & Ron's hair bows made by Belle & Bow Equestrian. We had raised a lot of money for the lip sync. Hailey's mom was great about helping us make the treats since she liked to cook. She rolled up her sleeves and threw on an apron and she didn't mind that her kitchen floor was covered in oats and her counters were sticky with mo-lasses. She also was awesome at helping us package the treats in pretty bags with labels she made on her computer. By the end of the two weeks of the show, we'd sold all but three of the packages and lots of bows, and made four-hundred-and-thirty-eight dollars. With Mom matching that, it was close to a thousand dollars.

I won four out of five classes with Tyler the first week. It was like I was tired of figuring out how not to win. But the whole time I rode I still felt numb, like I was going through the motions. It got to the point where I felt physically ill lead-ing Tyler into the jogs. I'd feel whatever I'd eaten that day climbing back up my throat and it was all I could do to keep it down. I fake-smiled at people who congratulated me. Martha asked me once or twice if I was okay. I said I was fine and she must have believed me. I guess people thought that, if anything, what was going on with my mother was taking its toll on me.

The summer had been incredibly dry, with a nearly record low rainfall, which Hailey, of course, thought was a plot by the gods to ruin her summer. All those weeks when she was trying to qualify and the sky stayed Crayola blue. But on Friday of the second week, with Hailey qualified and the numbers in the ponies dwindling anyway, the skies opened up. Rain in the mountains of Vermont took on a plague-like feeling. Instead of steady rain it came in massive intermittent torrents, with raindrops as big as your hand. If there was a flash of lightning or the rumble of thunder, the show would be stopped or perhaps classes canceled, but otherwise everything kept going. Enormous puddles sprouted up in the rings and rivers of water threatened to invade the aisles of the tents. At midday, it was so dark it could have been eight o'clock at night. Hektor furiously dug trenches outside the tent to keep out the water. The rain continued through Friday night and into Saturday morning. The rings were now nearly just one big puddle, no matter how many times the ring crew dragged the footing with their tractors.

We huddled under the tent, listening to the rain pounding on the canvas. Every so often we'd see a golf cart go by with its plastic covers up or a crazy person in their brightly colored rain slicker ride by on a drenched, steaming horse.

"I think we'll scratch Tyler," Susie told me. "You can still do Drizzle and Sammy, if you want."

"Do we have to scratch him?" I said. Maybe he would like going in the rain. Maybe it would be more of a challenge.

"I don't want him getting hurt or pulling a shoe, especially after the bruise he had."

I knew Susie wasn't going to change her mind. She usually let horses be horses, but it was like she'd been brainwashed to be overprotective with Tyler. I felt badly for Tyler. No one ever gave him a chance to see what he could do.

The rain stopped by the time the mediums went, but the ring was still a mess and lots of people had scratched. The few ponies that went did funny things like spook at the puddles or try to jump over them, often landing splat in them. Donald couldn't have cared less. He cantered straight through the slop, jumping better than ever. It was almost like Hailey rode better, too, knowing this was her chance to shine. By the time she was called on top in both jogs the sun was blazing again. Beaming, she led a mud covered Donald out of the ring.

By Sunday, the rings were dried out and the footing was good again. It was amazing how much rain the rings could absorb. The only reminder of the rain were the trenches around the tents, some fortified with sandbags, puddles around the grounds, and the still waterlogged tack. Some of the people who scratched rode; others who were going to leave on Sunday anyway decided to make an early exit, packing their trailers and hitting the road Saturday afternoon. Susie said I shouldn't bother showing Tyler on Sunday—she still didn't want to risk him getting hurt even though the footing was pretty much back to normal. Hailey finished second and fourth on Donald and was champion. I had gotten good ribbons on Sammy, winning the class she was second in, and ended up reserve champion.

On the last day of the show I didn't want to leave. Back at the stabling, people were in pack-up mode. Several barns had already left and many aisles of the tent were now empty. Big rigs lined up outside the tents as grooms hustled back and forth with hand trucks full of trunks and equipment.

I wanted to move in with the Mullins instead of going home to our modern, gleaming, and impeccably clean apartment and face Mom's surgery. Sometimes at home I left crumpled tissues around or glasses of water just to see how quickly someone came and whisked them away. The longest a tissue had survived outside of my room was twenty-two minutes. A glass of water had lasted sixty-three minutes, but it had miraculously moved onto a coaster after fourteen minutes. Of course I felt guilty about not wanting to go home. What kind of a kid wanted to stay with another family when her mother was about to have cancer surgery?

Chapter 41

WHEN I GOT HOME THE APARTMENT felt so quiet that I went straight to my room to unpack and turned on music. The barn was closed on Monday and I couldn't possibly stand being in the apartment all day so I asked if Lauren could pick up Hailey and then take us to the country club. It wasn't really where we wanted to be—that was the barn—but we still had fun swimming and drinking smoothies at the café. When I opened the car door at the barn the next day, though, everything felt right with the world. This was coming home.

The Pony Finals were now two weeks away. After the relaxed vibe at Vermont, the pressure started to build again. We practiced longer courses and tests for the Medal Final. Out of the ring, Hailey had been practicing her lip sync. Now she kicked into high gear. On Friday night, she had Jane and me over for a rehearsal. We made pizza for dinner using a pizza stone, and then we pushed the coffee table and chairs to the side of the TV room to create an open space like a stage. Hailey's mom, Anna, Owen, his snake in its travel cage, Milo and Chopper, Jane, and I sat on the couch. Hailey slid her phone into a dock and pressed play. She stood in the center of the room with her back turned to us. The music started and she tapped her foot to the beat. Watching her, I was thinking how I could never perform like Hailey. I could never stand up there in the TV room, let alone do it at Pony Finals in front of a huge audience. I could ride in front of lots of people but somehow that felt different.

When the lyrics began, she pivoted around to face us. She strutted around the room, pretending to groove to an imaginary jukebox. During a riff, she acted out playing the guitar. Her lip syncing was accurate, especially the few times Joan lets out a powerful screech. She finished with a dramatic toss of her head and we all clapped.

Her mom whistled. "Really good. I love it!"

Owen held the case with his snake tight. "I think it's stupid."

Hailey made a face.

Anna scratched Milo's ear. "I liked it."

Hailey looked at me and Jane. "Well? Someone who's not related to me?"

"Good," I said.

"Yeah, it was good," Jane echoed.

But the truth was it was just okay. I wasn't quite sure why. Maybe just because it was in her TV room and not up on stage. Maybe because she wasn't dressed up like she would be for the actual performance. Something was missing.

Hailey put her hands on her hips. "Good enough to beat Dakota?"

I shrugged. Should we tell her the truth? Hailey was always the one to tell us the truth. Didn't we owe her the same?

"I don't know," I said.

Jane held up her hand in the universal sign for so-so. "Maybe."

Hailey paced the TV room. "What else can I do? It can't just be okay. Is it the choreography? My lip syncing? The song?"

Mrs. Mullins slapped her hands on her thighs. "I think you need a guy."

Hailey squinted at her.

"The song is talking all about a guy... about the singer seeing this totally hot guy by the jukebox and trying to figure out how to make him, well, want to get with her."

Hailey covered her face with her hand, embarrassed by her mother's language, but Jane and I looked at each other and nodded. Mrs. Mullins was right. It wasn't working with Hailey all alone. Lots of acts had multiple kids with backup singers or groups. I could see it working much better with a guy.

"She's right," I said.

"Great." Hailey's arms fell to her sides. "Because there are *so* many guys to choose from at the shows. Maybe we can put an ad on Match.com. *Looking for hot teenage guy to be in lip sync contest.*"

"There's got to be someone we know." Mrs. Mullins looked at Jane and me. "Girls?"

"Um." I cleared my throat. Jane was going to freak out but the perfect person was obvious. "What about Alex?"

"Alex?" Jane's eyes were wide.

"He's coming to Pony Finals and he *is* cute."

Jane shook her head. "He'll never do it."

Would he never do it, or did Jane not want him to do it?

"You don't know that," Mrs. Mullins said. "It's a great idea. You should ask him."

Jane turned her head to the side. "I'm not asking him."

"I can ask him," I offered.

Hailey shrugged. "I guess if you don't mind."

"Of course. I'll do anything for you... and to beat Dakota." And I'd do anything to have a reason to talk to Alex. Alex had spent the two weeks we were in Vermont at home and then he'd been away at a big motocross competition. I'd heard from Jane that he hadn't done very well at the competition. I looked at Jane tentatively. "Is it really okay with you?"

She crossed her arms. "I guess, do what you have to."

Chapter 42

NOW THAT I HAD JANE'S begrudging permission, I had to get up the nerve to talk to Alex. I told myself that I was doing this for Hailey and it was no big deal. I found him the next day cleaning one of his bikes in the garage in back of the barn, where the tractor for dragging the ring was stored. He was kneeling down, gently sponging off the metal on his bike with as much care as we used on our ponies. I came into the garage quietly and he didn't hear me. I watched him for a few moments. Then I decided I better say something before he caught me standing there staring at him.

"Hi," I said.

"Oh, hey, what's up?"

He had a funny look on his face, like he was trying to figure out why I was there, or even how I'd known to find him there. (I'd asked Hektor.)

"I heard your race wasn't great."

He went back to working on his bike. "It's not just one race but yeah, whatever."

I felt dumb for saying race when I had no idea what you actually called what Alex competed in. "Sorry, I hate it when people who don't know about horse shows say stupid things like, how was your race? They ask me that all the time."

"It's okay. No worries." Alex traded his sponge for a brush and started in on the spokes of the wheels.

"So when's the next one?"

"A few weeks. After Pony Finals."

"Does Jane ever go watch? Or, um, your dad?"

"Jane—no, never. My dad—he's been to a few over the years."

"But you get dragged to horse shows sometimes... like you're coming to Pony Finals, right?" It didn't seem fair that Jane never had to go to Alex's competitions.

Alex shrugged. "Mom's going, so I guess I have to go, too."

"You sound about as excited as I am."

"You don't want to go?"

I guess he still didn't understand how I felt about Tyler so maybe we were even. "I like Pony Finals. I just don't want to show Tyler."

"Right. You'd rather ride Frankie, the pony who tossed you."

I flushed red. "I know it makes no sense. Anyway, about Pony Finals..." I explained about the lip sync and how we needed a guy for Hailey's act.

"Wait, you want me to be in her lip sync?"

"You don't have to sing or anything."

"Do I have to dance? I don't dance."

"No, you just have to pretend to be this cool guy she meets. Do you know the song 'I Love Rock and Roll' by Joan Jett?"

"No."

"I have it on my phone if you want to hear it." I took out my phone.

He motioned to it. "Is that the new one?"

I nodded. This was one of those dreaded moments when it hit me how privileged I was. I had tried to tell Mom that I didn't want a new phone, but she had insisted.

"You're really lucky."

"Sometimes," I said. "Do you want to hear the song?" I took it as a good sign he hadn't just said plain no. I pressed play and we listened. I snuck glances at Alex, to try to figure out what he thought of the music, and also just to look at him. The lyrics seemed to be saying things I thought about Alex and I had the strange feeling that he knew what I was thinking and maybe even didn't mind, or felt a little bit the same way, if that was even possible. But when the song ended, I told myself I must have been imagining things.

"Kind of cool, right?" I said.

"Yeah."

"We really need you to do it. It's the only way we're going to beat Dakota."

"Dakota Pearce?"

"Yeah."

"I don't like that girl."

"No one does."

"And doesn't she ride with Hell's Acres?"

"Yup." I chuckled. Alex might not like the horse show world, but he still knew all the players.

"Okay."

"Okay, you'll do it?"

"Yes."

"Wow, I thought that would take more convincing."

Alex shook his head. "Jane makes me out to be a total jerk, huh?"

"A little."

"We're just different. I don't hate her like she hates me. Well, not all the time anyway." He put down his brush and picked up the sponge again. "How's the pony detectives thing going?"

"Jane didn't tell you?"

Alex made a face, like no way would Jane tell him anything.

I filled Alex in on Janette and how she'd sold Frankie out of desperation to some man she didn't even know and how we'd figured out that Frankie had been a vaulting pony.

"I was kind of joking when I said you guys could be the pony detectives, but I'm pretty impressed."

I put my hands in my pockets. "Thanks. But I'm not really sure what to do now—how to find out who this guy was. I've tried looking for different circuses. I haven't been able to find out anything."

"I guess you could post again—see if he bought any other horses or ponies. She didn't know the man's name?"

"No, he paid cash. Posting's a good idea. Hey, maybe *you'd* make a good pony detective."

Alex held up his hands. "Being in the lip sync is as far as I'm going to go."

"Right," I said.

I had nothing else to talk to him about, but I didn't want to leave. And he didn't seem like he minded if I stayed. I thought about asking him to explain the motorbike world to me, but I never liked it when people who didn't know anything about horse shows asked me to explain the hunters to them. It was nearly impossible to do and anything I'd say made horse showing seem simple, which it wasn't at all. "Well, I guess I should go. I'll tell you if I find out anything more, though."

"Yeah," Alex said. "Do you have my cell?"

"Um, no."

"Put it in your phone."

He gave me his number and I entered it into my phone. Alex Hewitt. He'd given me his number—wasn't he essentially asking me to text him?

"Well, see you," I said.

He smiled. "Yeah, see you."

As I walked back to the barn, I took out my phone so I could look at Alex's name. Just seeing it there on the screen was enough to make me feel stupidly giddy.

Chapter 43

MOM HAD HER SURGERY THE week before Pony Finals. Dad and I sat in the surgical waiting room at the hospital. It was for all the people whose relatives were having surgery that day. It was strange to sit there and not know how serious the surgery was the people's relatives were having. Were they having emergency heart surgery or arthroscopic knee surgery? I tried to figure out by looking around the room. Would you read *US Weekly* if your husband was having heart surgery? Would you be able to work on your computer? Dad brought his iPad and a copy of the *The Wall Street Journal*, but he didn't use either one. I texted a few times with Jane and Hailey. I leafed through *Practical Horseman* and tried to read an article about grand prix rider, Tara Barnes, putting together a syndicate to buy an international caliber horse, but it was hard to concentrate. Every once in a while Dad would say something, but neither one of us really felt like talking.

Last time Mom had surgery, I hadn't been allowed to

come until after she was in recovery. Now Dad felt I was old enough to handle it. I'd been surprised when he'd said I could come with him if I wanted. So I was old enough to wait at the hospital while my mom had surgery, but I couldn't make any decisions about which ponies I wanted to ride. That made no sense.

Every so often doctors would come in and whisk relatives into a smaller room attached to the waiting room. After only an hour, the surgeon came in and called Mom's name. We bolted up from our seats, surprised since we had been told it would take several hours. We tried to read the surgeon's face for how the surgery had gone, but she didn't give us any indication. What did it mean that it was over so fast? Was that good news, or bad?

The small room had a couch and a chair. We sat on the couch; the surgeon sat in the chair and crossed her legs.

"Things did not go as we had hoped with the debulking surgery."

That was the last sentence I heard in complete clarity. The rest blurred together, as my mind spun. I started to get that panicky-can't-breathe feeling. "Tumors had not shrunk enough... even if we resected the colon itself... identified other tumors... best option at this point is palliative care."

Dad leaned forward in his seat. His head was in his hands and he was crying. Openly weeping.

It was like when I'd fallen off Frankie. Everything had been one way and then the next moment I was on the ground trying to figure out what happened. The whole world had shifted and I was a having a hard time catching up.

The surgeon waited patiently until Dad picked up his head. "So you just closed back up?"

The surgeon looked at me and then quickly averted her eyes back to my father. Perhaps I *was* too young to be there.

The words came in undefined chunks again: "Only option... if we resected the colon... in her weakened state... best chance for quality time."

"Okay, okay," Dad said.

He reached out and pulled me to him, almost too hard. It felt wrong coming from him—he was always so gentle. It scared me to feel him so scared. This was it, the moment we knew she would die. Still, did either of us truly believe it? Was Dad's brain doing the somersaults mine was, thinking, well, maybe they're wrong, maybe more chemo will help, maybe there will be a wonder drug that will fix her? Thinking, no, no, no.

When we went into recovery, Mom looked like someone else, someone not even qualified to be a ghost of herself. She was barely conscious and didn't really seem to know we were there. And this was all without having taken anything out of her.

Nurses came and checked all the beeping machines. At one point Mom looked at us, but she couldn't hold eye contact and returned to kind of staring vacantly. It was awful seeing her like that and I got the feeling that maybe Dad was realizing he'd made a mistake by letting me come with him. Soon, he suggested that we let Mom rest and I could go to the barn with Lauren and come back later, when Mom was more "up and about."

At the barn, everyone wanted to know how the surgery went and I just said we didn't really know yet. I couldn't bear to say any of the words the doctor had used. After the hospital, the smells of the barn that I usually took for granted smelled stronger: the sweet, musky smell of leather, the thick scent of horses' sweat in the July heat, and the rich aroma of manure. Everything looked wonderfully bright and it felt comforting to put on my half chaps and helmet.

The next few days were spent going back and forth to the hospital to visit Mom. She got better and was able to have conversations and ask me annoying questions about whether Tyler was ready for Pony Finals. But she still tired easily and slept a lot. The nurses helped her shower, but she still didn't look herself. She didn't wear her wig anymore, just one of those cancer-scarves tied around her head. It was hard to believe she could get thinner. Her eyes retreated into deeper sockets in her face and even her nose looked more angular. At some point, she and Dad must have discussed the situation. I didn't mind that I was left out of that conversation. Dad told me we didn't know how long it would be now, but it was months, not years. And only months if we were lucky.

She came home two days later. We moved permanently into the house in Darien. It was farther from her doctors, but I had the feeling she didn't need them in the way she had before. It was closer to the barn, which made it easier for me to slip out to ride. I also had the feeling that it was all planned out—if she died there we could sell the house and maybe put those awful memories behind us.

She set up camp on the couch in the living room. It hurt

for her to bend over or get up so she had a little table next to her with everything on it: phone, iPad, remote, box of tissues, glass of water, orange-colored bottles of pain meds with unpronounceable names.

As the week passed, Mom was able to do more things around the house and have visitors. It was strange to see her get better when we knew things were going to get much, much worse. Even though she was physically a little stronger, sometimes she'd look incredibly confused. Once I found her in the kitchen with the cabinet open. She said she was looking for milk. I pointed to the fridge, and she quickly said that of course she knew the milk was in the fridge. She didn't explain why she'd been looking in the cabinet.

Visitors often came when I was at the barn and they didn't stay long. Mom had to conserve her energy. They left all kinds of things that were supposed to bring her comfort. Books she didn't have the energy to read, photo albums that sat untouched, crystals with supposedly mystical healing powers. All those things seemed ridiculous, but I guess people just wanted to bring something.

She still took drugs to slow down the growth of the tumors, but she was deemed too weak for any more infusions. Every once in a while there would be talk of a medical trial, a not-yet-approved drug. Dad would fly into a fit of action, calling any influential people he knew who worked in medicine to try to get her enrolled. But nothing ever worked out.

We watched TV together, mowing through back episodes of shows we'd missed. Often while I watched I doodled, usually drawing Frankie's brand over and over again. The mystery of Frankie had taken a backseat to everything with Mom, but I was still intent on figuring it out. Sometimes I drew a picture of him or his blue eye, coloring it in with my pen. I started jotting down words: circus pony, blue eye, vaulting, moon, half-moon, triangle, triangle on top. Words flowed into my mind and I scribbled them all down, repeating some again and again. Moon, circus pony, triangle on top like a hat, top hat, big top.

I pulled back my pen and stared at what I'd just written. Big top. I sat up in my chair and said out loud, "Wait a minute."

"What's up?" Mom said.

"Frankie—his brand. I think I can finally read it!" I dashed out of the room to my own room where my laptop was. The triangle above the half-moon—what if it was actually a symbol for a big top? Maybe the circus Frankie was in had 'moon' in its name, or half-moon, or crescent moon. I went online and googled the words 'circus' and 'moon.' One of the first entries that came up was for the Circus of the Moon. I clicked on it, but the link was dead. I googled "Circus of the Moon." I scanned the list of hits. There was a listing for a novel. There was a store that sold handmade plates. At the end of the second page was a link to a short news item in the town paper of Bryn Mawr, Pennsylvania dated from a year ago. My heart charged in my rib cage as I clicked on the link and the town paper's screen appeared.

Chapter 44

THE SHOW WILL NOT GO ON

The Circus of the Moon, a small-scale circus, was due to make a stop in Bryn Mawr and many residents had purchased tickets after seeing advertising. But the circus never came to town. Proprietor Lincoln Morse had gone bankrupt and was no longer able to pay the circus performers or feed the animals, which included a bear, a lion, several birds, and one pony. Sources say that Morse did not adhere to any standards for ethical treatment of his animals. While sources also believe he may have sold the bear and the lion, Justin Hillerman, who worked as a roustabout for the Circus of the Moon, claims the birds and pony were simply let loose to fend for themselves. Attempts to locate Morse have been unsuccessful.

Mom poked her head into my room. "You lost me there. What's going on?"

I could barely tear my eyes away from the screen. "I think I just found out the circus Frankie came from."

"Circus?"

I nodded, realizing that I'd kept all the research I'd done on Frankie from Mom. "We found out Frankie used to be a circus pony."

"Really?"

Mom looked actually interested and it was enough to encourage me to tell her everything that led up to my finding the Circus of the Moon.

"Listen to this—" I read Mom the brief article. I found myself racing through it and made myself slow down. It was so exciting I couldn't help myself. It all finally made sense. Either Lincoln Morse, or whoever was in charge of the animals, was probably the one who wore the baseball hat. In the whole mess of Mom's cancer, there was the tiny gem of solving Frankie's mystery.

I finished reading. "Like the article says, he probably just let Frankie loose and that's how he ended up in one of Vi's pastures. Her farm isn't far from that area."

"And you figured all this out?" Mom had a hand on the doorknob. Standing for so long was probably making her tired.

"Well, Jane and Hailey helped, too."

But I had been the one to put together the pieces. I had stuck with it.

"I'm going to call Hailey and Jane and tell them."

"Okay," Mom said. "Come back in after and we'll finish the show."

"So they just let him loose?" Hailey said when I got her and Jane on conference call.

"I guess so."

"And he jumped into Vi's pasture?" Jane still sounded a little skeptical.

"Or wandered in... remember how she admitted that her fences were always coming apart and ponies were getting loose."

"I can't believe you actually figured it out," Hailey said. "I bet that Lincoln guy abused the animals."

"Yeah," Jane said. "That's why Frankie's weird about some things."

"You can't blame him," I said.

Our conversation drifted to Pony Finals. It was hard to believe that it was almost here. We'd have a few weeks left of summer and horse showing after, but Pony Finals still always felt like the end of something, in part because later in the fall we often moved on to bigger ponies, selling the ones we'd outgrown. The fall shows were always a time of people trying ponies for sale. It was a time of change in the horse world, of bittersweet endings and new partnerships.

"Is your dad going?" Hailey asked me.

"He might come later. I'm going with Susie."

"I think we're all on the same flight," Hailey said.

"Not me." Jane sighed dramatically. "Fourteen hours in the car with Alex."

Alex. My hand tightened on the phone. He said to let him

know if we found out anything more about Frankie. I'd text him after we hung up.

"You got your outfit for the lip sync?" I asked Hailey.

"It's awesome. You guys have to see it."

I heard Hailey's mom calling her in the background. "Coming!" she yelled.

We hung up and I went back into the TV room. Mom was on the couch. She hadn't heard me come in and I stood there, watching her. Her eyes were on the TV, but it wasn't clear whether she was actually watching.

I couldn't believe she would miss Pony Finals. Before her cancer, she never missed any of my shows. It hit me right then how much of my life she would miss. How everything, not just horse shows, would be without her. Breakfast, and homework, and bedtime. I wanted to yell out to the world that it wasn't fair. But I sank down in the chair instead, keeping it all inside.

Chapter 45

THE LAST DAYS BEFORE PONY FINALS dragged on. We didn't want to overschool the ponies—they needed to be sharp and fresh. But we still needed to practice. Susie had us do gymnastics and two days before the ponies were set to leave we jumped a big course.

I packed my bag days before in case I'd realize I was missing something. Mom sat on my bed while I packed. After I had packed my show clothes, I started going through some of my regular clothes, and soon we were cleaning out my closet, deciding what to keep and what should go. I often brought clothes to Darien instead of giving them away, and my closet was filled with things that didn't fit anymore or that I never really wore. We made a pile for Goodwill and, feeling inspired, Mom suggested I help her with her closet. We went into her room, which was enormous. She and Dad had a king bed with a ton of pillows on it and there was a couch on the side of the room. She had a huge walk-in closet and she sat on her bed while I pulled things out and brought them over for her to see. Mom was objective, never waffling on an item the way I did.

"Donate," she said when I held up a fancy dress she'd worn to some charity event. "It never fit me right. I bought it to go with..." She made a face like she was searching for a word. "These things..." She frowned and looked at her slippers. "Things that go on your feet."

"Um, shoes?" I said.

She laughed. "Yes, shoes. These shoes I loved."

I pulled out a scarf and draped it around my neck. "How about this?" It was an expensive brand and a pretty design.

"I got that in Paris. Your father bought it for me shortly after we found out we were pregnant. You should keep it."

I looked in the mirror. I looked all wrong in it now, but somehow I could see myself in five or ten years time, growing into its classy style.

"I want you to have some things of mine," Mom said.

It was the closest we'd gotten to talking about her dying, to talking about what was going to happen.

"You should have the scarf and there will be other things just for you, too."

Maybe she'd done more than clean out her closet—it would be just like Mom to have everything in order. I fingered the scarf still around my neck. I couldn't bottle my sadness and anger up this time and I started crying.

"It stinks you won't be able to come to Pony Finals," I said.

"I know," Mom said. "But I'll be there in spirit."

I twisted the end of the scarf around my hand. "Do you believe in that stuff? Spirits?"

"I don't know." Her voice sounded choked up. "I'd like to."

I'd always thought I'd have more time to figure out religion and the whole life-after-death thing. We didn't go to church or temple and so I only knew about the ideas of heaven and hell from TV and books. Susie sometimes used an animal communicator and she told us that the communicator could talk to animals that had died, too. But I still wasn't sure whether I believed in supernatural stuff. I thought that I'd figure out how I felt about whether there was a heaven and whether you could talk to the dead before I lost someone really important to me.

"I'd like to believe in it, too," I said.

"Then let's believe." Mom's voice sounded upbeat, like it could be that simple.

"Like believe people see each other again, and watch over people?" Mom had always been so practical minded, I was surprised she would go in for all this stuff now. But maybe dying could do that to you.

"Yeah, let's believe in all of it," she said.

"But what if it turns out not to be true?"

Mom smiled at me with tears in her eyes. "We'll be sad."

I climbed onto the bed next to her. The scarf was still around my neck. We snuggled close, like we never had before. I could feel her body against mine. Even though she was nothing but skin and bones, I could still feel the weight of her.

Chapter 46

THE LAST DAY BEFORE PONY FINALS, Mom decided she'd drive me to the barn. No one ever officially said Mom couldn't drive. It just seemed to be something she didn't do anymore, along with go for jogs, wear anything besides comfortable clothes, wear her wig, and put on makeup. Lauren was supposed to drive me, but she'd called because there was a huge accident and she was going to be at least an hour late. Dad was at work. He didn't go in often anymore, but he had decided to take one important meeting.

"This is ridiculous," Mom said, grabbing her keys.

"It doesn't matter if I don't go till later," I said. Everyone at the barn was willing to do whatever to make things easier for us. Without me telling them, they'd found out about the failed surgery and how it was just a matter of time.

Mom grabbed her purse. "No. It's the last day before Pony Finals and I, at least, want to drive my daughter to the barn."

Mom looked okay with her purse and keys and I wasn't going to tell her I wouldn't go with her. It was only a half-hour ride to the barn on roads we'd driven countless times before. She was weak, but she would be fine.

Once she was behind the wheel, Mom looked impossibly small and frail. She backed out of the driveway and I had the queasy feeling I should have come up with some reason why she shouldn't drive me. I sat upright in my seat, playing with my seat belt, and hoping she was up to doing this. We were halfway to the barn and she still seemed fine when we came to the four-way stop sign. She turned left instead of right.

"Um, Mom, you went the wrong way." I glanced at the gas gauge to check if it was low, but the gas station wasn't in that direction anyway. Had she forgotten how to get to the barn? How was that possible?

She increased her speed. "No, I didn't."

"Yeah, the barn's that way—" I pointed back in the other direction. "You were supposed to go right."

She leaned forward, close to the wheel. "I think I know how to get to the damn barn." Her voice had a hard edge, one I'd never really heard from her, even when she was angry. This tone was different than her angry or let down tone. It was like she was a different person speaking.

She was going too fast for the small road and we were going the wrong way. But what was I supposed to do? I tightened my grip on the seat belt, feeling like the ground was shifting underneath me again the way it had when we'd talked to the doctor after the surgery.

We came to another four-way stop. She braked and then just sat there. The car behind her honked and she shouted, "You moron, give me a sec!"

This wasn't my mother. Something was terribly wrong. I

felt terrified and confused. I had no idea what to do. There was no brochure they gave you for moments when your mother became another, unrecognizable person. She still hadn't budged, which maybe was a good thing. She wasn't fit to drive. Even if we made it to the barn, how could I possibly let her drive back alone? I'd have to make up some reason why she should stay and watch me. The car behind us honked again.

"Mom, are you okay?" I asked.

"Of course I'm okay. It's this maniac behind me. I'm going fifty for heaven's sake and then I've got you telling me what to do and where to go. If fifty isn't fast enough, he should pass me."

My head whirled. Mom thought we were going fifty when we were standing still? Things were worse than I had thought. Were the drugs making her crazy?

I rolled down my window and motioned for the car to go around us, praying that it wouldn't upset Mom. I could see the guy staring at us as he passed, trying to figure out what our problem was, and I just tried to ignore him. Mom's eyes were fixed straight ahead, like she couldn't take her eyes off the road, because we were moving. It made me want to cry, but I had to be strong. I had to figure a way out of this, for both of us.

"Good, now at least he passes me. You'd think fifty would be fast enough for that jerk." She peered at the odometer. As much as I wanted her to come back to her senses, I couldn't bear for her to realize it was on zero—that were were standing still.

"Oh," she said, quiet, more like herself, only sadder. She took her hands off the wheel quickly, like it was burning hot. "I don't know what's going on. I don't know where we are." She shook her head, like a confused, elderly person who had wandered away from a nursing home.

"It's okay. Let's put the car in park." I cautiously reached forward and put my hand on the drive shift. She seemed okay with that, so I slid it into park, like I'd seen her do a million times before. It felt strange to be doing it myself. "Let's put on the flashers." I pressed the hazard button. "And let's just relax. I think something's wrong with the car."

Mom nodded, latching onto this idea. "It could be the engine."

"We shouldn't drive it. I'll call Martha. She can come pick us up." It would take much longer for Dad to get here from the city. We needed help now. I didn't want to be alone with Mom when she was like this. What if she tried to drive again? I'd have to stop her.

While we waited for Martha, a few people pulled up next to us and rolled down their windows to ask if we needed help. Mom waved them away and I added that we were fine.

Finally, Martha pulled up behind us and I opened the car door quickly, hoping Mom wouldn't get out, too. "Something's wrong with her. Maybe it's the medicine. She took a wrong turn, then got all angry."

Martha went to Mom's door and tapped lightly on the window.

Mom opened the door. "Thank god, you're here. We think it's the engine."

"Could be," Martha said. "I can take care of it." She walked Mom to her car and helped her into the passenger seat. She pulled Mom's car over to the side of the road. People continued to stare at us as they drove by and I wanted to scream at them to mind their own business. I waited for Martha, not really wanting to be in the car alone with Mom. It was like Martha knew just what to do. Would all grownups? Or was she just very capable?

"It's going to be okay," Martha said to me as we walked over to her car. "You did the right thing calling."

"You are a godsend," Mom told Martha when Martha got in the car. She sounded like everything that had happened was completely normal when it was the most unsettling thing I'd ever lived through.

I sat in the back, shaking, not knowing what had happened to my mother. Had we lost her forever now, even though she might be right in front of us?

Chapter 47

AFTER WE HAD BEEN HOME for a little while, Mom returned to semi-normal. Dad rushed home, cursing himself for ever having left in the first place. He called her doctors, who explained that the tumors must have metastasized to her brain and it was normal to have dementia-like symptoms, especially out of her home environment. I could tell Dad wanted to kill the doctors for saying it was normal—there was nothing normal about a fifty-four-year-old acting like she was ninety-eight. It might be normal to them, but it wasn't normal to us. It was shocking, terrifying. I told Dad about the other times Mom had acted funny—the time in the kitchen when she'd been looking for milk in the cabinet and the time she couldn't think of the word for shoes. Dad had his own similar examples of things we'd both tried to ignore, but which were clearly signs. The doctors said it was best that Mom stay at home now, and to keep everything as routine as possible. Dad and Martha told me how amazingly I'd handled what had happened, but it didn't make me feel better. I wondered if I shouldn't go to Pony Finals, but Dad told me I should most definitely go. He'd see how Mom held up the next day or two and decide whether he could come.

The ponies left for Kentucky at the crack of dawn on Saturday. I flew with Susie later that same day. I was glad to get away for a few days, but it felt all wrong to be going without Mom and to be going at all given how she was doing. What if she died while I was there? Could it be coming that soon? Worse, though, was the gnawing feeling that my mom as I had known her already might not exist anymore.

* * *

Pony Finals wasn't just a horse show. It was a larger-than-life pony extravaganza, kind of like Disney cruise meets horse show. The Kentucky Horse Park had lots of rings—indoor and outdoor—multiple barns and a huge cross country course used for the biggest eventing competition in the U.S., the Rolex Three-Day.

Some of the big barns had been in Kentucky for an entire week showing in the regular horse show before Pony Finals started. Our ponies got there late on Saturday and we just hand walked them. Sunday we flatted them and rode in the schooling rings. Sunday was the last day trainers could ride the ponies and the schooling ring was full of trainers schooling ponies in draw reins and custom bits. Kitty was on Dakota's pony. In the corners of the ring, she overbent him, pulling in his nose and jabbing him with the spur of her inside leg. Susie never let us use draw reins. She said pulling a pony's nose to its chest wasn't the way to teach it to frame up and that ponies had to build up the neck and back muscles to carry their head low. She also rarely schooled our ponies, only if it was absolutely necessary. Besides the no trainers school-ing ponies rule, starting on Monday at noon, only the rider who was showing a green or medium pony could ride it or else you were disqualified from the whole show. The cut-off for the small and large ponies was later in the week because those divisions didn't go for a few more days.

Jane, Hailey, and I trotted and cantered around the schooling ring next to the ticketed warm-up rings. Susie had us school over a few jumps before it was our turn to go into the rings. The jumps in the ticketed rings were crazy, dressed up with brush and flowers. They were more elaborate and beautiful than nearly any regular show during the year and this was just the warm-ups. Of course Tyler couldn't have cared less. Susie looked at me and smiled. "He looks great. Let's quit with that."

I walked out of the ring and stood by the in gate to watch Jane on Frankie. Frankie was wired—his head was high, his eyes were wide, and his breathing bordered on snorty.

"Just try to keep him calm," Tommy told Jane. "Do the best you can. He needs to relax and settle in."

Jane picked up a canter and headed to the first jump. Frankie grabbed the bit and ran at the jump, crow-hopping it.

Jane pulled him up hard. Too hard. Over the past few weeks, Jane had been patting Frankie more often and gener-ally just riding him with more patience and kindness. It was as if what she'd learned about him had made her understand him better. He'd been going so much better and some trainers had even asked Tommy about him in Vermont. But all the good feelings Jane had developed toward Frankie seemed to have disappeared when she'd seen Ike on our way up to the ring. It was the first time Jane had seen Ike in person since he'd been sold. He was impeccably turned out with gleaming tack and fancy front boots that I'd only ever seen on grand prix horses. When Jane saw him her face turned pale. She shortened her reins on Frankie and the hurt on her face turned to a kind of bitterness and anger. Now, Frankie seemed to be paying the price as Jane yanked him up with unnecessary force.

"Easy, easy," Tommy said. "Pick up a canter, jump the line, halt, canter the next line, halt, all the way around the course. Try not to get upset. Just try to work through it."

I wanted to be on Frankie so badly. I had pushed my feelings about Frankie and how much I liked riding him aside because of everything with Mom. I knew she didn't want me riding him. But now, away from her again, I wanted to be the one riding him.

Jane was locking her elbows and bracing her weight against him. All it did was make Frankie go faster and get more scared.

"Okay, that's enough," Tommy said.

From what he didn't say, I could tell Tommy was frustrated with Jane, too. Jane kept her eyes down as she left the ring. She rode over to me and said, "I can't believe I have to show this pony." I thought she would say something about Ike, since we'd never talked about seeing him, but instead she said, "Did you know Maddie's pony, Enchanted, was sold?"

Enchanted was from Florida and was one of the other top mediums in the country, right up there with Tyler. Maddie was the daughter of Jen Stiller, one of the top pony trainers.

"But Jen made the deal so that Maddie gets to show him here." Jane shook her head.

Looking at her, I began to think this had to be the stupidest situation ever. Here I was, not wanting to ride Tyler and here Jane was, not wanting to ride Frankie. It would be my dream to ride Frankie in the greens, which went tomorrow, and if Jane rode Tyler in the mediums she'd probably be overall grand champion. He wasn't Ike, but he was as close as she could get.

After doing our ticketed warm-ups, we rode up the hill to the Walnut Ring, where the real competition took place. The Walnut Ring was enormous, like Yankee stadium compared to a town baseball field. It was where all the grand prix classes and other big hunter derby classes took place during other shows. We didn't get to jump in the Walnut before the classes, but it was open for riders to hack around to get the ponies used to it.

On the short end of one side of the ring was a mini derby field with grass footing and a hill. For some other finals and big classes at the Horse Park the course designer used the derby field for natural jumps. It had never been used as part of the Pony Finals. Some trainers had their riders walk their ponies around on it and Kitty and Lenny had Dakota gallop up the hill just in case this year the course designers used it. Susie said there was no way they'd use it—riding in the Walnut Ring was tough enough.

It was fun to look at all the different ponies and riders as I hacked around the ring. I recognized kids from our area, but there were plenty of riders I didn't know. I saw Tinley Haskell, who did a lot of catch-riding and winning. We only saw her in Florida because she was from South Carolina and did different circuits than us during the rest of the year. Tyler and Donald were fine hacking. Of course Frankie was on edge. Jane kept cantering him around and around. He was drenched with sweat, but didn't seem to be getting tired. As I passed the in gate I saw Emily coming into the ring with Ike. Just what Jane didn't need. I quickly searched the ring and located Jane down at the far end, but there was nothing I could do. There was no way she wouldn't notice Ike. Jane cantered Frankie down the long side toward the in gate as Emily moved Ike off into a floating trot. Jane pulled Frankie up like she'd had it.

Again all I could think was how crazy it was that we were both on ponies we didn't want to ride. I looked up at the big scoreboard, which would show each pony and rider's name and their scores. I imagined Frankie's name with mine next to it and a jolt of excitement ran through me.

As we left the arena, I heard Kitty telling Lenny she wanted their older pony jock to school Dakota's medium pony in the ticketed warm-up before the deadline passed. "One last tune-up," Kitty said.

That's when it hit me.

By the time we headed back to the barn, I had it all worked out.

Chapter 48

AFTER THE PONIES WERE PUT away and we'd cleaned our tack, we went over to pony land. Inside the tent miniature jumps were set up in a course. There was also a bouncy house and an obstacle course. Some small pony kids were skipping over the jumps, playing horseless horse show. One stopped at a little oxer and pretended to smack her pony with an imaginary crop for refusing the jump.

We decided to go in the bouncy house. Hailey and I jumped as high as we could while Jane sat on the floor with her arms crossed.

"I have a way we can turn that frown upside down," I said to her, feeling giddy and lightheaded with the idea of my plan.

"Yeah, right," she said. "There's nothing anyone can do. I have to watch Emily ride Ike and Maddie ride Enchanted while I'm stuck on a circus pony."

I jumped closer, jostling her. "What if you rode Tyler and I rode Frankie?"

"Why would you ever want to do that?" Jane said.

Hailey stopped mid-jump. "Have you lost your mind?"

They were both staring at me. I was still jumping, smaller pogo type jumps now.

"I don't like riding Tyler," I said.

"Yeah, and I don't like chocolate," Hailey said.

"I don't," I said, coming to a standstill. Suddenly it felt weird that we were in the bouncy house and not jumping. "I didn't want to buy him and I've been making mistakes on purpose so I don't win." I started bouncing again and felt like I could bounce all the way to the top of the tent. Why had I waited till now to tell my best friends the truth?

"Really?" Jane said.

I was sort of surprised that they hadn't guessed—I mean Hailey had totally seen through my feelings for Alex.

"That time you went off course at Fairlee?" Hailey asked.

"On purpose."

A few of the younger pony kids burst into the bouncy house, all braids, ribbon belts, and giggles. Jane crawled out. Hailey and I followed.

The three of us walked in silence out of pony land. I desperately wondered what they were thinking. Suddenly I worried that they were mad at me, furious even. I mean, who got the top pony in the country and then *tried* to lose? Outside, I said, "I'd much rather ride Frankie. I know you hate riding him but I love him. It's like finally people see what I can do right, instead of just seeing whatever I do wrong. And I like working with him. So, what if we swapped? What if I rode Frankie and you rode Tyler?"

"Me? Ride Tyler?" Jane shook her head in disbelief.

"Right, how exactly would that work?" Hailey said.

"Just like I said. I show Frankie in the greens and Jane shows Tyler in the regulars."

"Uh, minor details? Your mom—" Hailey looked at me and then turned to Jane. "—and your dad?"

"Yeah, I don't think my dad would go for that and your mom never would."

We walked past the pens where Danny and Ron had dogs up for adoption. They were all new dogs—Peanut and the others had found good homes already. We stopped to pat Cheeky, a hound mix with long ears and a speckled coat.

I laid out the beauty of my plan. "Tomorrow in the warm-up ring before we do our ticketed rides, we switch ponies. Then they'll have no choice—we ride each other's ponies or we're disqualified." Susie wanted us to school early, before the models started, so if all went according to my plan, I'd be modeling Frankie and Jane would be modeling Tyler.

"You're serious," Jane said, gaping at me.

"Yup. Your dad likes the way I ride Frankie."

"But your mom buys this amazing pony for you and then you don't show him at Pony Finals? She'll think I made you do it. She'll hate me."

Cheeky licked my hand and I rubbed behind one of his floppy ears. "We'll say it was by accident. That we forgot the rule."

"That makes no sense—why would we switch?"

He leaned into me more as I scratched him. "We could say I was just helping you out because Frankie was being bad... Okay, or say they find out we did it on purpose... it's your way of finally showing your dad how much you want to have a good pony to ride every once in a while."

"And your mom?" Hailey said. "You're really going to do this *now*?"

It was as tactful as Hailey got, alluding to the fact that this might be the last show my mother was alive for. But in a crazy way, that made it even more important to me that I do this show on my terms and not wait for her to no longer be here for me to follow my heart. "She'll finally see this isn't what I want. I don't want a pony like Tyler."

Jane took a deep breath. "I have to think about it."

"Okay," I said. "Think about it, because we have to decide soon."

Chapter 49

THE NEXT MORNING WE LED the ponies out to the ring. We had been strangely quiet in the barn. I'm sure Susie and Martha thought it was just because we were nervous. They didn't know the real reason we were acting odd.

In the schooling ring, a few riders were flatting their ponies. There were two trainers I didn't recognize in the ring. I said a silent thanks that it was trainers from the Midwest or West Coast and not Hugo, Kitty, or someone else we knew. I locked eyes with Jane. We had only a few minutes till Susie and Martha arrived in the golf cart. Tommy was over at the annex ring watching a few auction ponies go. He would learn the news secondhand.

This was the moment.

It felt like the biggest decision I had ever made in my life. I couldn't quite breathe, but it was a different kind of couldn't breathe from the panicky kind. It was an excited breathlessness, like the time I'd turned off on to the trail.

We walked the ponies toward each other and I handed

Jane Tyler's reins. She forced a nervous smile and handed me Frankie's.

"Oh my god, I can't believe we're doing this," she said.

Hailey had hopped on Donald and gathered up her reins. "Me neither. You guys are in deep doo-doo."

"We'll be in deep doo-doo together." I glanced at Jane one more time to make sure she was still in. Until we were on the ponies we could still forget the whole thing, but she didn't look like she was having second thoughts.

I slid the reins over Frankie's head and put my foot in the stirrup. I hoisted myself into the saddle, feeling Frankie under me, and suddenly everything felt right. That feeling only lasted a split second, though, because Kitty walked into the ring. She saw Jane on Tyler first. She stopped right where she was and a girl cantering by had to circle so she wouldn't hit her. Kitty still didn't move. She looked like she was trying to figure out if what she was seeing was for real since it could be the biggest shake-up of Pony Finals since Hillary Friedman was disqualified for schooling someone else's pony two years ago.

I could see the thoughts going through Kitty's head: would she be the one to get the best pony at Pony Finals disqualified? Or would she help out Susie, and figure out what was going on?

Before Kitty could say or do anything, Susie and Martha pulled up in the golf cart. Susie caught sight of us and flew out of the cart before Martha had even come to a complete stop. She busted into the ring looking like she was about to scream, but then she must have realized she didn't want to draw attention to the situation in case there was a chance of keeping it under wraps and fixing it. She glanced around the ring to survey who else was there and noticed Kitty.

"What are you girls doing?" Susie said. "Is this some kind of joke? Get off now!"

"It's too late," Kitty said. "I saw them."

Kitty had made her decision, or maybe she'd never been considering whether to help out Susie in the first place. Either way, it didn't matter because we'd made our choice.

"I want to show Frankie." I sat up taller. "I don't want to ride Tyler. And Jane doesn't want to ride Frankie. She wants to ride Tyler, so it's okay."

"It's okay? You don't... you can't... *your* mother and *your* father..."

I'd never seen Susie so flustered or angry. Her face was red and as she spoke she was gesturing wildly with her hands. "Oh my god, girls, do you know what you've done? You're probably both disqualified because *you're* entered on Tyler and *you're* entered on Frankie so even if you wanted to switch you can't."

Jane's mouth fell open as she realized Susie was right but I followed up quickly. "I changed the entries yesterday afternoon."

"You did?" Jane said.

I gave Jane a reassuring nod. After Jane had said she was in, I'd gone to the office and made the changes.

I saw Susie relax a little, her shoulders lowering. At least we weren't disqualified. But then it was like she remembered that even if we weren't disqualified, she had a huge problem on her hands.

"Regan, your mom bought you the best pony in the country—what's going on?"

I looked down at Frankie's braids. Martha had come into the ring. "I think I know," she said.

I met Martha's eyes. She didn't look mad. She almost looked sympathetic. "Regan never wanted the pony."

"Is that right?" Susie said.

I nodded and let out a breath that I'd been holding since Mom had first told me she wanted to go look at Tyler. I thought it would feel awful to have everyone know the truth and it was scary, but good, too.

"Why didn't you say so?"

"Because she couldn't," Martha said. "Her mother wanted the pony."

Susie sighed and turned to Jane. "And you?"

I spoke up for Jane. "She's sick of making up ponies and then not getting to show them at big shows."

"I don't need to show them for a whole season or anything," Jane added. "I just don't understand why I couldn't have had Ike for Devon."

Susie rubbed her eyes like she was still hoping this whole scene would just go away. "You guys are going to have a lot of explaining to do to your parents."

Kitty listened to our whole conversation, not even pretending to mind her own business. I bet she was still trying to figure out how she could get Tyler disqualified.

I reached out and scratched Frankie's neck. "But can we ride them?"

"I don't know about that yet," Susie said. "Tommy will probably want Frankie to go, but I don't know if your mom will want Tyler to show if you're not on him. It's not like he's got anything to prove."

I felt a sharp pain at Susie's words. What if I had gotten Jane into this whole mess and then Jane had the nice pony pulled out from under her just like always?

Chapter 50

SUSIE LET US SCHOOL THE PONIES, but she barely said anything to us. It was like she was still in shock. Tyler went perfectly with Jane. She looked beautiful on him and gave him a smooth and soft ride. If she showed him, she'd have a really good chance of winning. It made it all the more painful to think about her not getting to ride him. I tried to push aside the terrible pit that was growing in my stomach as the initial excitement at making my own choice receded and all I was left with was the fear of having to tell Mom what I'd done. I had a flashback to the car when she'd made the wrong turn and how she'd spoken to me in that horrible tone of voice. That wasn't my real mom. That was the cancer talking. But would I be able to talk to my real mom?

I tried to concentrate on giving Frankie a good ride. I needed to show Susie that I was good with him. And I desperately needed to practice if there was any way I was going to show him in the Walnut Ring tomorrow and make it past the first jump. I'd ridden him well, but that was at home. I'd never even shown him.

When we got back to the barn, Jane gave Tyler to Martha. I helped Jane untack Frankie and get him put away.

"My dad is going to kill me," she said as she worked on Frankie's saddle mark, rubbing his back with a rag.

I brushed Frankie's other side, putting all my effort into it. "My mom is going to *kill me.*"

"Your mom is going to kill *me.*"

I looked at Jane over Frankie's back. "Your dad is going to kill *me.*"

We both stared laughing. Jane tossed the rag into the grooming box. "What are we going to do?"

Thankfully Jane wasn't blaming me for getting her into this mess. She didn't hate me. But I *was* to blame. "It was all my idea. I can tell your dad that I convinced you to do it, which is the truth."

"I'm not letting you take the fall for it." Jane picked up a brush. "No, this is good. He's finally going to know how I feel—just like you said."

"And same for my mom."

But we both knew we were trying hard to convince ourselves.

After Frankie was put away, I went to Tyler's stall. Martha was trimming his nonexistent whiskers. She whistled when she saw me, like people do when you've done something really bad or really crazy.

"I know. I'm in big trouble."

"I didn't think you had it in you." Her lips were curling up slightly—it seemed like she was smiling, which wasn't exactly the reaction I had expected.

"I didn't either."

Martha switched off the clippers. "Good for you."

"Really?"

"Well, I'm not sure I condone your tactics, but good for you for doing something besides the self-sabotage thing."

"You mean going off course..."

She ran her hand over Tyler's muzzle, checking for any missed whiskers. "And missing distances."

"I can't believe you knew."

"I can't believe no one else did." Martha rubbed under Tyler's jaw. He leaned toward her. I felt badly that I didn't like him more—he deserved a kid to love him. He was just a ticket to a blue ribbon for everyone who rode or took care of him. Martha looked at me with concern. "It'll be okay, kiddo, whatever happens."

"I just have to get my mom to let Jane ride Tyler," I said.

Martha nodded. "Yup, you do."

Chapter 51

BEFORE SUSIE COULD TELL ME I needed to call Mom, I went out by the manure pile and called her. The medium model was today and we needed to know whether Jane would be showing Tyler. I wanted to be where no trainers or riders would be—the only people were grooms dumping wheelbarrows.

"Hi, sweetie, how's it going?" Mom's voice was fake-chipper, which was only making this harder. She'd probably been asleep when I called and was now pretending she was feeling much better.

"Um, okay." I tried to gauge how with it she was. Which mom was I talking to?

"What's up? Is something wrong? Is Tyler okay?"

I wiped my forehead with my free hand. It was already hot out and heat seemed to be steaming off the manure pile. Maybe I should have picked a better location, but it was too late now to find some place else. "Something *is* wrong. I did something that's going to make you really mad."

"Oh, I can't imagine that," Mom said. She sounded like her old self, only maybe nicer and more Zen.

"Yeah, well, I talked Jane into switching ponies with me."

There was a short silence. "What do you mean, switching ponies?"

I made it sound like we were riding bareback or playing sit-a-buck, not showing at the country's biggest pony competition. The barn announcer came on the PA with an announcement about the pony auction and I had to wait until he was done to speak again. "I didn't want to show Tyler. I want to show Frankie."

Mom listened as I told her about my plan and Susie finding us in the ring and how if we didn't swap ponies now we'd both be disqualified. By the time I was done, she was still quiet. Finally she said, "I'm sorry, honey. I got crazy—the cancer made me crazy."

I wasn't sure if she was talking about buying me Tyler, or what happened in the car the day she tried to drive me to the barn. It was hard to figure out how lucid she was now. "Mom, I can ride Frankie well. I really want to. And Tyler can still show with Jane. He'll be grand champion—I'm sure."

"Of course you can," she said. "You're going to do great."

Dad got on the phone next and I told him everything that I'd told Mom. "Did she understand what happened? What I did?" I asked him. I wasn't sure. Maybe it was all too late. Wouldn't old Mom be more upset?

"Yes," he said, but I couldn't tell if he was lying.

"So I can ride Frankie?" This was too easy. It felt all wrong. There was supposed to be a fight.

"Just do me a favor and don't get hurt," he said. "I'll be there late tonight. Wendy's coming to stay."

I walked back into the barn to hear Jane having a similar conversation with her dad, only it sounded more normal, punctuated by anger and accusations. It was how my conversation with my mother should have been. It felt crazy to be jealous of people having an argument, but that's exactly how I felt.

"What pony you ride is not your choice," Tommy said. "You don't get to ride ponies like Tyler."

"It doesn't have to be Tyler. I just want to be able to keep a pony I bring along for a big show every once in a while."

"So this is about Devon," Tommy said. "When someone's ready to cut a big check I can't exactly say, wait, hold on, Jane wants to show at Devon. I know you just paid a lot of money, but you wouldn't mind skipping Devon, would you?"

"Why not? Jen Stiller did it with Maddie and Enchanted."

"Which is stupid. What if the pony gets hurt? Deal's off."

"Then maybe I quit," Jane said. "Maybe you should find another rider."

I got goosebumps listening to Jane. She was so brave. I guess all those reject ponies had made her really tough out of the ring, too.

"That's what you want? Quit riding?"

"No. I just want one big show every now and then on a pony *I* made. I want one shot to get the top jog and pose for the pictures and see the article in *The Chronicle* and think, I made that pony a winner. Not see a picture of another girl grinning with *my* pony and *my* trophy."

Jane's voice was loud now. Not angry, but full of conviction. Tommy was the quiet one. Then they were both silent. Since I couldn't see them I wondered what was happening. Had Jane or Tommy stomped off? Were they staring at each other? My stomach ached as the silence stretched—I had caused all of this. I was about to go tell Tommy it was all my fault and to give Jane a break when I heard his voice again.

"Okay, I get it."

"Really?"

"Yeah. You work hard with these ponies. We could get you a big show—I'm not saying every big show, but a big show, now and then."

"Oh my god, I never thought you'd see my side! Dad!"

They must have been hugging because their voices were muffled, but then I could make out, "You're a great rider. I'm sorry I haven't let you enjoy that much."

Tears pressed at my eyes again. They were happy tears for Jane and the way she and her dad had gotten to understand each other, but they were jealous, angry tears, too. Had Mom and I gotten the same chance to understand each other, or had it been too late when I'd tried to make her see what I wanted?

Chapter 52

I STOOD OUTSIDE THE WALNUT RING before the green medium model, more nervous than I could ever remember being at a show. I'd defied my dying mother, shook up my barn and my best friend's life, and started the whole horse show gossiping. Now I needed to prove to everyone it had been a good idea. I had to prove that I could ride a green pony, and Jane had to prove that with the right pony she could win big under pressure.

I saw Ava Higgenbotham as I was standing outside the ring.

She glanced at Frankie. "So it's true you're doing him instead of Tyler?"

"Yup." I waited to see what she would say, bracing myself, even though Ava was usually nice enough.

She smiled. "That's cool."

The announcer called for my section of the model to enter the ring. Frankie was still a little on the skinny side, but it was amazing how far he'd come from the pony who had arrived back in April. Jane and the grooms had worked hard on getting him clean and clipped and, once we'd learned that we could show the ponies, Jane and I had spent the remaining time before the model applying the final touches. We'd used white horse spray paint to make his hocks gleam brightly and baby oiled his muzzle. The braider had woven in a fake tail— it wasn't as beautiful as Tyler's custom tail, but it looked full and pretty.

I was third in line going into the ring and led Frankie down the long side. The judges were finishing up with the group in front of us, who stood their ponies in a line parallel to ours on the other side of the ring. The all-weather footing, groomed to perfection, gave just the right amount under my feet. It was really hot out, but the moment I was in the ring I forgot all about how much I was sweating under my coat and shirt.

Unlike Tyler, who knew how to model, Frankie was nervous and skittish, looking around the arena as if he was watching for someone to give him a clue to what was going on.

"It's okay," I told him, patting his neck.

Compared to riding, it would seem like a model class was pretty easy. But strange things could happen. Ponies refused to stand still; they spooked or reared. Last year one of the top ponies laid down and tried to roll, scoring zero, and no chance at an overall ribbon. There was far more talent, and art, to winning a model than it looked like, especially with a green pony that didn't have an auto-pose mode. Everything had happened so fast that I'd barely even had time to practice modeling with Frankie.

I led Frankie a few steps forward and then asked him to halt. He came to a stop with one foot more forward than the other. I tried asking him to move his one foot backward so it would be in line with the other by pressing on his shoulder. When he put it back down it was too far back. I decided to circle and start all over. The judges were still finishing up with the other group so I had time. I halted him again, making sure to leave enough room between me and the bay pony in front of us. At the back of the line a pony was skittering sideways, head raised, and I hoped it wouldn't set off a chain reaction and unnerve Frankie completely. This time I got him to set his feet nearly square with his hind end under him.

I stood in front of him, letting him relax for a few moments. The trick to a model was timing. It didn't do any good if you had your pony standing perfectly and the judges were looking at the pony four down the line from you. So I let Frankie veg while the judges finished scoring the other section. It felt like it was taking a long time for the judges to finish and the pony in the back was still acting up. Frankie swiveled his head to look behind him. I tried to persuade him to look back at me. Finally, the other section led their ponies out of the ring and the three judges walked over to our group. The judges spread out with two starting at the front of the line and one starting at the back. When the first judge was one pony away from me, I took the squeaky cat toy out of my breeches' pocket and used it to get Frankie's attention. I held it out in front of his nose and squeezed it. His ears perked up and he stretched his nose out to reach it. But then he started to fidget and I just knew he was about to move his feet again. The cat toy maybe had been too much for him. I stuck it back in my pocket as he shifted sideways, crowding his feet too close together.

The first judge was finishing scribbling notes on her clipboard about the pony in front of me and would be judging Frankie in a matter of seconds. Should I circle Frankie and try to get him back in place in time for the judge to look at him? Or try to work with how he was standing now? The way he was standing made his chest look sunken and narrow and his hind end was trailing behind him. I had no choice but to circle him. Just please, I thought as I went to line him up again, please let him stand up square.

The judge, a woman in a navy pantsuit and a scarf with bright colors on it, was waiting for us, which was never good. I smiled quickly at her, a sort of apology, and tried to set Frankie up. She immediately went to stand in front of him and started evaluating him, letting me know that she wasn't going to wait till he was standing perfectly. Frankie was acting fidgety and I just knew I wasn't going to get him standing well. Then, I thought of how he'd halted so well on the lunge line. He'd pulled up into a perfect square halt and didn't move until we told him too. I had nothing to lose so I said, "Brrr."

Frankie glanced at me out of the corner of his eye. I issued the command one more time with a little more confidence in my voice and Frankie set himself up square as could be. He looked at me again, and I swear he was saying, "Good enough?"

I rubbed my fingers together in front of his nose to get him to keep his ears up. The judge jotted notations as she walked around him. She scrutinized his neck and body, hind end, and back legs. She spent a decent amount of time looking at him, which probably meant she didn't think he was an absolute dog. For ponies with terrible conformation—an old bowed tendon or sickle hocks—judges would just quickly assign a low score and move on. After all, they had hundreds of ponies to look at and score. They only deliberated over the nicer ponies.

The two other judges followed her and Frankie continued to stand still.

After the judges had looked at each pony in line, we were asked to jog our ponies down the middle of the ring. I decided to use a voice command again, saying "tr-ot." He listened and jogged down the middle even though the bay pony was skittering and spooking up ahead. The judges finalized their scores, adding or subtracting points for movement. Finally, we were excused from the ring.

We gathered by the in gate, all eyes turned to the scoreboard. Hektor tossed a fly sheet on Frankie as the ponies' names and scores appeared.

Frankie had scored a seventy-nine. Not bad at all. The best ponies scored in the high eighties or low nineties. Seventy-nine wouldn't earn him a ribbon in the model phase, but it was good enough to keep him in the hunt for an overall ribbon, especially since he was a good mover and, if he went well, could score a ribbon in the under saddle phase. It would be great to go into the jumping phase with a good shot at an overall ribbon. But I was getting ahead of myself. One step at a time—I had to remember, nothing was a given with this pony.

Chapter 53

THE MEDIUM GREEN UNDER SADDLE went after the model. Some people pulled their ponies front shoes to make them move even better, and I saw plenty of ponies walking up to the ring with their little blue booties on to protect their feet before they got into the ring. Susie and Tommy didn't believe in pulling shoes. They said you never knew what might happen—maybe a pony would come up lame.

The class was called to order. I decided to use the voice commands again along with my leg aids. In the first direction, Frankie stayed calm at the trot and I was able to get some really good passes in front of the judges. He shot forward a little when I asked him to canter, but I was able to get him to settle back down. In the second direction he became even more relaxed, giving me a better canter departure. We were excused and the next group invited in.

When the scores were posted, Frankie had gotten an eighty, a seventy-seven, and an eighty-two, which meant I was standing seventeenth out of the seventy-one medium greens going into the jumping phase. In the greens, even more than in the regulars, a good round could shoot you up into the overall ribbons. Many ponies spooked, added a stride, missed a lead change, or even stopped.

The regular medium model went after all the green models and under saddles were finished. Jane and Hailey were in the same section. I watched Jane and Hailey's section. It was so much more fun to watch Tyler, although I did see several people leaning close and whispering as Jane led him into the ring. I wondered what they were saying. Perhaps that I couldn't handle the pressure? But I didn't even care—it felt right to be showing Frankie.

Tyler drew the highest model scores of the day so far, averaging a ninety-three. On the other end of the spectrum, Donald scored an average of seventy. "At least I broke out of the dungeon," Hailey said, which is what we called scoring in the sixties.

By the time all the green and medium models were over, it was nearly time for the pony auction to begin. Most of the ponies up for auction were young: three, four, and five-year-olds. Sometimes trainers would auction off an older pony they were having a hard time selling. Tommy had spent the morning before evaluating the younger ponies. He'd had Jane try several later in the day, and he planned to bid on a few. Jane liked one in particular, a fancy three-year-old roan mare.

Jane sat next to her father, with Hailey next to her, then Anna, and finally me. Just before the auction was about to start, Alex slid into the open seat next to me. I'd seen him around a little since we'd been in Kentucky, but this was the first time we'd talked.

"Hey," he said. "Did I miss anything?"

"Not yet."

The first pony was brought into the ring and led around while the auctioneer gave a little background on it. Then the bidding began. Some of the young ponies spooked at the crowd, the noise, and the lights. The few older ones didn't seem to care. Next to Alex, I was self-conscious about every little thing I did, like how I breathed or if I crossed my legs. The first pony Tommy bid on was a gorgeous five-year-old dapple gray with really good breeding, but he stopped bidding when the price reached over ten thousand dollars. He made a few half-hearted bids on another pony, but let someone else win the bidding.

At one point, Alex leaned over to me and said, "My dad bought me one of my first ponies at this auction. You know, I actually kind of used to like riding."

"That's hard to imagine," I said.

The auctioneer asked for final bids on a cute bay pony with a huge white blaze.

Alex said, "I used to ride all the time, like Jane does. I was actually pretty good."

There were only a few bids on the bay pony. People must have noticed something when they tried it. Either it had a bad attitude or a soundness problem. It went for just twelve thousand dollars.

The auctioneer started the bidding on the next pony. It

was an older pony with a lot of miles. It would be a good teacher for the right young kid and a few hands went up.

"Why'd you quit?" I curled and uncurled my program in my lap.

"Because of my dad, but I said it was just because I didn't like it. I've never really told anyone that." Alex glanced over at Tommy, who was busy marking up his program.

"Well, we already have a few secrets, right?"

Alex smiled. "Yeah."

The bidding dropped off quickly on the older pony. Nobody was going to overpay for age and experience. The final bid was seven thousand. A good deal for someone.

The roan was next. The auctioneer gave his little speech about the pony: "Next up we have American Icon. This 14.1 hand pony is a Virginia Pony Breeder's Association registered half-Welsh half-thoroughbred gelding. At four years old, this fancy pony is ready to be a made into a winner."

"You've really got guts, you know." Alex elbowed me. "Pulling the greatest switcheroo of all time?"

I chuckled. "I guess so."

"I'm glad you did. Jane deserves a shot on a pony like Tyler and you didn't want to ride him anyway."

At first, a few trainers bid on the roan. Soon several dropped out and it was just Tommy and Hugo. The price reached $20,000 and Hugo raised his hand. He looked like he could have been at a fashion show in his dark sunglasses and carefully gelled hair.

"Twenty thousand. Do we have twenty thousand, five hundred?"

I leaned forward to look at Tommy. He sucked in a deep breath. All of us sitting next to him were watching his right arm to see if he'd raise his hand. $20,500 was a lot of money for Tommy. Hugo was probably bidding for a wealthy customer and could go higher. I was surprised Tommy was even bidding on a pony like the roan. He usually only bid on the diamonds in the rough, the ponies no one could see the value in.

"Twenty thousand, five hundred?" the auctioneer repeated. "This kind of breeding does not come around often, folks."

I checked Jane—her fists were clenched. Maybe this would be the pony she'd bring along and be able to keep for a show like Devon, Pony Finals, or Indoors.

Tommy raised his hand. "Twenty thousand, five hundred."

It continued back and forth by five-hundred dollar increments until the price reached $23,000. The last bid was Hugo's.

"Do I hear twenty-three thousand, five hundred?"

Jane was at the edge of her chair, chewing on a fingernail.

"Twenty-three thousand, five hundred," Tommy called out.

The auctioneer asked for twenty-four thousand and we waited. Hugo's face was impossible to read, giving no indication of whether he would go higher.

"The gentleman in the back? Do I hear twenty-four thousand?"

I stared at the auctioneer. Why couldn't he just say it already? Why couldn't he just call out, "Sold!" He tried to get Hugo back in, asking once more for $24,000. "This pony is going to be a future Pony Finals winner, no doubt about it. Well-bred, good attitude. This pony has all the makings of a winner."

More silence. $23,500. I couldn't believe Tommy was going to shell out so much.

Hugo shook his head and finally, the auctioneer banged his mallet. "Sold!"

Jane stood up and screeched. Then she reached over and hugged her dad.

Chapter 54

THE AUCTION HAD BEEN a fun diversion, but the next day it all began again—the pressure, the nerves, the intensity. Pony Finals was supposed to be about kids horse-showing and having fun and it was, but there was also no denying how seriously everyone took it, from the riders to the trainers, to the parents. As much as everybody pretended otherwise, it was about winning. The kids wanted to achieve something they would remember forever, the trainers wanted to prove their programs were the best, and the parents wanted it for their kids, but for themselves, too. Everyone there had put in endless hours of training and gobs of money to get to this point and they wanted to have something to show for it.

I had dreamed of courses all night—winding, difficult courses where lines were set on the half-stride, jumps were spooky, and in-and-outs loomed higher than the maximum height allowed. In one of my dreams the designer had used the derby end of the ring and built a kind of miniature circus that you had to ride by and, of course, Frankie was terrified and wouldn't go near it.

Dad had arrived late the night before and we'd had break-fast together at the hotel although I couldn't eat anything but buttered toast. He said Mom was doing okay. I wasn't sure I believed him. The large greens went first so we didn't have to get to the show until nine. Before the medium greens, every-one gathered at the in gate to look at the course. There were no impossible parts like in my dreams, but it still looked in-timidating. Especially since I'd be on Frankie.

The course started across the diagonal going away from the in gate over an eight-stride line of two wall jumps with birch colored rails. The eight was a little flowing and since it was the first line and going away from the in gate, I'd need to make sure I got up it okay. When Frankie got tense, his stride shortened. Then it was another line across the diagonal. This one had double jumps where you could choose the option of jumping the left or the right jump. Both were the same mate-rials and height so it had more to do with whether your pony drifted one way or another. The second double jump was a hedge in the shape of a V that might be a little spooky to some ponies. After that line, you turned to go back up the middle of the ring over a two-stride. The two-stride wasn't spooky—it was two simple white gates. But the long approach on its own might trip up some riders. The last line was three jumps in a row. The distance between the first two jumps was ten strides—almost too long to even bother counting. Then it was six strides to the last jump.

I watched the first few rounds before going to the schooling area to get on Frankie. I didn't want to watch others because it just made me more nervous. If someone made a mistake I'd worry I'd do the same thing and if someone was really good I'd feel like there was no way I could be as good.

When there were twenty rounds before me, Martha gave me a leg up onto Frankie and I walked him into the schooling area where both Susie and Tommy were waiting for me.

Frankie felt pretty good for the first part of my warm-up. I loosened him up and then we started jumping over a vertical. Tommy stood on one side of the jump and Susie on the other. Susie did most of the coaching. Every once in a while Tommy would add something.

"Remember to be subtle with your aids," he reminded me. "Don't ride him any differently than you did at home."

As I was processing what Tommy was saying, another girl who was ahead of me in the order crashed her pony into the oxer she was schooling over, sending the rails flying.

"You chased him to no distance again!" her trainer was screaming at her. My stomach sank as I noticed he was wearing a baseball hat. "If you do that in the ring you're going to be on the ground!"

Frankie took notice of the crash, but it seemed to be the man yelling that set him off more. Frankie had earplugs to keep the noise of the announcer and the crowd from bothering him, but he must have felt the vibrations or seen the trainer's body language because he raised his head and picked up speed at the canter.

"Just try to work through it," Susie said. "Don't make a big deal, see if he can get over it."

I took a deep breath and tried to relax, letting Frankie know that there was nothing to be worried about. A few trips around the schooling area and he still felt agitated. Susie had me jump a lot of small jumps, trying to get him to smooth out. It felt like nothing was working.

"They're on the thirty-eighth in the order," the in gate guy called. Which meant I had only five more trips till I was in the ring.

The girl on the pony who stopped got him back over the oxer a few times and her trainer said, "We better go with that."

The girl nodded and headed out of the ring. I hoped with him gone Frankie would relax, but he was still keyed up. I jumped a few more jumps with Frankie wanting to rush and be quick in the air.

I heard Susie say to Tommy, "I'm not sure we're going to get him to calm down now."

Susie told me to let him walk. She came closer and said, "We can try a few more but we need to head up."

"I don't want to jump him out here any more," I said. "I think it's better to let him chill out and see if he can start over in the ring."

Of course the ring wasn't just the ring—it was the Walnut Ring. He'd been in there to hack and for the model, but it was now filled with brightly decorated jumps. But giving him a chance to de-stress seemed like my only shot. On the dreaded long walk to the Walnut Ring, I gave Frankie lots of rein and tried to let him forget about what had happened in the schooling ring.

At the in gate, I stood Frankie as far away as possible from where the trainer with the baseball hat was giving last minute instructions to his rider. Another trainer was talking with a rider who'd just come out of the ring, explaining where things had gone wrong. The girl was breathing heavily, her face red. Dad was up in the tent watching with Hailey and Jane.

Hektor worked on cleaning off Frankie while Susie and Tommy talked to me.

"This is a lot for this pony," Susie said. "So whatever happens in there, just do your best to deal with it."

I nodded. "And Jane was supposed to be on him..." Right then the fact that I was riding him seemed crazy. I had no experience with green ponies and I'd only ridden Frankie a handful of times.

Tommy frowned. "You know why I asked you to ride this pony that first day?"

I shook my head.

"I felt sorry for you and I couldn't think of anything else to do for you." Tommy placed a hand on my leg. "And then you rode the hair off him. You rode him better than my own daughter. You ride this pony best of anyone. Do you think I'd let you be on him now if I didn't think you could give him a good ride? No way."

Hektor painted Frankie's hooves and wiped my boots. I couldn't see all of the ring. Every now and then I'd see the pony on course come into view. It went out of view again and I heard the crowd groan.

"Did he stop?" I asked Susie.

"Don't think about that. You know your course?"

"Yes."

"If something goes wrong, just keep a clear head. Don't fall apart and don't give up."

The rider came out of the ring, head down and crying. A score of forty was announced, which meant she had one refusal.

The girl who'd crashed in the schooling ring was next to go, and then it would be my turn. Her trainer told her to smack her pony with her crop and when she did, he shot forward.

I tried not to watch what I could see of her round and instead kept my eyes on the braids near Frankie's withers.

"Regan, you're in next," the in gate guy called. "Mia in two, Taylor in three, Sophie in four."

At a loud crashing sound, I looked up to see the pony had stopped at one of the few jumps I could see, and as predicted by the trainer, the girl was on the ground. She was unhurt, though, and stood up as her trainer shook his head and sent the groom in to help her. One of the jump crew had caught the pony and handed him to the groom.

"Great," I mumbled. I would have been nervous anyway, but did the two ponies in front of me really have to have disaster rounds?

"Clear head," Susie reminded me.

Right. I couldn't fall apart before I even got in there. I thought about Mom. About watching the video of my round with her when I got home and her seeing what a great rider I really was. This was what I'd wanted. I'd done things I'd never thought I'd do for this very moment and now I had to make it count.

The girl trailed her groom and pony out of the ring. I looked past them and went into the ring.

"Good luck!" Susie called after me.

Chapter 55

"AND NOW ON TO OUR NEXT green pony, Visions of Blue, owned by Thomas Hewitt and ridden today by Regan Sternlicht."

Hearing my name paired with Frankie's gave me an extra little shot of adrenaline. I took a look around the huge ring, which instead of looking smaller with the jumps in it, somehow looked even grander. The jumps were decorated with bright flowers, each looking like a display in a florist shop window.

I eased Frankie into a trot and before I could even ask him he broke into a canter. His stride felt ragged and uneven. I'd never find the distances this unbalanced. I half-halted him and tried to get some sort of consistent rhythm to his canter. I sat down in the saddle for a few strides and then rewarded him by lightening my seat. I felt him settle in a little and the canter rhythm felt better, which was good because I was headed to the first jump. Sighting the jump, Frankie quickened again. It took all my will not to pull hard on the reins as we headed, above the pace, to the wall with the birch rail and enough brush to fill the back of a landscaping truck. I had to let Frankie keep going to make the eight strides and we landed from the line going too fast.

I half-halted and took a deep breath and perhaps I was imagining it, but it felt like Frankie almost did, too. He had come back to me. I found a nice distance into the line across the diagonal, choosing the left side of the double jumps. Frankie didn't spook at the hedges, but he did overjump them. He burst forward eagerly on landing again and I knew we would be chipping into the out of the line if I didn't use the bend to slow him down and fit in the strides.

I tried to use the curve of the line, bending out and asking him with a light half-halt to slow down. If I acted desperate, he'd respond desperately. I used my seat bones lightly touching down in the saddle and my upper body to tell him we needed to back down a notch. Two strides passed, then three. Was I getting his stride short enough? Or would we be eating the out of the line? Four strides. I saw the distance coming up. It was going to be too tight. Frankie wasn't backing off enough—he was going to run right through the distance. Without really thinking about it, I murmured, "Brrr." If I had thought more about what I was doing I might have realized he could have slid to a screeching halt. Instead, he seemed to understand I didn't mean halt—I just meant slow down. He eased back and we were a little deep to the second hedge, but it wasn't a total chip. I turned back up the middle to the two-stride, finding a nice distance in. I turned to the last line, the ten to the six. I was a little deep again coming in, but it ended up helping make the other two jumps work.

I landed to Susie and Tommy's whoops confirming what I couldn't tell by feel—that he'd jumped well, getting his front end up even when we were deep.

As I rode my closing circle I did a mental replay of my trip. A few deep distances and I'm sure Frankie looked a little nervous. But no big mistakes, which hopefully meant I wouldn't be in the dungeon. I had done it. I'd turned in a solid round on a difficult pony in his first time at Pony Finals. I couldn't wait for Mom to see my trip.

"Really good job," Susie said as I came out of the ring.

"Great ride," Tommy added. "You really finessed the hedge line."

The scores came up on the board. Seventy-six, seventy-eight and eighty-point-five. I had moved into ninth place.

Dad was waiting in the tent with Hailey and Jane. He hugged me tight and said, "That wasn't easy, was it?"

"Not at all. It was hard to keep him together. I felt like at any moment I might lose his frame of mind."

"You rode him so awesome!" Jane said. "So much better than I would have. I probably would have left out strides everywhere. You were able to get him to fit it in."

I would order the official video later, but Hailey's mom had taken a video herself and quickly uploaded it to her Facebook page. I called Mom, hoping we could watch it together while on the phone. But Wendy said she was sleeping. She said I should try back later. Something in her voice made me worry that later wasn't going to be a good time either.

I walked away from the tent, just wanting to be alone for a moment. I'd wanted so badly to share my ride with my mom. When I'd jumped the last fence I'd immediately thought about what she'd say when she saw it. How proud she'd be of me. I'd nearly forgotten that Mom wasn't Mom anymore.

I walked off a little ways, not wanting everyone to see me upset and near tears. I just needed a few moments to get myself back together. I saw Dakota sitting in her golf cart. Her back was to me but there was no mistaking her hair. She was on the phone and her voice sounded upset. "But you said you'd be here. Mom—" She hung up a few moments later and dropped her head into her hands.

Her parents couldn't come to the biggest show of the year. My mom had come to every show, no matter how sick she was, until she physically wasn't able to. Dakota's parents were never at a show—choosing their charity work above their daughter. For the first time ever in my life, I felt a little bit sorry for Dakota.

Chapter 56

AFTER EVERYTHING THAT HAD happened over the last few days, I was even more excited than ever for the lip sync. I don't know about Jane, but I needed a non-horse night where I could focus on nothing else but cheering Hailey on.

Jane and I helped check people in as Kim Kolloff, the event organizer, rushed around taking care of last minute details. The sound system and microphone needed tinkering and the stage lights were too bright. It was strange to see riders out of their show clothes. I almost didn't recognize Ava Higgenbotham with her hair down.

Before it was time to start, Jane and I slipped backstage to wish Hailey good luck. She looked killer in her leather pants and leather jacket. Her black spiky mullet wig looked almost like her real hair and she had on tons of black eyeliner just like Joan Jett. Alex was wearing jeans and a white T-shirt with the sleeves rolled up. We'd put fake tattoos on his biceps.

When it came time for the event to start, I settled into my seat up front with Dad, Jane, Susie, Tommy, and Mrs.

Mullins. I missed Mom and wished she were there. She would have cheered so loudly for Hailey. It hurt so much that I couldn't even just pick up the phone and call her. Dad and I tried back later and she'd gotten on the phone and said a few words, but she wasn't old Mom. I hoped it would be better when we got home. At the same time I realized I was now doing what the doctors had been doing—hoping. Wendy said maybe texting would be good so I texted a few times and she answered, but I had the feeling Wendy was the one writing back.

Mrs. Mullins pointed to the judging panel. "Oh my god, there's Donna Dames!"

Donna had a few number one hits back in the eighties and she was also a huge animal lover, which was how she'd agreed to be the celebrity judge for the lip sync.

"I love you, Donna!" Mrs. Mullins shouted out.

The seven-to-nine age group went first. The first act was two small pony kids doing a Rihanna song. They hopped around the stage, their cuteness making up for pretty lame choreography and lip syncing. Anna and Jill were also cute doing their Kelly Clarkson song. In the ten-to-fourteen age group category, Charlie Frisch kicked it off with a song by Justin Bieber and everyone was in hysterics because he looked a lot like him.

Dakota went toward the end. She did Beyoncé's "Single Ladies," which figured. The crowd quieted down, just like they did when a good horse entered the ring. Everyone knew she was the one to beat. She was wearing a really tight mini dress and her hair was dyed blue. She was a good dancer and

I hated to admit it but she had good choreography. People started whistling and cheering as she strutted around the stage. After what I'd witnessed, maybe I didn't hate her quite as much. But I still wanted Hailey to win.

There was one more act before Hailey. It was actually really good, three sisters wearing long sparkly dresses and wigs doing a medley of Supremes' songs. The crowd got really into it, but I was so nervous for Hailey and Alex, I was only half watching. I hoped we were right about adding Alex and it wouldn't look stupid. The group finished to loud cheers and whistles.

As they left the stage, the announcer said, "Next up we have Hailey Mullins doing 'I Love Rock and Roll'."

Hailey walked onto the stage with purpose, followed by Alex. She didn't acknowledge him, pretending that he wasn't there. She stood in the middle of the stage, arms crossed. Alex stood off to the side. I could feel every girl in the crowd take in the sight of him. I inched forward in my seat as the music started. Alex turned his back to Hailey and pretended to put coins into an imaginary jukebox. He hunched over the juke-box, tapping his foot to the beat.

I meant to keep my eyes on Hailey, but I kept looking at Alex. He looked so unbelievably hot in the jeans and white T-shirt. I never would have guessed from the way he liked to disappear for hours into the woods with his bike that he would be comfortable in the spotlight, but he seemed relaxed on stage. I could tell that a lot of girls in the audience were noticing him and wondering who he was, if they didn't already know. Hailey was singing about how he was going to be going home with her. He spun around and they locked eyes dramatically. She strutted over to him and circled around him. She moved away from him again and then toward the end of the song, she motioned to him and he walked toward her. Even though I knew it was pretend, I felt jealous of Hailey. For the finale, she threw her arms around Alex possessively. The crowd went crazy as Hailey did a quick bow.

For a second I thought I saw Alex look at me, but the lights were so bright on stage and dark in the audience that I couldn't be sure. Anyway, why would a fifteen-year-old be looking at me, when he could probably get any girl in the audience?

Hailey and Alex left the stage and Kim Kolloff came on to tell everyone that it would be a few minutes before the results were announced.

"Do you think she won?" Jane asked over the buzz of the crowd.

"God, I hope so," I said.

Jane rolled her eyes. "I hate to say it but Alex was good."

Mrs. Mullins leaned over and grabbed my arm. "She was great, wasn't she? We were right about needing a guy."

Finally, another woman came on stage and handed Kim Kolloff an envelope. "First of all I'd just like to thank our contestants—you were all amazing! Tonight we've raised so much money for Danny and Ron's and we have you to thank for that. I'd also like to thank our judges, especially the amazing Donna Dames, who have the nearly impossible job of scoring all these awesome performances!"

The clapping quickly faded out. We all wanted to get to the results.

"Okay, let's get to what you've been waiting for..."

Of course we had to wait through the results for the younger age group. Anna and Jill were second in the seven-to-nine age group. Finally, it was time for the award for the ten-to-fourteen age group.

"In third place with an eighty in choreography, a seventy-eight in lip sync, and an eighty-three for overall performance is Ainsley Light."

If Ainsley, who had done a so-so version of a Nicki Minaj song, placed third, Hailey had to be in the top two. Surely it was down to Hailey and Dakota. I exchanged a hopeful look with Jane, who held up crossed fingers and said, "I can't believe I actually want my brother to win."

"In second place with an eighty in choreography, an eighty-two in lip sync, and an eighty-six in overall performance... Dakota Pearce!"

Jane and I squealed, but then I pressed my finger to my lips. Hailey hadn't won yet and you never knew what could happen. Dakota came out to give a bow. She smiled, but it was fake. I had another pang of feeling sorry for her. She had no one there for her and here we all were cheering for Hailey.

"And now, our winner in the ten-to-fourteen age group, with an eighty-seven in choreography, an eighty-seven in lip sync, and a ninety in overall performance... Hailey Mullins."

Jane and I stood up and cheered. I yelled so hard my throat hurt. Dad, who always seemed calm, also stood and pumped his fists in the air. He and Hailey's mom high-fived. We stood and cheered through the whole award ceremony. Even though Jane, Hailey, and I were best friends, a lot of time in the ring we had to compete against each other. This time we could root for Hailey as hard as we wanted and it was totally genuine.

Hailey ran down from the stage into the stands. She grabbed my hands and we did a silly dance, jumping up and down.

"Oh my god, I won! I did it!" Hailey pulled me close and whispered in my ear, "We smoked her butt!"

"I know! You were awesome!"

I had just let go of Hailey—she was now hugging Jane—when I heard Alex behind me. "Hey, what about me? I think I had a little something to do with it."

I turned to Alex. I was about to tell him he was awesome, too, but instead he reached out and hugged me. My face pressed into the cotton of his white T-shirt, which smelled wonderfully of his sweat. He was a head taller than me and he felt stronger than I'd ever imagined he would. We stayed there, hugging, for what seemed like a moment longer than friends normally would. And when he pulled back, he looked at me like he might kiss me. I'd never kissed anyone before, so I wasn't sure how I knew that was what might be about to happen but I just knew it—I guess it was instinctual. Maybe he was embarrassed by letting his emotions overtake him, because he turned away and hugged Hailey. I watched him hug her and he let go quickly. It was nothing like what had happened between us.

"Isn't this awesome?" Jane was tugging on my elbow, trying to figure out why I looked like I'd just seen a ghost. Something had happened between Alex and me—that was for sure.

To cover up, I said, "Yeah, I'm almost in shock."

Chapter 57

HAILEY AND I WERE IN THE spectator tent. Jane would be coming in the ring any moment now. As much as I didn't want to ride Tyler, it did feel a little strange to be watching while Jane was out there riding. I was still in my breeches and show shirt, because I'd had the small pony model and hack that morning with Drizzle.

The class was called back in reverse order so Hailey had gone early. She had a really good round with Donald, but her scores had still only been high-seventies. He didn't move well enough or look smooth enough for her to break into the eighties, which meant she was finishing way out of the ribbons. But she had won the lip sync and that was big. She hadn't raised the most money and gotten the golf cart but that didn't matter. Ava Higgenbotham had raised over $20,000. We'd raised a lot and it was great that Ava had raised so much more since it all went to Danny and Ron's.

Jane had won the model and the hack with Tyler, which put her in first place, but also gave her the dreaded task of going last in the class. Going last was hard for anyone, but Jane always wanted to go first when she could. Now, all eyes were on her. Would she keep the lead, or be known as the biggest choke of this year's Pony Finals? To make things even more tense, coming in second to last was Ike.

"I'm really nervous for her," I told Hailey.

"Don't be. This is Jane."

I was glad Hailey was so confident in Jane. I still couldn't help but feel like all the pressure might get to her. The greatest riders ever had been known to make the ultimate mistakes. In the live stream of the Medal Finals, McKayla Crowne, who was called back on top in the second round and was favored to win, jumped up the neck, knocking her out of the ribbons completely.

If Emily made a mistake with Ike that would at least help relieve some of the pressure for Jane, but of course Emily was having a really good trip. She was halfway through the course and I could see Jane, Susie, and Tommy at the in gate, watching and waiting for Jane's turn.

Emily turned to the in-and-out. She was a little tight to the in, but Ike still jumped well. She rode the last two lines and finished to whoops from her trainer. Scores of eighty-one, eighty-three, and eighty-five flashed on the board. "That moves Impromptu into the top spot with our last of the one hundred and eighty medium ponies competing here today at the in gate."

There was no leeway for Jane—she would have to lay one down to beat her, or lose to the pony she had made up.

Jane walked into the ring on Tyler, and Hailey and I

wordlessly turned our full attention to them. Everybody in the tent was watching, too—riders, trainers, parents.

"Now on course, our last to go, Woodland's Tried and True, owned by Regan Sternlicht and ridden today by Jane Hewitt."

My arms felt stiff and my stomach unsettled. I was more nervous for Jane then I would have been if I were the one walking into the ring on Tyler. Jane had to be perfect to win. Not one tight distance. Not one change in tempo. She couldn't be good or good enough. Then people would say she couldn't handle the pressure, or that she wasn't such a good rider after all. The medium championship and the overall championship were on the line, as well as the admiration of everyone watching. But most importantly, she had to show her dad that she could do it.

She stayed at a walk for a few moments longer than most riders had. I wasn't sure if it was from nerves or confidence.

She eased Tyler straight into the canter, a seamless transition, and headed to the first jump. The expansive arena only made Tyler look more impressive, like seeing a movie star on a big screen instead of on your TV.

She met the first jump right out of stride and Tyler curled around it, rounding his back and snapping his knees up in perfect form. Sometimes when you were watching someone ride a great trip you felt like at any second things could change and the rider could miss a distance. But, as Jane continued, I knew there would be no missed distances. She nailed every jump and Tyler didn't put a toe out of place. Jane had time to style in the air over the jumps, giving Tyler a generous release. As they landed off the last jump, Susie and Tommy erupted in whoops. Everyone in the tent clapped, too, although some I'm sure had been hoping Jane would make a mistake.

Jane brought Tyler down to a walk, patting his neck and giving him his head.

The scores lit up the leader board, confirming what we'd all just seen.

"Wow," Hailey said as we read the numbers: eighty-eight, eighty-seven, and ninety.

Even the announcer had excitement in his voice as he said, "Top scores of the day for Jane Hewitt and Woodland's Tried and True, giving them the win overall in the medium pony hunters."

As she left the ring, Jane threw her arms around Tyler's neck. That photo would appear in the next issue of *The Chronicle*.

Hailey and I ran from the tent to the in gate, where Jane was being mobbed by people congratulating her. A reporter from *The Chronicle* waited nearby.

I broke through the crowd. "That was amazing! Best round ever!"

Jane reached out to me. "Thank you, oh my god, thank you!"

Chapter 58

JANE POSED FOR PLENTY OF PHOTOS that day. She was medium pony hunter champion and overall grand champion. Hailey had made the top thirty.

The small ponies finished on Friday and the large ponies went on Friday and Saturday. I did really well with Drizzle, placing third in the model, tenth in the hack, fourth over fences, and fifth overall. Jane rode a large pony for another trainer and placed fourth overall. On Sunday, we all had the Pony Medal Finals. I rode Sammy and got called back for the second round, but finished just out of the ribbons. Jane rode Coco and had a really good round, except for a few strides when she cross-cantered, which killed her scores. I knew Jane wasn't happy because on the right pony she could have won, but at least she had done so amazing in the hunters.

Hailey did the best out of all of us, making the test of the top ten, and finishing fourth. The test asked riders for a halt, a trot jump, and a few tight roll back turns and Hailey nailed every hard part, but then was deep to the last jump. I could tell Susie was disappointed because otherwise Hailey might have had a shot at winning and while having a rider win the Pony Medal Finals wasn't the same as having a rider win the Medal or Maclay Finals, it was still pretty cool. Tinley Haskell ended up winning.

It was hard to get on the plane home after all the buildup and excitement. But, for the first time in a while, home was where I wanted to be.

If you've never had someone you know well die of cancer, if you've never been there seeing them over the last few weeks, it won't really make too much sense how it happens. You'll think how could a regular, healthy person get so sick that they just fade out and finally die? But it's like that person keeps replacing themself with someone else, a sicker, lesser version of themself till they're just gone. Mom got weaker and weaker. She slept more and talked less. A hospital bed was installed in the downstairs sunroom and soon she never left it.

It was tradition that every year after Pony Finals we'd have Pony Finals video night at Hailey's. Jane and I would sleep over and her mom made us mango smoothies. We would watch our rounds and basically just relive it all over again.

This year, though, Mrs. Mullins had been asked out for a third date by a guy she'd met at the café at her hospital. After all her online dating, she'd met him as they commiserated over the poor selection of sandwich bread. He'd been visiting his mother after her hip surgery and he was dentist. He didn't have much hair, but he had really good teeth.

Mrs. Mullins made us smoothies, then spent the next half

hour running between her bedroom and the TV room getting our advice on what she should wear. Her first outfit was a black dress. It looked good, but we decided it was too much. He said they were going out to dinner, but she didn't know how fancy the restaurant was. We settled on black pants, cute little heels, and a rose-colored sweater that she'd just gotten on sale.

The doorbell rang but it wasn't her date yet. Milo barked and ran to the door. It was the teenage girl who lived next door who was coming over to "babysit" us. Her name was Bronwyn and she was nice, even if she didn't know anything about horses. Sometimes she'd tell us about her boyfriend— we loved that.

Mrs. Mullins poured Bronwyn a smoothie and asked her how her summer was going. Bronwyn was working as a counselor at a creative arts camp. Bronwyn was into arts and crafts stuff. Sometimes she'd wear a shirt she'd sewn herself or bracelets she'd beaded and she was always trying out for some play or another.

The doorbell rang a second time and Milo barked again.

"Some watch dog," Mrs. Mullins said. "An intruder wouldn't ring the doorbell." She smoothed back her hair. "Do I look okay?"

"You look fine," Hailey said.

I added, "You look really nice."

She let the dentist in. He leaned down and let Milo lick his face, which I thought was a very good sign. He was wearing jeans and Mrs. Mullins gave us a quick look, which I took to mean she was grateful she didn't go with the dress.

"Okay, Bronwyn, I won't be back late. Hold down the fort. Girls, have fun. Sorry I'm missing out."

"Bye, Mom," Hailey said.

We spent the next hour playing the videos over and over while Bronwyn read a book in the kitchen and made us trail mix with pretzels, raisins, nuts, and chocolate chips. Sometimes rounds on video looked worse than they felt in real life because you had more time to see every little blip like a rider's jiggling leg or a pony's flattened ears. But Jane's round on Tyler was absolutely flawless. She sat back on the couch as she watched.

"Did it feel as good as it looked?" Hailey asked her.

"Pretty much, yeah. After the first line I just knew we were going to nail it."

Hailey looked at me. "Are you going to show him again or sell him, or what?"

I shrugged. "I'm not sure." I didn't want to show Tyler, but selling him didn't feel quite right either. Dad and I hadn't talked about it yet. It was one of the many things that got pushed to the *after* pile. It was just a question of how soon *after* would come.

I was critical of my round with Frankie, but I was still so proud of how he'd gone.

"He would have totally run through that last hedge with me," Jane said.

Tommy had gotten some calls on Frankie after Pony Finals and people were coming to try him next week. I thought about asking Dad if maybe we could buy him instead and I could finish out his green year and then show him in the mediums next year, but I didn't want to push my luck. Still, I couldn't imagine him not being in the barn—I really understood what Jane went through time after time.

We watched the Pony Medal and Jane was bummed about her cross-canter.

"Next year you'll make the test," I said.

"Dad wants me to qualify for the Medal/Maclay Finals," she said.

If she rode in the Medal Finals, Jane wouldn't be able to ride in the Pony Medal Finals and you couldn't ride in the Pony Medal and the Medal at the same show. It felt like Jane might be leaving us behind—would we still be best friends if she was doing the big eq and we were still in the ponies?

The doorbell rang again and Milo leapt up, barking.

"I hope my mom didn't have a date from hell," Hailey said. "He probably told her he has three other wives or something."

But why would Hailey's mom ring the doorbell at her own house? Before I could say that out loud, we heard someone come inside. I recognized Dad's voice and I just knew.

In the kitchen, I saw Dad first, before he saw me. He was trying to be strong, I could tell. But when he saw me, his face crumpled into tears. I ran to him and we hugged for a long time. He didn't need to tell me she was gone.

I didn't officially get to say good-bye to Mom. There was no scene where TVMG tells her mother she loves her. Mom never held my face in her hands and told me to have a wonderful life. And we never got to have the real conversation about riding Frankie and how I never wanted Tyler in the first place. I guess I could have said those things to her when she was sleeping or unconscious during that last week. I could have also whispered good-bye. But I didn't. The closest we ever got to saying good-bye was the day we talked about spirits and stayed on her bed together for hours. Maybe Dad or friends like Wendy officially had their good-bye moments, but that day was mine. I just didn't know it at the time. At first I was mad that I didn't have a more powerful good-bye moment, but then I realized it made more sense this way. That last day when we snuggled on her bed, she gave me something she'd never given me before—her. And that was better than any other kind of good-bye. And anyway, what girl should ever have to say good-bye to her mom?

Chapter 59

I LOOKED EVERYWHERE FOR SIGNS from Mom that she was watching over me. I thought I might feel her at the funeral, but all I felt was sadness there. I thought I might feel her when we got back to the apartment in the city. A few times I kept looking at my phone and the time was always something thirty-three, but I couldn't figure out what thirty-three meant or why Mom would be trying to say something to me through the time of day.

I felt some relief in the fact that everything in life kept on going. It felt wrong in a way, but comforting, too. She was dead, and here we were, still living, still eating breakfast, still getting dressed. Dad and I were surviving. Maybe we weren't exactly okay, but we were here.

Dad made me go to a support group even though I swore I had Jane and Hailey and that was all the support I needed. There was one for kids who'd lost a parent to cancer that ran at the same time as a group for spouses, so when Dad told me he was going, I couldn't really say no. And even though just being in a support group was cringe-worthy in itself, there was something different about talking to those kids. Hailey and Jane would always be my best friends, but no matter how hard they tried they couldn't understand what it was like.

Like she had promised, Mom left me some things. That scarf and a few other pieces of her clothing and jewelry, most for when I was older. Dad gave me a beautiful framed photo of her to put in my room. She also left me a small package with a beautiful leather dog collar inside. There was a short note: *For when the time is right. Find a dog that needs you. XOXO, Mom.*

I guess I could have been mad that she didn't leave me a longer letter filled with poignant memories and maybe advice for all the things I'd face without her help: dating boys like Alex, falling in love, applying to college. But I liked her short little note, too. It felt less like an ending. Like maybe I would meet up with her again, or somehow our conversations would continue, even if it was just me talking to her, or thinking about what I'd say to her. At first I thought the short note was the sign. Then, it began to feel like not enough of a sign.

I wouldn't get a dog right away. It felt better to wait and like she said, find the one that needed me. Maybe finding the dog would be the sign. I drove myself crazy for months afterwards looking for signs, and they never came or never felt right. Then I was really angry that there was no sign. Why couldn't she bother to send me a sign that was recognizable? Like a sign in big flashing lights that I couldn't possibly miss. Would that be too much to ask from my dead mother? What other things was she so busy with?

I thought about how she'd said we'd be really sad if there wasn't a way for people to reach each other through their spirits, and I refused to believe that the reason there was no sign was that she wasn't able to talk to me. That just seemed too cruel to be possible. So I kept looking for signs.

I decided not to show at Indoors, even though all my ponies were qualified. I just needed a break from it all. Some people would have thrown themselves into their riding even more and I didn't stop riding—I rode every day—I just didn't want to go to a show without Mom yet. Who would braid my hair and tie in my blue ribbons? Maybe when I did show again, I'd start wearing my hair up instead. Still, for now, I couldn't handle coming out of the ring and not seeing her there, which I knew was ironic since so many times I wished she hadn't watched me so intensely. Dad and I decided to ask Jane to show Tyler at Harrisburg and Washington. Tommy hadn't sold Frankie yet and since he didn't have enough points for Indoors, I rode him a lot at home.

One day in November after Indoors was over, I hacked Tyler when no one was around. Susie was taking a much-deserved week of vacation, Hailey was at her voice lesson, and Jane and Tommy had gone to look at a possible eq horse. I was all alone in the ring.

After only a few minutes of warm-up, I took him out around the ring. I turned off onto the path into the woods. There was no one who would be mad at me now for taking him trail riding. Since Mom had died, Tyler had gotten to be more of a horse again, getting turned out in the big field where he loved to roll in any dirt he could find. His preferred state was filthy, which was pretty funny considering he was such a fancy pony.

The woods were different in the late fall. The tree branches above were bare and leaves crunched under Tyler's hooves. He perked up, happy to be out on the trail. I trotted off right away. I couldn't wait to get to the field. I almost wondered if it was still there. Or if it had been some kind of magical mirage. Tyler wanted to canter. He pulled at the bit. I let him canter. He loved being out in the woods. It was like he came to life underneath me. Maybe he'd been born into the wrong world. Maybe his true calling would have been as an event pony.

We reached the edge of the woods and the field opened up in front of us. We kept cantering, picking up speed. I pushed Tyler forward even more. We were near galloping, and it felt amazing. I didn't mind that the cold air burned my face a little and stung my eyes. Tyler's breath was visible as he puffed.

Finally, I brought him down to a walk.

"That was fun, wasn't it?" I said.

He sighed in agreement.

I looked out over the field. It was so quiet and beautiful, just Tyler and me out in nature. I couldn't exactly say that I felt like Mom was watching me. But I felt that, in the end, Mom had understood me more than I realized. I would continue to figure out what I wanted and who I was. That would include what to do with Tyler. I had thought being myself was a place I needed to get to while she was still alive so she could witness it. But my whole life I would be figuring out who I was and changing all the time.

I gave Tyler a pat and picked up a canter for one more spin around the field before we headed back to the barn.

*

About the Author

KIM ABLON WHITNEY lives with her husband and three children in Newton, Massachusetts. In addition to writing fiction, she is a USEF 'R' judge in hunters, equitation, and jumpers and has officiated at the Washington International Horse Show Junior Equitation Finals, the Capital Challenge, the Winter Equestrian Festival, Lake Placid, and the Vermont Summer Festival. As a junior, she showed in the equitation, placing at the USEF Talent Search and USEF Medal Finals. She later competed as an amateur in the A/O jumpers, winning top ribbons at WEF, Lake Placid, and Devon on her self-trained off-the-track Thoroughbred. To learn more about Kim and her books, please visit www.kimablonwhitney.com.

Want to read more about the show circuit from Kim Ablon Whitney?
On the next page is an excerpt from
The Perfect Distance, available on Amazon.

Chapter One

"NO! NO! NO! What did I say about making a move at the last minute?"

Rob's voice was so loud, I could hear him all the way up at the barn—over a football field's length away. What I couldn't hear was the response from whomever he was yelling at. I hoped it wasn't Katie.

I led Tobey out of the barn and up to the mounting block. Behind me, my dad gave Gwenn a leg up onto Finch.

"Thanks, Juan," she said. Even though I'd heard all the riders call my dad by his first name a million times before, it still sounded strange.

As I swung my leg over the saddle, my stomach started to tie up in knots. It was the first day of boot camp, which was what we called the weeks of training before the finals. This was when Rob got tough—tougher than usual, that is.

Tobey swished his tail and stomped a front hoof as I tightened the girth. He was really girthy so I had to tighten it only a hole or two at a time.

"Hold on," I told him. "We're going."

I gathered my reins, and Gwenn and I headed down to the indoor arena. West Hills was set on a hill, with the main barn, two impeccably groomed outdoor rings, and take-your-breath-away grand prix field on top and the indoor arena and half-mile galloping track down below. With all the well-kept buildings and manicured grounds, the farm was insanely gorgeous.

"Have a good lesson, girls," Dad called after us.

The door to the arena yawned open, but we didn't go in yet. That was rule number one of riding at West Hills: *Wait until Rob tells you to.* And it applied to most everything.

Rob had left the sliding door open because the early-September-still-summer sun was beating down on the metal roof, heating the indoor like a sauna. But since most of the finals took place indoors, we practiced inside no matter how hot it was. Rob stood in the middle as Katie cantered a circle around him. Tara was standing on the side of the ring.

Rob stood five foot ten, had rusty brown hair, and was a little on the beefy side. He had great posture—he never slouched or slumped. No one knew his age for sure, but we guessed that he was around forty-five. If you saw him on the street, you probably wouldn't think much of him, but in the horse show world he was basically God. Parents sent their kids from all over the country and paid a fortune for them to train with him. He was notorious for being tough on his riders, but as much as we griped about him, we all knew it was worth it because he was the best.

"How did that feel?" he asked Katie in a deceptively moderate tone. A tone I knew all too well.

Katie answered softly, "Not so good, I guess."

Knowing what was coming next, I cringed for her and for how many times I'd been in her situation.

Suddenly Rob's voice boomed again. "Jesus Christ, Katie, have some conviction! Speak up! It was lousy. You were completely out of control."

Rob paused. The worst was hopefully over—once he'd exploded, he usually calmed down.

He continued in a saner tone, "The course is all parts that make up a whole. You have to ride it in parts and put the parts together. You got going and didn't stop to take a breath or collect your horse the whole way around. Again. And this time, for God's sake, get it right."

Katie cantered off the circle to start over. Her face muscles were tensed, like she was trying to hold it all together. I watched in silence, thinking: *Please don't mess up.* Because the more upset Rob got now, the tougher he would be on me. But also because Katie was my best friend at the barn and probably my best friend, period. If we hadn't met at the barn, I'm sure we never would have been friends. Other than riding, we really didn't have much in common. But horses had brought us together, and we'd found that even though we were from completely different backgrounds, we got along well.

Stretch's nostrils flared with each stride and he expelled the air in forceful snorts. His neck glistened with sweat, and where the reins rubbed against him was white with foam.

All in all, Katie was a pretty bad rider, but she got away

with a fair amount because of Stretch. Stretch had won the finals a record five times and was Rob's best horse. He was practically a legend in the equitation world. He was pure white and was so easy anyone could ride him. In fact, Stretch would probably jump a course with a monkey on his back. When you jump, you have to tell your horse where to take off from. The correct spot to take off from—not too close to the jump and not too far away—is called the right "distance." If you're good at judging the distances and telling your horse where to take off from, people say you have a "good eye." Katie had what people called "no eye." Luckily for her, Stretch had a good eye of his own, and even when Katie didn't see the perfect distance, a lot of the time Stretch did. He was also known for being able to make a really long distance look good—hence the name Stretch.

Katie's father was a big-time New York City litigator, and he paid six figures a year to lease Stretch. Many of the eq riders at West Hills leased horses from Rob. Some riders even came specifically to ride with Rob because of his amazing stock of proven eq horses. I, however, rode whatever Rob gave me. For the past three years that had been Tobey.

This time Katie managed the course without any major faults. She kept cantering after the last fence because that was rule number one-A: *You're not done until Rob says you're done.*

"Okay, let him walk," Rob said. "Good enough . . . for today."

Katie barely had to tug on the reins and Stretch dropped back to a walk.

"The one thing I want you to think about is being subtle," Rob told her. "When you see the distance, don't make a big move for it. The judges never want to see that big move. Understand?"

"Yes," Katie said. "Thank you, Rob. Thanks a lot." Rule number two: *Always say please and thank you.* The rules weren't printed up and handed to you when you arrived at West Hills, but if you had any sense at all, you learned them quickly.

Rob turned to Gwenn and me. "Come on in, girls."

I took a deep breath and tried to ignore the butterflies attacking my stomach. After all, I had lived through boot camp and the finals plenty of times before. But it didn't matter. I could do the finals a hundred times and I'd still be fighting my nerves the whole way through. And at seventeen, this was my last chance.

Gwenn had headed into the ring. I realized I hadn't budged.

"Francie?" Rob said. "Would you like to grace us with your presence?"

Here goes everything, I thought, and pressed Tobey forward into the ring.

*

The Perfect Distance is available on Amazon

Made in the USA
Lexington, KY
12 October 2015